PRAISE FOR
THE CADDIE WHO PLAYED WITH HICKORY

"John Coyne knows his golf history, its characters, and the game. He spins a story that includes a mysterious character, a hero, a romance, a semi-villain, and a classic golf match into a believable tale."
                    —Dr. Gary Wiren, noted golf teacher and former director of
                              research and learning for the PGA of America

"John Coyne spins a tale so involving, the reader is in enjoyable suspense about the outcome of every putt."
                    —Jerry Dudek, director of development, Evans Scholars
                              Foundation/Western Golf Association

"Coyne can take all that is esoteric and nuanced about golf . . . and make it not only intriguing but a seamless part of the narrative; it's all but impossible not to be captivated."
                                        —*Piedmont Post* (California)

"I enjoyed the book so much (and also his first golf book) that I am hoping that Coyne has another 'caddie' book in his bag. The first two were so good that a trilogy seems a natural."
                                        —*GolfBlogger.com*

THE CADDIE WHO
PLAYED WITH HICKORY

ALSO BY JOHN COYNE

NOVELS

The Caddie Who Knew Ben Hogan

Brothers & Sisters

Child of Shadows

Fury

Hobgoblins

The Legacy

The Piercing

The Searing

The Shroud

GOLF INSTRUCTIONAL

Playing with the Pros

New Golf for Women

Better Golf

COLLECTIONS (EDITED)

Going Up Country: Travel Essays by Peace Corps Writers

Living on the Edge: Fiction by Peace Corps Writers

THE CADDIE WHO
PLAYED WITH HICKORY

JOHN COYNE

THOMAS DUNNE BOOKS
ST. MARTIN'S GRIFFIN   NEW YORK

THOMAS DUNNE BOOKS.
An imprint of St. Martin's Press.

THE CADDIE WHO PLAYED WITH HICKORY. Copyright © 2008 by John Coyne. All
rights reserved. Printed in the United States of America. For information, address
St. Martin's Press, 175 Fifth Avenue, New York, N.Y. 10010.

www.thomasdunnebooks.com
www.stmartins.com

The Library of Congress has catalogued the hardcover edition as follows:

Coyne, John.
    The caddie who played with hickory / John Coyne.—1st ed.
        p. cm.
    ISBN-13: 978-0-312-37244-6
    ISBN-10: 0-312-37244-2
    1. Hagen, Walter, 1892–1969—Fiction.   2. Golf stories.   3. Caddies—
Fiction.
    PS3553.O96 C33 2008
    796.352—dc22

                                                            2008003997

    ISBN-13: 978-0-312-56091-1 (pbk.)
    ISBN-10: 0-312-56091-5 (pbk.)

First St. Martin's Griffin Edition: May 2009

10 9 8 7 6 5 4 3 2 1

For all my fellow caddies at Midlothian Country Club

ACKNOWLEDGMENTS

I DECIDED TO WRITE ABOUT WALTER HAGEN BECAUSE HE IS THE most important person in golf history we have never heard of. In his wonderful biography *Sir Walter: Walter Hagen and the Invention of Professional Golf,* author Tom Clavin writes of the gathering of PGA professionals and other golf luminaries at the Traverse City Golf and Country Club in August 1967. It was a dinner to honor Hagen and to celebrate his seventy-fourth birthday. Over three hundred people came to pay their respects to the man most responsible for the creation of America's professional golf tour. At the banquet, Arnold Palmer, then the reigning king of the PGA, said, "If it were not for you, Walter, this dinner tonight would be downstairs in the pro shop, not in the ballroom." In its story the next day, *The New York Times* called Hagen "the father of modern professional golf."

During the 1920s Golden Age of Sports, Walter Hagen earned more money from playing golf than Babe Ruth earned from baseball or Jack Dempsey made as heavyweight boxing champ.

Along with the great amateur Bobby Jones, Hagen was the most successful and well-known golfer in the world.

Hagen first played golf when clubs were made with hickory shafts and had names like cleeks, mashies, and jiggers. He lived long enough to compete with steel shafts and persimmon woods, and saw the game move from the exclusive preserve of country club members to being a popular sport that was played by "Arnie's Army."

In writing this novel with Walter Hagen as a central character in a story set in the Midwest of 1946, I have relied on two excellent biographies of The Haig: first and foremost, Tom Clavin's *Sir Walter: Walter Hagen and the Invention of Professional Golf* and *Sir Walter and Mr. Jones* by Stephen R. Lowe. I also read, and recommend, Hagen's own book, *The Walter Hagen Story*; as well as *Links of Life* by Joe Kirkwood, a golf trick shot artist who traveled the world with Hagen as they played in tournaments and golf exhibitions.

For information on the history of hickory clubs and how to repair them, I am indebted to Bob Kuntz for his instructional manual, *Antique Golf Clubs*. For instruction on how to play with hickory clubs, I turned to *Golf Fundamentals* by Seymour Dunn; *Sixty Years of Golf* by Robert Harris; and Bobby Jones's own history, *Down the Fairway*, written with O. B. Keeler. For background information on the Professional Golf Association of the period, there is no better history than Herb Graffis's *The PGA*.

For their editing and research assistance, I'd like to thank my fellow golfers (and hickory enthusiasts) Denis Nolan, Randy Jensen, Ralph Livingston III, and my brother (and former Midlothian caddie) Tom Coyne.

I also want to thank my agent at Trident Media Group, John Silbersack, and my golf editor guru at St. Martin's Press/Thomas

Dunne Books, Peter Wolverton, who had faith enough in me to say, "Let's write another caddie book."

And, as always, all my thanks to the best editor in the world, my wife, Judy Coyne, who wrestled this plot into prose.

1

As I've grown older I have come to realize that what is most important to me is not what I daily forget but what I remember. And what I recall from years ago comes back to me so intensely that I imagine I can reach back through time and distance and change with a few words, a gesture, or even a smile, the lives we all once lived.

This fantasy enriches my days but also troubles me with its what-ifs. I will let you decide if I was wrong—"needlessly romantic," as Clare always said—or if I was the only one who fully understood what was happening that summer of 1946, the summer when the great Walter Hagen came back to Midlothian Country Club to play the last important golf match of his life.

It all began at seven o'clock on a hot Sunday morning in June, when Harrison Cornell walked down the country-club drive and into my life. I spotted him as he crossed the bridge below the second green, four hundred yards from where I sat on a low concrete wall above the caddie shack, at the top of the members'

wide gravel parking lot. He was keeping to the far left edge of
the narrow blacktop drive and moving fast, as if he were late for
an important appointment.

What I first noticed was his walk. There was none of our
usual caddie lope, that slow, camellike cadence most of us had
mastered as a way of pacing ourselves to handle two loops a day
around the golf course. No, Harrison's stride was so long and
smooth that from a distance it looked as if he were gliding over
the ground. As he approached me, he said in a soft British voice
as smooth as his stride, "Excuse me, young man, could you tell
me where I might find the caddie master?"

He took off his panama and ran his fingers through his fair
hair. It was humid that morning and sweat glistened on his forehead and temples. His jacket was too heavy for the warm weather
and his tie was worn and frayed. He wore heavy black brogans
with thick rubber soles.

For a moment I didn't—couldn't—say anything. I was too
busy taking him in, and he repeated his question, politely. I
stood and saw that we were the same height and build, just under
six feet and thin and wiry, though I was "black Irish" and he
resembled one of those pale English gentlemen you see now
mostly in old black-and-white movies on TV.

I took him to be in his early thirties, although he was weath-
ered for a man that age, and I wondered what had happened to
age him. Seeing him there in the country club parking lot, I
would never have guessed that he had once been a fighter pilot,
a war hero, and a wealthy man.

"Harrison Cornell," he said when I stood. He smiled shyly,
extending his hand. It was the charm and warmth of that first
smile that captured my friendship. During the long Illinois
summer, whenever my feelings for Harrison faltered, whenever
I thought he was just another loser who had ended up looping at

a country club, his smile would bring me quickly back to his side.

"I've come for the Hagen exhibition this August," he added. I nodded, watching his soft blue eyes. They were eyes that asked for forgiveness before he had done anything wrong.

"You want to caddie in the exhibition?" I asked. He seemed nothing like the older men who sometimes came out to the club looking for a quick loop. Since the war ended, and the ammunition factory near Blue Island closed, we were getting lots of guys looking for work.

Still, most of the caddies were kids like me, and even I was getting too old for the job. I had gotten out of high school that spring. Mom and Dad wanted me to stop caddying and work full-time on the family farm, or go downtown to the Loop and try to get a job "pushing a pencil," as Mom always called office work. But I had told them, and myself, that I would spend the summer deciding what to do with the rest of my life.

"I hope so," he said. "I guess it all depends on your caddie master." He looked in the direction of the caddie shack and asked with that sad smile, "Is that his office?"

I nodded. "His name's Jimmy Leamer. We call him the Professor." I guessed then that he didn't know much about the modus operandi of caddie yards, but I was wrong about that, as I was wrong about a lot of things when it came to Harrison Cornell.

"Well, I'd best go introduce myself." He smiled again quickly, shyly. "Thanks for your help. And your name?" As he waited for my answer, he turned his head so that his left ear was closer. Later, of course, I would learn how he had lost some of his hearing when his Hawker Hurricane went down over Germany.

"Tommy," I said. "Tom O'Shea."

"Thank you, Tom. You've been very helpful. I hope to see

you again." With one hand, he carefully and unhurriedly slipped on his hat, almost as if he were doing a bit of stage business. It was all very grand for someone who looked like he slept in his clothes.

"If you're caddying here this summer you'll see enough of me," I told him.

"You're a looper?"

I picked up my golf cap and showed him the #1 badge pinned to it. I wanted him to know right from the start that I was the top caddie. It had taken me seven years of working every summer to make it to number one at Midlothian, and when anybody came looking for a job I made sure they knew who I was. The caddie yard was a tough place and if you wanted to survive you had to claim your space.

His eyes went from the badge to my face. "Ah, well, I've stumbled on the best source of information." He smiled once more and then nodded toward the book beside me on the wall. "What are you reading, if you don't mind my asking?"

I held up *It Was Good While It Lasted,* by Henry Longhurst.

"I met Longhurst once," he offered. "A charming man, a great raconteur. May I ask why you're reading him?" His accent, his whole manner of speaking, seemed so out of place in the middle of the Midwest.

It wasn't Henry Longhurst who interested me, I told him. I was reading the book to learn about Walter Hagen.

Harrison Cornell nodded and then asked if I was planning to caddie for Hagen.

"That's right," I told him.

Cornell looked thoughtful for a moment, and then, just as I thought he might speak, he nodded goodbye and walked down the slope to the caddie yard as though he had been doing it for years and knew exactly where he was going and what he had to do.

I settled down on the stone wall again and went back to reading Longhurst's account of golf in Great Britain before the war, including a match at St. Andrew's between Hagen and Henry Cotton, while I waited for my number to be called.

Kids were going out. They kept streaming up from the shack with caddie cards in their hands, running across the gravel parking lot, then around to the back of the pro shop, where they'd pick up their players' bags from Bill Vicars, the assistant pro, and walk around to the first tee, where they would wait for their players to arrive. It was the everyday caddie ritual at the club.

While the Professor hadn't yet given me a loop, I wasn't worried about grabbing a bag. Most of the early players on Sunday were old guys and hackers—members who weren't good golfers—and as the number one caddie, I was never sent out with any of them.

So I was surprised when my kid brother Mike came running up from the caddie shack to say that the Professor wanted me. It wasn't yet eight o'clock.

The caddie shack was only two rooms in a cinder-block building, one of which was a wired cage where the Professor worked, selling Cokes and candy, keeping safe our brown-bag lunches, and taking calls from the pro shop when Vicars wanted a caddie. Later in the day, when we all came off the course, the Professor paid us out of a tin box whatever we had made looping that day. The other room had a few benches against the walls, giving caddies a place to go when it rained or to stretch out and nap during the heat of a slow summer day.

The Professor and Harrison Cornell were standing together in the sun outside the office. They looked as if they were old friends who just happened to have met up by chance at this dead-end corner of the world.

Like Cornell, the Professor was wearing a jacket and tie, and a wide-brim straw hat. But the Professor's tie was new and his shirt was pressed and clean. Jimmy Leamer always dressed for work, even though he spent his days handling the likes of us, a bunch of ragamuffins. He showed off his dignity like the neatly folded white handkerchief in the breast pocket of his seersucker sports jacket.

The Professor was laughing about something Cornell had said. He had one of those quiet laughs that came easily, though I had learned the hard way that his good-natured ways were only on the surface. He wasn't someone to mess with.

Cornell, too, was smiling, as he leaned forward and whispered again to the Professor. I was to learn that this was Cornell's way. Whatever his point, he made it as though he was dealing you a card from the bottom of the deck.

"Tommy," said the Professor, spotting me. He stepped back into the office, moving carefully on his bad leg, and grabbed a white card off a stack, scribbling the name of my player as he introduced Harrison Cornell.

"We met," Harrison interjected. "I interrupted this young man's reading." He smiled as if we were the best of friends.

The Professor handed me the caddie card, saying, "Higgs and Frazier are going off as a twosome. Take Cornell with you and show him the course." With that, he looked over at Harrison, explaining, "Tommy's my best kid."

Knowing that I was about to bitch about Higgs and Frazier, the Professor quickly added, "I'll get you a good loop this afternoon, Tom." Then, before I could protest, he stepped back inside the caddie office and closed the door in our faces. I might have banged on it to make my case, but then Cornell spoke up and thanked me for doing him a favor, and said he was sorry to ruin my Sunday morning with a bad loop.

I waved off his apology. It wasn't his fault, I told the stranger. Though I wasn't looking forward to caddying for a hacker, I knew that the Professor must have had a good reason for wanting me to show Harrison Cornell around Midlothian Country Club.

2

WE PICKED UP OUR PLAYERS' BAGS AT THE REAR OF THE PRO SHOP and walked to the first tee. We were the only caddies on the wooden bench, set under a maple tree. Vicars was at the scoring tent. He had pinned the day's big white score sheets to the green board, and then went walking back and forth to the pro shop beneath the men's locker room, getting scorecards and pencils and arranging them in neat stacks on a small metal table. A few members were down on the range banging balls out to their caddies and, closer to the clubhouse, a twosome of early-morning players was practicing on the putting green. It was quiet on the tee, warm and pleasant. It was one of my favorite times of summer, early on a weekend morning before the rush of players and the heat of the long and busy afternoon when the golf course would be full of members. It was at times like that, early in the day, when I thought the country club belonged just to me.

From where we were sitting in the shade of the maple, I could see the length of the rambling three-story white colonial club-house. Built on the rise of a hill, the clubhouse overlooked the width of the golf course, which fanned out below, its holes stretching away like the slender fingers of a young woman's hand. When Midlothian Country Club opened in 1898, the clubhouse was called one of the most beautiful in America; as I walked across the course in the early mornings on my way to work, the mansion loomed larger and larger as I went closer, a paradise out of place, like Shangri-la in *Lost Horizon*.

Harrison got up from the bench and walked to the iron railing where we'd stacked the bags. From there he had a clear view of the front nine and a few holes on the back side. Closer to us were the eighteenth and ninth greens, just below and in front of the clubhouse itself.

I turned around on the bench to watch him as he stared down the length of the first hole, a par-4. He stood with his hands lightly on his hips, leaning back on his left foot, as if he were a member deciding what club to play.

I knew then that he was a player. There is something about the way a person acts around a golf course that tells you whether he plays the game. It's like people with dogs, or jockeys with horses. Cornell seemed to relax now that he had clubs handy and a golf course in sight. I understood how he felt. Even when I caddied at another club in a pro-member event, all of it might be new and strange, but once I was standing on the first tee I relaxed. Whatever way a golf course might be designed, I was at home on any eighteen.

Harrison turned from the view and walked back to where I was sitting.

"Do you play yourself, Tommy?"

I nodded. "I play to a two," I said slowly to show him he wasn't dealing with some ordinary caddie, then added, "and last month I won the Illinois state high-school golf championship down in Champaign."

"You're a real player, then," Cornell exclaimed. "Are you the best out here?"

"There's a member's kid, Drew McClain, who's pretty good. Club champ."

"Have you played him?"

"Sure, all the time."

"Who's the better?"

"Well, tee to green, I'd say he is, but I've got him beat on the greens."

"That's grand. The game of golf is all about making those three-footers." Cornell sat down beside me and asked, "Is he your age?"

"He's a couple of years older than me. Goes to Yale. He's on their golf team."

"Yale, is it?" He seemed impressed. Next, he smiled. I learned to call it his anticipating smile as he thought of a story he wanted to tell. "You know Bobby Jones went to Harvard, but never played on the golf team."

"That's impossible. He was a U.S. amateur champ when he was a kid. How could he not make the team?"

"Oh, he was good enough. One day at Harvard he took on the whole six-man team and beat their best ball. No, the problem was that by the time he was at Harvard, he had already graduated from Georgia Tech with an engineering degree. He'd used up his college eligibility. So, instead of playing for Harvard, he traveled with the team as their manager, helping to carry their clubs, running errands for the others—and all the while he was the U.S. Open champ." Cornell shook his head, as if marveling at Jones's career, and then asked me my college plans.

"I just got out of high school. I might go to college in the fall," I said vaguely, then added, "once I put away some dough." I nodded toward the clubhouse. "I have a job inside during the winter. I work the bar in the men's locker room. It's good money." Talking about the future made me uneasy and I slipped into silence. I knew—as I guessed everyone else knew—that at eighteen I shouldn't still be caddying. To me, and I suspected to all the members, it meant I was already some kind of failure. "I'm only hanging around to the end of summer so I can caddie for Hagen," I added, hoping that would help justify me in Cornell's eyes.

He didn't say anything right away, just watched me as if I were a tricky downhill six-footer he had to make.

"If you go to school, what would you study?" was all he said.

"I don't know. Medicine maybe." I shrugged and looked off. I was embarrassed by all my big dreams.

"Medicine. That's grand. Good for you." Cornell tapped me on the shoulder, as if I'd already graduated and become a doctor. Then, dropping his voice, he asked abruptly, "Those our gentlemen?"

Glancing around, I saw Frazier and Higgs come out of the men's locker room. They were stepping carefully on the metal spikes of their golf shoes as they crossed the concrete terrace and then walked down the steps. Once they reached the gravel path that led to the first tee, they picked up their stride, though both men were pushing sixty and neither moved with much speed.

"That's them." I grabbed Higgs's bag and walked toward the right side of the men's white tee markers with Harrison coming after me, saying under his breath, "What's Frazier's game?"

"He drives about one-sixty, hits everything with a big banana slice, and he cheats. He'll want you to read his putts and pull his clubs. Walk slowly. He doesn't like to be rushed."

I swung Higgs's bag off my shoulder, set it down by the men's wooden tee marker, and pulled out his driver, a MacGregor Ben Hogan. It was the only new club in his bag.

Harrison stared into his bag and studied Frazier's woods.

"He plays Hagens." The way Cornell said Hagen's name caught my attention. I watched him pull the socket-head driver from the bag. Walter Hagen's name was scripted in white across the top of the black laminated wood.

"Well, he doesn't play like Hagen," I joked. Then, wanting to show him that I knew what I was talking about, I added, "Those Hagen woods are made of Strata Block. Because of the war, they couldn't get persimmon."

I kept showing off, explaining how Hagen had been the first golfer to mass-manufacture clubs, and how he had designed his irons himself in Florida before his company was bought out by Wilson. "Hagen's the one who came up with the compact blade that everyone uses."

"Have you ever seen Hagen play?" Cornell asked, ignoring what I rattled off about Hagen's company.

"Only in films," I had to admit.

Cornell was still examining the Hagen driver. He placed the club head on the ground to get the look and feel of the shaft, then lifted the wood with his right hand and felt its weight in his fingers.

"You've seen him," I said, knowing that he must have, or he wouldn't have asked the question. "Where was that?"

"Down in Bermuda, I caddied for him in a Red Cross exhibition."

"You caddied for Hagen?"

"In forty-one, Hagen played in a Bahamas benefit organized by the Duke of Windsor and his wife. Hagen, Jones, Sarazen, and Tommy Armour; they all played in that exhibition. I paid for the privilege of caddying for Hagen," Cornell said. Then our two players arrived and he added quickly, "I'll tell you about it sometime," in a way that suggested he had a lot to say.

3

It wasn't until the third hole that I had a chance to talk to Cornell again. On three, we walked ahead to forecaddie on the top of the rise while Frazier and Higgs went back to the tee. Cornell came up beside me and set down his bag. He was breathing hard and I knew then that he wasn't a real caddie. No looper would be winded after only two holes. He took out a cigarette and lit it with a kitchen match, striking it with a flip of his thumbnail, a trick that always impressed me. Then he asked me if I had figured out why Frazier sliced his drives.

"Oh, I don't know," I said, laughing at the absurdity of the question. "Maybe it's because he doesn't get off his right side and swings outside-in. Maybe it's his weak left hand, or because he tees up too far forward." I shrugged. "Take your pick."

He smiled, suggesting that he knew a lot more than I did about the mechanics of a golf swing. You have to remember, this was in the age before great players like Ben Hogan came along to write *Power Golf*. Only a few golfers had written books; Ralph

Guldahl and Bobby Jones were the ones that I knew of. Also, we didn't read books to learn the game. What we knew, we picked up from being around the course and watching good players. Ignorance about the swing, however, never kept me from spouting off as if I knew exactly what I was talking about.

Cornell exhaled a thin, straight whistle of smoke and nodded. "Everything you say is true," he replied. He watched Frazier tee up, but I kept my eye on Cornell. "Every player has half a dozen things wrong with his swing. Instead of worrying about all of them, you need to fix the one fault that will cure the others." He looked at me. "Do you know who gave me that piece of advice?" Without waiting for an answer, he went on: "A pro named Claude Harmon. Do you know of him? He lost last year to Nelson in the PGA semifinals and now he's off in New York at a rich country club called Winged Foot. A marvelous player, but a better teacher. You know, great golfers are rarely great teachers."

"What are you?" I asked, baiting him. "A player or a teacher?"

"Neither. I'm a caddie." He smiled, acknowledging my taunt. "In fact, by the end of today, members are going to call me the best caddie at this club."

I started to laugh. The caddie yard was full of kids with attitude, and though Harrison Cornell was no kid, it was oddly reassuring to know that he could be as cocky and brash as the next guy.

"How 'bout a small bet," he said next. "I'll wager two dollars I can cure Frazier's slice before we make the turn. And for good measure I'll add another fifty to seventy-five yards to his drives."

Cornell's cigarette was limp in his thin lips and whiffs of smoke curled up past his eyes. I grinned at the claptrap of his challenge. Caddies were always betting on everything and anything, so I was happy to take his money. I knew that he might straighten out Frazier's swing for a few holes, but there was no way he could keep him from slicing. Last year, Frazier had spent a C-note taking lessons from our pro, Red Denison, who couldn't cure the Doc's slice.

I told Cornell I'd take his bet but only for the drive on the eighteenth. Frazier had to clear the creek and keep his ball in the fairway.

"How far is the creek?" Harrison asked.

I pointed across two fairways toward the eighteenth hole. From our high point on the ridge of number three, we could see the finishing hole and where the creek crossed the fairway.

Cornell pulled a scorecard from his pocket and studied it before saying, "Quite all right." He slipped the card back into his pocket. "It's a wager."

We heard the whack of Doc Frazier's drive and both of us spun around as a high banana ball flew down the left rough and sliced back into the fairway. The ball carried the ridge but landed less than 160 off the tee.

Frazier had a terrible swing, and there was no way, I told myself, that this old guy could fix it in one round of golf.

For the rest of that first nine, Cornell hung tight to Frazier, talking to him between shots, gesturing, smiling, having a swell time, it seemed. And yet I saw no improvements in Frazier's drives, or any other parts of his game. Cornell did help on the greens by reading Frazier's putts, and that impressed me. Even a good caddie usually needs several rounds to learn a course's greens.

On the front side at Midlothian, there are only a few holes with forecaddies, so I didn't have a chance to twit Cornell about Frazier's slice until we reached the ninth.

"You can't rush these things," Cornell explained. "It's all up here." He tapped his temple, smiling as if he had it all under control. I was grinning, too. For all his fancy British ways, Cornell was just another small-time hustle, I decided. He was like all the other guys who blew into the caddie yard, looped a few times, and then, on a big Sunday payday or after an outside tournament, got a crap game going behind the handball court and took all the little kids' money, before moving on.

I looked back at the ninth tee. Higgs had the honors, having won the par-3 eighth hole with a double bogey.

"I'm trying to get him to trust me," Cornell volunteered, explaining his golf-instruction strategy. "I'm telling him stories about the pros I knew down in the islands. I'm telling him how I clubbed players like Hagen."

"Was Hagen as good as they say?"

Cornell didn't respond immediately. It was as if he was thinking of what he might say, and then he answered, "What Hagen could do was read you. That's what made him such a great match player. Do you know the story about him and Mike Brady at the 1919 Open at Brae Burn?"

"Hagen won the play-off. It was his second win; his first was here at Midlothian in 1914," I answered. "He beat Chick Evans."

Cornell nodded, agreeing, and then went on talking as if he wasn't impressed at all by what I knew. "Brady was favored to win that Open; he was from Boston and knew the Brae Burn course. The Open was medal play and Brady had finished and was in the clubhouse when Hagen reached eighteen. Hagen has a six-foot putt to win outright and he starts to putt, then backs away and glances around, and asks, 'Where's Mike?'

"There are almost fifteen thousand spectators waiting for Hagen to make the final putt, to win or force a play-off, but Hagen stops and tells the tournament officials to go straightaway to the clubhouse and bring Mike Brady down to watch him make the putt and win the U.S. Open. Damn cheeky of him, I'd say.

"Hagen waits in the middle of the green in the twilight of the day. He stands there leaning against his blade putter with his legs crossed, wearing a white silk shirt, a fancy silk tie, plus fours, and white golf shoes. He waits until Mike Brady arrives at the green."

"Hagen didn't make the putt," I said.

"True enough. And maybe the Haig knew all along that he couldn't make it. Maybe it was all gamesmanship. If he made it, he would have humiliated Brady by having him stand there and watch, and the next time they played, Brady would still be humiliated. And if he missed, as he did, he'd still have proven to Brady that he wasn't afraid of him.

"The play-off was the next day, but Hagen goes out that night with the entertainer Al Jolson, who was in Boston with his troupe. Hagen is up most of the night and he's due on the tee the next morning. So, he goes back to his hotel towards dawn, takes a bath, dresses up in his fine knickers and a fancy bow tie, then drives his Pierce Arrow over to Brae Burn for the play-off. Brady is already there. He has been hitting balls for almost two hours.

"On the first tee, Hagen tells everyone that he has been out all night with the great Al Jolson. He wants Brady to know he has been drinking and carrying on and not even thinking about the play-off.

"Brady wins the toss and starts to take a few practice swings and Hagen leaves the tee and jogs into the clubhouse grill and grabs a drink. He's showing Mike Brady, and everyone else, that he's so unconcerned about the match that he can have a drink before he tees off.

"They both par the first hole, and on the second tee, when

Brady is taking more practice swings before driving off, Hagen walks over and whispers to Brady that he should roll down his shirtsleeves before the gallery sees that the muscles in his arms are quivering. 'They'll think you're afraid of me,' Hagen tells him nicely.

"Brady rolls down his shirtsleeves and duck hooks his drive into the thick trees on the left side of the hole. It's the end of the match. Haig is three up before they make the turn." Cornell swung his bag onto his shoulder. Doc Frazier was on the tee.

"It sounds like you were there yourself. What was the Haig like when he wasn't playing golf?" I asked, realizing that Cornell wasn't faking it after all.

"Hagen?" As Cornell moved toward the fairway, he said over his shoulder, "As far as I'm concerned, Walter Hagen is a worthless son of a bitch."

4

WHEN WE WALKED OFF THE NINTH GREEN, BOTH PLAYERS GAVE US their putters and went up into the clubhouse to have a drink in the men's bar and I led Cornell over to the back side. I dropped my bag beside the men's tee and stepped over to the water fountain for a drink. When I returned, Harrison was standing by the tee markers almost as if he were at attention, studying the layout of the hole. I interrupted, asked why he had called Walter Hagen a worthless son of a bitch.

You see, at Midlothian, Hagen was the caddies' hero. Like us, he'd grown up in a small town—in his case, in upstate New York. He'd caddied at the Country Club of Rochester and gone on to win the 1914 U.S. Open here at our own course. It was Hagen's victory at Midlothian that had changed his life; from it he went on to win the British Open four times in eight years, five PGA championships, and another U.S. Open, finishing his career with eleven majors.

But besides his own wins, his real contribution, after Midlothian, was to create a new career on the links: the professional touring golfer. Hagen was the first American to play tournaments and exhibitions around the world. He made more money than any other professional athlete, more money than his friends Babe Ruth and Jack Dempsey, in what was called the Golden Age of Sports.

"Playing great golf doesn't make you a great person, Tommy; you know that well enough," Harrison replied calmly after I made my defense of Hagen.

"The Haig was a good guy, too," I answered. "When he won the British Open for the last time, he gave his entire winnings to his caddie." That was the kind of gesture any caddie would remember.

Cornell smiled. "The kid's name was Hargreaves. Hagen called him Sonny. He caddied for Hagen in that Open and some Ryder Cup matches." He let his mastery of details sink in. Then he added, "Let me tell you another story." He stopped again, making me wait while he lit a cigarette. "This happened at that Red Cross benefit match organized by the Duke of Windsor. You know the Duke used to be the King of England, right?"

"He married a divorced woman, an American, so he had to abdicate," I answered. I might have been a midwestern farm boy, but I read newspapers.

Cornell nodded. "In nineteen forty, Churchill sent him off to be governor-general of the Bahamas. Hagen and Jones, Gene Sarazen, Tommy Armour, they all knew the Duke of Windsor in England. They followed him to the Bahamas in the winter months to play golf. The Duchess—Wallis Simpson was her name—organized fund-raising matches to support the Red Cross and the war effort. One of the ways they made money was auctioning off the right to caddie for the pros. That's when I paid three hundred dollars to loop for Hagen."

"So, you're not a real caddie," I said, trying to find out who he really was.

"I am now," Cornell shot back and took a long drag on his cigarette.

I didn't press him further. I didn't want to embarrass him. I felt sorry for the guy, thinking how once he must have been a country-club member, hanging around English royalty and famous golfers, and now he was looping for a living.

Frazier and Higgs were stepping out the side door of the clubhouse, just behind the tenth tee. They were talking and laughing over something, having a fine time in the bright, sunny Sunday morning, and Cornell forgot about his story and me and turned his attention back to his player.

Frazier's drive off ten split the fairway and carried to the right of the left-side bunker, which I knew was 180 from the men's tee. His drive was straight, though it did fade slightly before it reached the bunker that jutted into the fairway from the left-side rough. The ball landed safely and ran a dozen yards farther on the wide, flat fairway. Old Doc Frazier couldn't have placed it better if he had walked out and dropped his ball. There was a stunned moment of silence as the two players comprehended the drive, and then Higgs swore and congratulated Frazier, who was looking over at Cornell, grinning wildly at his caddie. Frazier picked up his tee and went striding off as if he had been hitting drives like that all his damn life.

There is a quick way to fix a slice, as anyone who plays golf might know. It is not by simply closing the face of the club at the address. By doing that, a player is only rotating the hands and not really closing the face. I had watched as Frazier addressed the ball. He had put his driver down and then moved the face from square to closed before setting his hands, doing it the right way.

I rushed after Cornell and asked him what had happened.

Had old man Frazier just gotten lucky one time with his wood?

Cornell shook his head and whispered, "He exhaled." He took a deep breath, then demonstrated what he meant.

Now, players know you have to take a deep breath before teeing off. Cornell hadn't told Frazier anything new.

"You take a breath, right," Cornell went on, "but I told him not to swing until he had exhaled that breath. So he did, and he didn't tighten up."

"That's all?"

Cornell shrugged. "There's more, there's always more, but learning how to breathe is enough for now. That's the secret with golf: keep it simple. Remember what Claude Harmon said—correct one fault and cure a dozen others. Right?"

As he spoke, he went toward his player's ball. I stopped beside Higgs's drive, which was in the left-side rough, short of the bunker. I knew that by now Doc Frazier had told Higgs how his caddie had fixed his swing with a little gimmick, and Higgs, I'd guess, was thinking to himself, What has Tommy O'Shea, the number-one caddie, done for me? Besides the possibility that I'd lose my bet, Harrison Cornell was making me look bad with my player.

The back side, I realized, was going to be a long nine holes.

Doc Frazier didn't hit all his woods on the back side dead solid perfect, as we have learned to call a great shot. The banana ball came again on fourteen, but that was all for the good as his drive worked itself around the tight dog-leg right par-4, leaving him a mid-iron to the green.

I watched as Frazier listened closely to Cornell before he played every shot. For example, on the short par-3 fifteen, Frazier got over the front bunkers with his 5 iron. The ball jumped safely to the left side of the hole and onto the fringe. Higgs drove onto the green (somehow) so I gave him his putter, pulled his driver for the next hole, dropped my bag at the forecaddie for sixteen, and walked up to the edge of the green and waited there for Frazier to play. He was twenty yards away, and with the pin cut on the right side of the green, he had plenty of room. All he had to do was get his ball on the putting surface and let it run to the cup.

"I hope this caddie isn't charging Doc Frazier for a playing lesson," Higgs commented, coming to stand with me as we watched Frazier get set for his second shot. All these minilessons were slowing down our round, which was upsetting Higgs but working for Frazier. He was keeping the ball in play on every shot, and he wasn't blowing putts. Cornell had already cut ten strokes off Frazier's game and we hadn't finished the round.

"Who's this guy, anyway?" Higgs asked.

"I don't know, sir. He just came out this morning." I told Higgs how I had spotted Cornell coming down the drive and told him where the caddie shack was located. I told him how the Professor had asked me to show him around the course.

"Well, he knows the game," Higgs summed up. "Hell, he's turning Frazier into a scratch player."

With that, Frazier played his pitching wedge in one smooth motion and the ball came out of the short grass and landed softly. It ran across the wide green, slowed down going against the grain, but nevertheless ran straight for the cup.

"Shit!" Higgs exclaimed. "He's going to hole the sonovabitch."

And he did. It was the first time Doc Frazier had ever birdied fifteen.

Now I knew I was going to lose my bet unless Frazier got all excited on eighteen and tried to kill his drive, which happens even to the best of players when they get excited. And Frazier still wasn't the best of players.

The doc was too unathletic to swing the club with any ease or grace, but Cornell had him tighten his back swing and that kept him from losing the club at the top. He widened Frazier's stance, turning his left foot out for better balance, and strengthened his grip by moving his left hand over the shaft so that he was seeing three knuckles when he addressed the ball.

All this was simple enough, small adjustments, tinkering with Frazier's basic swing, but somehow Cornell had made them into a Christmas present for the doctor and it had totally changed his game.

When we reached eighteen, I walked down the hill with Cornell to stand by the forecaddie at the wooden bridge over the creek. I swung the bag off my shoulder and asked Cornell, "Should I pay you now or later?"

"Golf's quite a funny game," Cornell said, shaking his head.

I watched as he fished the last cigarette out of the pack. He crumpled up the Chesterfield package and slid it into the pocket of his jacket, then lit the match with his thumbnail again.

It was after twelve o'clock and Cornell hadn't taken off his jacket. I could see he was sweating more and he didn't look good. Caddying eighteen had worn him out and I was feeling sorry for him again and hoping that Frazier would clear the creek with his drive so I would lose the bet and pay him two bucks. He looked like he needed the money more than I did. I looked up toward the tee, which was tucked into a cluster of oak trees. The tee was at the top of the rise, and we could see, from where we were standing down by the creek, just the heads and shoulders of the players. It was only by the way they ducked their heads that we knew when they were teeing off.

"You can be the greatest player in the world," Cornell went on, speaking softly, "but if you don't have faith in yourself out here on the fairway, you're all alone." He stopped talking, as if he were lost in some memory, then simply shook his head and went on slowly: "That's why Hagen was such a fine player. He could make those three-footers when it counted. Mike Brady was damn good, but he couldn't match Hagen's ego." He gestured with his cigarette. "You know what I mean, lad?"

I nodded, not really knowing, but expecting him to go on. Which he did.

"I once read an interview with Hagen," Cornell said, "about how he approached the game. He wasn't afraid of losing a tournament, because he knew he would come back and win again. There are a hundred stories of him doing just that, coming back when the other bloke thought he was dead and buried."

I was about to ask Cornell how any of this added up to Hagen's being a son of a bitch, when I saw Frazier step to the tee. I told Cornell to turn around and watch his player.

Remembering that drive, I would say that it was Frazier's best ever at Midlothian. His ball cleared the creek, split the fairway, and carried 190 to land safely, leaving him a short lofted club to the green.

I opened my wallet and pulled out my money. When Cornell tried to wave me off, I told him no, among caddies all bets were paid. "It's our rules," I said, and he took the money and nodded thanks. Maybe he remembered he did need it.

When I went down to the shack after we finished, the caddie yard was quiet, with most of the kids still out on their early-morning rounds. I bought a Coke and leaned against the wire mesh of the Professor's office and told the caddie master everything that had happened with Cornell.

The Professor was sitting inside the cage. His chair was an old white wicker piece that he had scavenged the summer before, when the House Committee bought new furniture for the terrace.

He now spent most of his days in that chair, reading library books and smoking cigarettes, his crippled right leg stretched out straight.

It was his leg that had kept him out of the war, and kept him working as our caddie master all those years when I was growing up.

"Where's Cornell now?" he asked when I finished my story. He took a sip of coffee, which we all knew was laced with vodka.

"He's with Frazier, working on his putting."

The Professor leaned forward, grinning.

"You don't know who Harrison Cornell really is, do you?"

"Yeah, he's a caddie at Midlothian," I tossed off. If Harrison Cornell really was somebody, the Professor would tell me, after he enjoyed his moment.

"I knew him in the Bahamas before the war," Leamer began. "I was working at the club where he was a member. Member's son, really. He came from old money." He started slowly, as if he had a long story to tell. "As I said, that was in the thirties. He was a helluva player, and he had just gotten married to one of the Thorne girls. They were a wealthy British family." He shook his head, as if caught up again in that moment in time. "He was a scion. Did they teach you that word in high school, Tom?" The Professor smiled. He had false teeth that were too big and too perfect for his small mouth, but the smile was genuine.

"What happened to him?" I asked, impatient with the vocabulary lesson.

"What happened? I have no idea. The war, I guess." He shrugged. "When Harrison Cornell walked into the caddie yard this morning, you could have knocked me over. I hadn't seen him in six, seven years. When I knew him in the islands . . . God, he was handsome. Like a movie star. None of those people had a worry in the world. They played golf and tennis every day, then danced all night. But Harrison." He stopped and shook his head and took a long drag on the cigarette. "He told me the Germans got him. His plane was shot down over France and he spent a couple years as a POW."

"He said he caddied for Hagen once in a Red Cross fundraiser," I said, going back to the part that interested me.

The Professor paused, sipped his laced coffee, then shook his head and said, "Well, that might have been. I was gone from Nassau before the war broke out."

"Is he still married?"

The Professor gestured with his cigarette, indicating that he didn't know. "She was a beauty, that girl," he said.

"You could ask him?"

The Professor raised his eyes without raising his head. "He'll tell us whatever he wants to tell us, Tommy."

"I'll find out," I told him, being cocky again.

"Who's going to tell you, O'Shea?"

"I've got connections."

The Professor laughed. It was a running game between us about who could find out the most gossip about the members. The caddie master had his elbow braced against the arm of the wicker chair and his right hand raised, holding his cigarette in his thin fingers. The smoke drifted up and, without moving his hand, he flipped off a thick length of ash with his little finger. In a louder voice indicating that he was finished with gossip, he told me, "Tom, run up to the kitchen and use one of your connections to get me my lunch. When you get back, I'll give you a loop and get you out of here." He waved me away. "Hurry up. I'm hungry." He smiled, as if he was doing me a favor, and added, "Go ahead, you'll get to see your girlfriend."

5

THE PROFESSOR WAS TALKING ABOUT CLARE FARRELL, AND SHE wasn't my girlfriend. I just *wanted* her to be my girlfriend. She was a summer waitress at the club, nineteen, and going to Smith College on a scholarship. Clare was the reason why I didn't mind going up to the clubhouse kitchen to pick up the Professor's lunch.

Clare and I had been train mates for most of our high-school years, riding the Rock Island line from Midlothian south for a half hour to Joliet, where I went to the boys' high school, Joliet Catholic, and Clare attended the all-girls' St. Francis Academy.

Clare, with her waterfall of red curls and her steady evaluating gaze, was the girl of my dreams. But there was, as my mother would say, a fly in the ointment: Drew McClain. Drew and I arrived at the club as kids, but Drew was a member's son and I was a caddie. Through our teen years we came up against each other in local teen golf matches, high-school-team competitions, and whatever other games came our way as young bucks on the same small piece of turf. We stayed friendly, but now it was different—now there was Clare. Getting the Professor's lunch, however, could give me the chance of a fresh encounter.

I crossed the parking lot, walking around the circle drive behind the clubhouse, where members dropped off their golf bags, then passed the pool, already crowded with the people who swam and played tennis and never went near the golf course.

The pool and small pool bar were new that year. The whole area was set back from the clubhouse, with a tiled deck and white metal tables shaded by big umbrellas in green and white, the club's colors.

And yes, there was Clare, working the tables in her black-and-white uniform. Her long red hair was pulled up and off her shoulders on the warm day, and she was laughing at something one of the mothers had just said. As she turned from the cluster of women sitting together under umbrellas, she spotted me over the low shrubbery that encircled the pool and her face blushed with surprise.

She waved, just a finger wiggle really, but her smile, her gesture, the sheer sense of her being there, a few yards from me across the tile deck, left me happy and surprisingly sad. There she was, everything I wanted in the world, but somehow beyond my grasp.

When Clare was in her last year at St. Francis Academy, she had asked me to her senior prom, and we had, as we used to say back in the forties, made out that night for the first time in my dad's Chevy. But then she had gotten a scholarship to Smith and gone away to college and out of my life. It was almost as if she'd never looked back. She was home for the summer and working at the country club, but it wasn't the same between us. She had changed and she wasn't very much interested in our midwestern ways.

On her way back to the snack bar, she floated through the green and white umbrellas and the members stretched out on chaises and the club's enormous MCC beach blankets, and walked over to say hello. The inside of the pool was painted green, and with the water behind her, it looked almost as if she were rising from the ocean's floor.

"Hello, O'Shea," she tossed off. "Been loopin'?" She smiled like she knew she was the most perfect thing in the world. "I saw you coming up eighteen with Higgs. Isn't he a terrible hacker? You must really be in the doghouse with the Professor."

As we walked—she on one side of the shrubbery, I on the sidewalk—she asked what I was doing in her territory.

"The Professor sent me on an important mission," I said.

"Oh, you mean get his lunch?" She laughed. Being a smart aleck was another part of her charm, but more than once she had said to me, "Look, Tommy, I'm too much trouble. Get yourself a nice girl. Why don't you date my little sister? Kathy's nicer than me and she thinks you're cute."

"What are you doing tonight?" I asked, ignoring her kidding.

"Working."

"Late?"

"It depends."

Sunday nights were never late at the club. They were family nights for the members and early dinners with the kids.

"I'll take you home if you need a ride."

"Thanks, I have a ride."

"Ah!" I said. "A pleasure ride in the little MG for you. Well, that's a lot sportier than my old Chevy."

"Stop," she said, and now she was serious.

We had reached the end of the walk that edged the pool deck.

"See ya," I said. "And tell your buddy Drew we're teeing off at nine."

"Bye," she answered, then added as I walked off, "Don't be a jerk, Tommy. It doesn't mean anything."

But it did. Drew would be taking her home in his MG after she got off work, and, of course, they wouldn't go straight there. They'd stop on Cicero Avenue and have a hamburger at Corsi's, and then maybe go hang out at the new miniature golf course on 137th Street. I didn't know exactly what they'd do, only that I wouldn't be there.

I went up the back steps of the clubhouse and through the kitchen door into the help's dining room. The small, unadorned space was jammed with waitresses, waiters, busboys, all the kitchen staff eating lunch before the afternoon shift.

I never thought much about the clubhouse employees. Caddies and grounds crews, those of us who worked in the sunlight—we always thought we were the important help at Midlothian. So, although I waved to a few people I knew, I didn't stop to talk; I just made my way through the crowded dining room, thick with cigarette smoke and loud voices, and into the kitchen itself, with its long work tables and metal racks.

In front of the gas stoves I found Sandy wearing a cook's hat and white apron. A cigarette drooped from his thick lips. Sandy was a tall, thin black man with long arms, a full gray beard, and a sweet smile. When he saw me his dark eyes brightened. "Looking for your girlfriend, Tommy?" he said, affecting an Irish brogue that amused him more than it amused me. The word *girlfriend* sliced a tiny bit off my heart. As he laughed, he assembled the Professor's lunch, a plate of fried chicken, mashed potatoes, and overcooked green beans, all from the steaming trays.

The plate he held had green trim around the edge and MID-
LOTHIAN COUNTRY CLUB and an M fashioned from golf clubs in
the center. He poured brown gravy over the potatoes, covered
the dish with a metal top, and spun it over to me.

"Don't forget the bread," he said, still smiling. "The Professor
likes his bread and butter." Then he leaned forward and asked,
"You making any progress with Miss Farrell, Tommy? Or are
you just having wet dreams?"

A few of the kitchen help overheard him and broke up
laughing.

I pulled several slices from the loaf of white bread and tossed
them on top of the metal cover, picked up the butter, took
kitchen silverware from the bin, and a white monogrammed
cloth napkin from the stack. Then I headed out the back door,
but before I left I turned around and gave them all the finger.

I walked back the way I had come, hoping that Clare would
be poolside again, but the women sunbathers had retreated to the
locker room to dress for lunch, leaving only a few teenagers to
horse around, cannonballing off the high dive now that there
were no adults to stop them.

The members' kids were okay for the most part; over the
years I had caddied for them in father-son events and
mother-daughter tournaments. I even had a favorite—Valerie
Driscoll, the teenage daughter of Dr. Driscoll, who had just lost
his wife to polio.

The year before Mrs. Driscoll got sick, I had caddied for her
when she won the club championship. When she was presented
the ladies' trophy on the first tee, she had singled me out to the
crowd of members, saying that she would never have won if she
hadn't had Tommy O'Shea picking her clubs, reading her putts,
looping for her. It was the greatest day I had ever had as a caddie.

After she died in the iron lung, Doc Driscoll had sent Valerie back east to prep school. I hadn't seen Val in months, but as I walked past the pool, she jumped up from a chaise where she was playing hearts with a handful of girls.

"Tommy, hi, I'm home," she called out and came over to me, wrapping herself in a bright green and white country-club beach towel as she ran.

I rested the Professor's plate of food on top of the wide hedge and smiled as she approached. I always thought of members' kids as just being kids, but I saw that Valerie had grown up that winter. She was almost my height. What had changed most about her, I realized, was her face. At the end of last summer, it had just been sweet and round. Now that she had matured, she resembled her mother in a haunting and heartbreaking way. Her thick blond hair was cut short in a pageboy that curled against her cheeks, and her bright brown eyes sparkled in the sun.

"You've grown like a tree, Driscoll," I said as she came closer.

"Is that what you think I look like?" She wrinkled her nose in the same way her mother had whenever she misplayed a shot.

"A pretty young sapling," I added quickly.

She rolled her eyes. And then she did something extraordinary: she uncurled the long towel from her body, stood up on tiptoe, and spun around, as if doing a ballet move, but actually showing herself off.

It was obvious that she had grown up.

Though I wished that Clare would come by and see us chatting, I knew it wouldn't be good for me to get caught gawking at a member's daughter.

"Great to see you, Val," I said, picking up the plate of food, backing away.

She made a face again. "I'm taking up golf," she announced.

"That's what you said last summer, Driscoll." I started down the path.

"I'm serious," she declared, following me on her side of the low hedge. "Will you caddie for me?"

"I'll caddie for you and your dad anytime." I tossed back another smile as I kept walking. As I reached the end of the pool and went along the clubhouse's circular drive, I looked around. Valerie Driscoll was still standing there wrapped in her big country-club towel, still watching me. Her blond hair sparkled in the bright summer sun. I stepped over the concrete wall and went down the path to the caddie shack, down to the world where I belonged.

6

MONDAY WAS CADDIE DAY AT THE CLUB, WHEN THE BAG RATS played golf. That summer, McClain and I had a game on Mondays, unless he was playing away in a pro-member, and then I was usually caddying for Red Denison, our pro.

McClain could play anytime, but he preferred to play with me. "I like taking your money, O'Shea," he always said.

Also, he knew about my thing for Clare, so he'd add something about using his winnings to take her out.

No matter what he said, I never reacted, and that pissed him off. I never said a word even though there was a lot I could have told him, especially about what his mother thought of his dating the country-club help. Caddying one Wednesday morning, I had heard his mother tell Mrs. Bradshaw, "Once he gets back to school he'll meet some nice girls and that will be the end of this Farrell child." Walking behind them, I heard Madge Bradshaw say nicely, "Well, Clare did earn a scholarship to Smith College. And she is a lovely young girl."

"Oh, Madge, I'm not talking about being smart or pretty." In a lower voice she added, "You do know, she's a mackerel snapper."

At our Monday game, Drew teed up on the first hole and stepped away from his ball. He swung the club loosely, warming up, smiling, looking like he was on the top of his world, while waiting for the caddies ahead of us on the fairway to play their second shots.

McClain always dressed up when he played, even on Caddie Day. On this overcast morning he wore light-gray pants, white buck golf shoes, and a long-sleeve linen shirt. Clothes meant a lot to him; as he said to me more than once, "Dress like a hacker and you'll play like one."

I stepped away and watched him loosen up. He was tall and slim with fair skin, a quick smile, and bright, perfect, white teeth. When he wanted to, he could be charming and friendly with anyone. I saw how the members' wives watched him as he walked by, saw how their eyes lingered.

Looking back, I now realize the reason he played with me was that he needed a friend. Drew was a kid frightened by his parents and the future they had planned for him. I also realize that Clare must have understood something of that, for she was drawn to him because he was so afraid. It is a powerful emotion, a woman's need to take care of someone.

But in 1946, when I was eighteen, all I knew was that he was a helluva player, better than our pro, and to beat him on any given round I had to catch a few breaks and make some putts. Still, I couldn't resist taking him on. I kept challenging him because I needed to beat him, to prove that while I was a farmer's boy from the other side of the road, I was as good a golfer as any member's kid. Of course, the fact that he was dating "my girl" also had something to do with it.

"Looking for a caddie?"

Glancing up, I saw Harrison Cornell. He was wearing the same strange outfit as he had worn the day before, only he hadn't shaved. When he smiled, his teeth flashed in his stubbled face.

Drew looked at me. He hadn't seen Cornell arrive the day before, though I thought the word might have circulated through the men's bar and locker room about how this new caddie had turned Doc Frazier's game around.

I introduced them, and Cornell brightened at the mention of Drew's name. "I've heard all about you," he declared, reaching to shake Drew's hand.

"From whom?" Drew asked, surprised.

Cornell nodded my way. "Your good friend here."

"You don't say." Drew shook his head, stepped up to his ball, and said, "Okay, O'Shea, two bucks Nassau. One press a side. That's your poison, right?"

Nassau was our usual game, betting two dollars on the front side, two dollars on the back side, and two dollars for eighteen. It started to get expensive when a press was added, doubling the bet.

As Drew set his feet and looked down the fairway, Cornell moved beside me and whispered, "Take a deep breath." The smile was gone from his face.

On the tee, Drew took another practice swing.

I took a deep breath.

"Another," Cornell whispered. "Slower, deeper, and shake out your arms."

Thinking of how he had helped Frazier's game the day before, I followed his advice and felt the tension leaving my shoulders. As I did, Drew swung fast and hard and hit a hook deep into the long rough down the left side of the fairway. He had hit his drive a little more than two hundred yards.

McClain banged the driver's head on the wooden marker as he walked off the tee. Then he stepped over to his bag and slammed his driver into it, swearing all the while.

I moved to the tee, taking my time, breathing deeply. Behind me, I heard Cornell say to Drew, "Walter Hagen had the best mind-set in the game when it came to missed shots. Hagen always knew he was going to miss a few, so it never bothered him when he knocked a drive into the rough." He paused. "Good advice, don't you think?"

I glanced over. Drew was staring at the caddie as if Cornell had said something obscene. Smiling, I called over to Cornell, making a joke at McClain's expense, "That's why everyone thinks Drew is another Hagen; he's never in the fairway."

It always amused me to see Drew pissed off, and that relaxed me even more. My drive on the first tee showed it. I hit a perfect one. The ball carried 265 and down the center of the fairway.

When I walked back to my bag, I saw that Cornell had already swung it onto his shoulder.

"I can't afford a caddie," I told him.

Cornell waved me off, saying that he had nothing else to do. Then he nodded toward Drew and said that he wanted to see the Yalie play. I wasn't surprised at that. Everyone at the club stopped to watch Drew hit a ball.

Drew was charging down the fairway, headed for his drive in the deep rough. Behind him was little Rich Fugener, carrying his bag. Drew always had a caddie, even on Caddie Day.

"I looped for his folks yesterday afternoon," Cornell said, walking beside me. "Lovely people."

I didn't say anything. I knew that Cornell had something to tell me. I heard it in his voice.

"Who's this girlfriend of his?" Cornell asked next.

"You mean Clare? His old lady was talking about her?" I asked, surprised.

"Clare Farrell, that's right," Cornell answered, "A mackerel snapper, I gathered."

"Aren't we all," I answered.

We reached the crest of the rise and paused to let Drew play his shot from the deep rough. Ahead, I saw my ball safely in the middle of the fairway, leaving me a mid-iron to the two-tier first green.

"Do you know her?" Cornell asked, but before I could answer, he said quickly, "Of course you would, working here. I'm told, as you Americans say, she's a hot tomato."

I busied myself flipping through my irons as if trying to pick a club. I felt Cornell's eyes on me. My guess was that the Professor had been talking.

"She attends Smith College, I believe."

"You know a lot, Cornell. You don't need to quiz me." I turned to watch Drew play out of the long grass.

Cornell was also watching Drew, and as he did, he took out a cigarette and commented, "The Haig had a great routine when he played from the rough. If it was a difficult shot he'd walk right up and play the ball, but when he had a shot that looked tough from the gallery, but really wasn't, he'd ham it up, move around, fret over the lie, get everyone thinking he was dead, and then, of course, he'd hit a great recovery and the gallery would go crazy." Cornell nodded toward Drew. "Is that what your boy is doing?"

"He's not my boy," I answered, and already I was thinking that if Drew was in the long grass, I had the hole won.

"You better not be thinking you have the hole won," Cornell said, standing beside me.

"You think he's going to make it out of that cabbage?"

Cornell shook his head as if he had heard all this before.

"When you're playing match, you need to keep pressing."

Across the fairway, Drew pulled a club and set himself to play.

"He's going for it," I said with some relief, knowing that there was no way he could manage that shot.

Drew widened his stance and shortened his grip. He had a bad lie and a bad stance, and even if the ball had the length, it was likely that he'd catch one of the two side bunkers guarding the green.

Drew took a half dozen more practice swings, cutting through the long grass that kept catching the hosel of the club.

When he played the iron, he drove hard with his left arm and did not turn the club over or finish the shot. He fell back from the simple force of his swing as we might see happen to someone like Tiger Woods, hitting from the heather at the British Open.

It was a superb shot. The ball cleared the rough, rose perfectly into the bright sky. From the moment it was hit, I knew he would reach the green; the only question was whether the ball had come out too hot and would run across the putting surface and into the thick grass beyond the green. But somehow he had hit the shot high enough that when it landed on the front tier of the green, it bounced into the rise, checked up, and rolled to a stop below the flag, within ten feet of the cup.

"Dammit!" I said.

Cornell stuck the cigarette into his mouth so that he could applaud Drew's recovery. Drew raised his club in recognition of Cornell's applause, and Cornell lifted his straw hat to him and tipped it back.

"Now that's a shot," Cornell declared.

I walked ahead to my ball, looking toward the green and thinking of which club to play. I needed to get inside Drew's ball. The first hole at Midlothian is not difficult. It's member-friendly, as we say around country clubs. Two green side bunkers clamp the sides and leave the approach wide open. Anyone with a decent drive and a good mid-iron is putting for a birdie.

Cornell swung my bag off his shoulder. I had a dozen clubs in my bag, all of them discarded by members, not one of them matching.

"You have a wooden-shafted blade putter," Cornell said approvingly. "Just like Bobby Locke."

"Who's he?" I asked, staring at my irons and thinking that I might hit a hard 8 and let the ball land in the front portion and roll up to the pin on the back half of the green.

"Bobby Locke's the best putter in the world. A South African. You'll be hearing plenty about him once he comes over to play the tour. He says he learned how to putt from Hagen back in thirty-seven, when the Haig played exhibitions in South Africa."

Cornell paused and looked at my ball, and then at the club in my hand. I was swinging the 8 iron, getting a feel for the shot. When our eyes met, I told him how I was going to play it. He nodded slowly, thoughtfully. Like any good caddie, he knew better than to cast doubt in my mind by saying that I had the wrong club and was playing the wrong shot. But he couldn't contain himself.

"What about hitting a seven?" He pushed his panama up on his forehead, as if to give himself a better view of the target. "The crew watered this morning. The greens are soft. Your eight might check up on you, like it did your boy McClain's ball."

I didn't see the groundskeepers watering, I told him.

"They did, around five a.m."

"You were here at five?"

Shrugging, Cornell said that he had never left the course. The Professor had let him sleep in the caddie shack, stretched out on one of the benches.

"I'm a little low on funds," he explained. "My discharge pay hasn't caught up with me." He went back to telling me which club I should hit.

His point was that it was a better percentage shot to finesse a 7 than to hit a hard 8. I'm sure he didn't say "finesse" back in the forties, but that's what he meant. I stared at the green where Drew had already arrived and was waiting for me to play up.

"Look," said Cornell, pointing at my ball. "Feel around it with the club. See how soft the lie is? Hit the seven and take a divot and you'll get backspin; the ball will hold."

I studied the shot, the lie, and looked again at the green. "Okay." I pulled the 7 and played the shot, driving down on the ball and taking a slab of soft wet fairway. I hit a great shot. High and dead on the stick, it landed two yards beyond the pin and spun back to the cup, leaving me a tap-in for my birdie. By the time Cornell and I walked up to the green, Drew had missed his putt and conceded mine. He was one down walking to the par-3, second hole.

On the second tee, Cornell handed me the 4 wood. That summer I had been hitting a strong 3 iron into the two-hundred-yard hole, hitting a draw that would land short of the green, on the high right side of the fairway, then cascade down the slope and onto the putting surface. The whole length of the hole fell away from the tee, but the green itself sloped from back to front, and, as we know, it's always better to be below the cup and putting uphill. So, on this hole, I wanted to come up short.

I usually played late in the day when the wind was down in that tight corner of the course. And this is also important to know about my game: I hit my long irons low, which gave me more distance than most players got, and my ball had a lot of topspin. Those were the days when balls were made of rubber thread wrapped around a rubber core and the ball would run.

I took the 4 wood from Harrison and waited for him to explain his thinking. If I caught the wood on its screws, I knew, I'd fly the green and end up in the bunker or in the long grass behind the hole.

"Play it way forward off your left foot," Cornell instructed quietly. "Open your stance and weaken your left hand. Play a big fade. And do this: pick a spot about five yards in front of you, and in the direction you want to hit the ball. Focus on that spot and don't look up. Keep it simple." With that, he moved my bag away and stepped to the far side of the tee markers.

Drew was standing by the ball washer, watching the two of us, his face all screwed up. Just seeing his confusion made me feel a lot better, and I did what Cornell had said, aimed at a spot five yards in front of the tee; I stared at it and not at the green, and hit a little 4-wood fade that carried onto the left side of the green, landed softly, and spun to a stop below the flag, leaving me an uphill fifteen-footer that I managed to make. Drew pressed his shot to get inside mine and pulled it left into the patch of thick straw-grass. It took him two shots to get out of the rough. He was two down to me in the match as we headed for the third tee.

7

"WHAT'S WITH THIS GUY?" DREW ASKED ME THE FIRST CHANCE HE got, on the next tee. Cornell and little Fugener had gone ahead, up the rise to the forecaddie position. With my birdie on two, I still had the honors, and I stood back from the markers and swung the club, thinking of what Cornell had told me about relaxing before teeing off. At eighteen years of age, I found that surprisingly hard to do.

The problem was that I knew I couldn't outdrive McClain, and I couldn't keep myself from pressing on my drives. Also, I knew it was placement on three that mattered, not distance, but when you're a kid all you want to do is bang the ball.

Placement on three meant that I wanted to keep myself on the high left side of the fairway and get it out about 250 so that I'd have a view of the green. The third fairway fell off dramatically to the right on the other side of the ridge, funneling down into the only fairway bunker on that hole, 253 yards from the tee on the right side. All the trouble on number three was to the right, unless you hit a big hook and knocked it out-of-bounds and into the backyards of the members who had homes along the left length of the fairway.

Drew never worried about placing his ball. He could unleash a drive far enough that he took the bunker out of play and had only a short iron for his second shot into the green.

Usually Drew never paid much attention to whoever was caddying. But standing on the tee, getting ready to play, I could tell by his tone that Cornell was bugging him.

"I don't know much about him," I said. I repeated what the Professor had told me, then summarized how he had turned Doc Frazier's game around in eighteen holes. That was every caddie's dream scenario. We all lived the fantasy that we could improve our player's game just by looping for him, that we had the innate wisdom, based on hundreds of rounds, to cure any member's bad habits and turn a hacker into a player.

"What did you tell him about me?" Drew wanted to know.

"I told him you were an asshole," I said and teed up my ball.

Drew swore back at me and I smiled and hitched up my left pants leg, as I saw all the good players do so that the fabric wouldn't tug on the backswing. I looked down the fairway and, as Cornell had instructed, picked a spot a half-dozen yards ahead of me and focused my attention on it. Years later I would learn how Chicago home pro Jack Grout had taught Jack Nicklaus the same trick, but that summer of 1946 it was Cornell who taught me, as well as almost every member of the club, that simple technique to establish the correct ball-flight line.

"Oh, also, he told me that Clare Farrell was too good for you." I said that as an afterthought, and in doing so I broke my concentration and hit a bad slice that cleared the ridge, but then went hard right and deep into the rough, way off the fairway.

"Another of your educated fades," McClain needled as he

stepped over to drive. I had used that phrase once before with Drew, when I cut a 6 iron into the fifteen green and left myself a five-foot birdie putt. I didn't tell Drew that I had mis-hit that shot; we never admitted mistakes to each other.

Drew's drive found the fairway and was long enough, straight enough, and high enough on the left side that he could see the green. From where my ball had landed, short of the bunker and deep in the rough, I was playing blind. Cornell had already reached my drive when I tramped up to him through the thick rough. I slid my wood into the bag and stared down at the ball, nestled in the long grass.

"I'm lucky I found it," Cornell answered, sighing in a way that suggested caddying for me was nothing but trouble. "That was the most god-awful swing I've seen you make, Tommy," he declared.

"Thanks," I said, trying for enough sarcasm to make him back off.

But he wouldn't.

"You swung that wood like you were back on your farm cutting hay," he said next.

"Hey, no one is forcing you to loop for me." I jerked the 5 iron out of the bag.

"What are you doing?" Cornell asked, sounding curious.

"I'm playing my five." I nodded toward the ridge beyond the bunker. "If I can get the ball up onto the rise, it will run halfway to the green."

"No, don't." Cornell reached into the bag for my wedge, and with his other hand still holding his cigarette, he gestured toward the fairway. "Play it out there safe." He waved again with the cigarette, letting a thin curl of smoke circle in the still air. "Think about it for a minute," he instructed. "It's a poor percentage shot to hit from the thick rough—uphill and over the bunker. I don't think you're strong enough to wrestle the ball out of this grass."

Of course, today we're used to seeing pros on television hacking the ball out of deep rough and making spectacular shots, but in 1946, I wasn't Hogan or Porky Oliver—two of the tour's stronger players—and I didn't have the muscle mass or the equipment to whack the ball from the weeds. This was decades before pros bulked up, long before technology changed the game and gave everyone recovery clubs. Cornell was right. I was being dumb and reckless trying to hit the mid-iron.

"You've got McClain two down, Tommy. Let's make par. He'd have to birdie to win."

"That's not what the Haig would do," I told Cornell. "He wouldn't play it safe."

That stopped Cornell. He took a long drag on his cigarette and then nodded. "You're right. He wouldn't play it safe. He'd go for the green." And then he asked an odd question: "Did you ever play with hickory clubs?"

I shook my head, puzzled by his question.

"It's a different game with hickory; it's harder, really. Hagen played with hickory most of his life, as did Bobby Jones. Golf was a better game, I'd say, with hickory clubs. It was a tougher game."

"It's tough enough as it is now, with steel."

"Playing with hickory, the problem was torsion. The clubface would twist naturally away on the backswing, then twist again on the downswing. It took perfect timing to be square at impact and Hagen's roundabout swing worked best with hickory." Cornell paused for a moment, then added, "You should learn how to play with hickory, Tommy. It will improve your game."

He looked down at the ball again and gestured toward the lie.

"Playing from here, Hagen would use a long iron, what they

called in the age of hickory a mashie iron; he'd hit the green, you can be sure." Then he smiled that warm smile of his and said simply, "But you're no Walter Hagen. And you're not playing hickory-shaft clubs." He handed me the wedge and pulled the bag away, instructing, "Hit your ball into the fairway and let's see if we can salvage something from getting yourself into all this trouble."

I took the wedge and played the ball out safely. I was still away. Drew had climbed the slope and was standing beside his ball, waiting for me to hit again.

Cornell gave me the 8 iron. I still couldn't see the green from where I stood in the fairway, but I had caddied enough times to know, from the tips of the trees behind the hole, trees that shaded the fourth tee, just where to aim the 8 iron. Cornell reminded me to take my time, telling me that I had plenty of club. I followed his instructions and hit a beauty. Without seeing the green or even the flag, I knocked the ball within five feet of the cup. Once again Drew had to bear down to get inside of me.

He didn't. He pressed on his short 9 iron into the small green and the ball came out hot and flew over the back edge, leaving him a fast downhill chip that he misplayed and hit too hard. He had a ten-footer coming back, which he made.

With Cornell telling me to play my uphill putt three inches to the high side, and to imagine hitting the ball past the hole, I drilled it dead center. The ball chunked in with that familiar winning sound that all golfers love to hear. Drew stormed ahead of me, still two down, heading for the fourth tee.

We played the next two par-4s with matching pars and then on six, a long par-4 that borders 147th Street, I knocked my 4 wood second shot into the left green side bunker and misplayed my sand wedge, leaving my ball short of the putting surface. Next I tried to get cute and play a Texas wedge off the thick fringe that had been watered overnight and I left the putt way short. I two putted to lose the hole.

On the seventh, the longest par-5 on the course, Drew would let it all hang out and try to carry the bunker on the left side of the fairway. Doing that, we both knew he could reach the green in two and be putting for an eagle. The hole is forgiving in that on both sides the rough is short, and in 1946 there was little tree trouble. It was a tempting hole for big hitters; they all felt that they could risk missing the fairway just to get some distance off the tee.

The shot for me, always, was to aim for the left edge of the fairway and work the ball left to right, which was my natural swing. The only problem was that it was the low side of the fairway and water drained down into that shallow trough. I wouldn't get much roll, especially when the grounds crew had had sprinklers on all night. McClain drew the ball so that if his drive landed on the high right side and got a good kick off the ridge, it would run another twenty yards.

While Drew teed off, I walked to the water fountain in the cluster of trees behind the halfway house and Cornell followed me. While I was drinking, he told me to slow down my game.

"You're playing too fast," he said, lowering his voice. "It's not your natural tempo." He nodded toward McClain, standing on the tee. "He needs to play fast. That's his rhythm, not yours. Take your time between shots. Walk slower." Again he nodded toward Drew. "Go at your own speed and you'll unnerve your young friend."

"Are you playing or what, O'Shea?" McClain shouted over at me, as if on cue.

Cornell smiled, swung my bag onto his shoulder, and ambled over to the tee.

Drew was tapping his driver head on the wooden tee marker when I moved up to stand beside him. His drive had gone just where I'd thought it would.

The tees at Midlothian were old-fashioned: small, high platforms that rose above the fairways. They were ministages that gave a player a sense of dominance over the holes. On the par-5s, a player would naturally reach for the driver and go for distance.

I pulled my driver from the bag and Cornell said, "I noticed this back on one. Where did you get it?"

"From an assistant pro who left the club last year."

"It's a George Izett club," he said.

"The shaft is true-tempered and stiff. The weight is fourteen ounces," I told him before he could ask. "The loft is eight degrees."

"That's too much club for you. You're not built to be swinging a telephone pole." He slipped it back into the bag. "Hit the spoon," he instructed.

"I can't clear the bunkers." I had never hit a 3 wood off the tee at seven. I looked down the hole. The hole was wide open with only a few trees on the left and right sides. I saw the flag in the distance, tucked behind several bunkers; beyond the green was a row of tall elms that guarded the driving range on the other side of the tree line.

Ignoring my comment, Cornell continued, pointing down the fairway. "Aim for that low spot to the left of the bunker."

He was talking about hitting the 3 wood 230 into an area marked ground under repair. There had been drainage problems at that spot for several weeks and the grounds crew had roped off a patch of fairway the size of a baseball diamond.

"Drop it in the middle of that swamp," Cornell said, handing me the club.

I didn't protest. After the second hole, I had decided to play golf his way. I teed up my ball and hit a good 3 wood. The ball landed in the middle of the diamond and stuck in the mud.

Drew charged off the tee, laughing at both of us, and headed for his drive fifty yards beyond my ball. Coming off the tee, Cornell fell into step with me, then slowed his pace so that I had to walk slower.

"Okay, what gives?" I asked when McClain was out of hearing.

"You're in ground under repair. You get to move the ball. You get a good lie and you hit the 2 wood. A good wood and you're on or close. Drew's going to hit a 4 wood or maybe a 1 iron. Either way, if you nail your shot, he'll press."

When we reached my drive, Cornell walked into the soggy ground under repair, plucked up my ball, and tossed it to me on the higher, dry fairway. He then went farther down the fairway to a spot where he could clearly see the green. I dropped the ball three times and it kept rolling back into the depression. Finally I placed it carefully, giving myself a lie that was good enough to use the 2 wood.

I couldn't see the flag but I knew, from the elms behind, where the green was, and I nailed my shot. My ball moved naturally from left to right, hit on the downward slope of the fairway, and kicked forward. I knew it was there even before Cornell signaled me that I had hit it onto the green.

I walked up the ridge as Drew played his second shot. He pressed a 4 wood trying to match my second shot and pulled the ball way left, knocking it into the bushes beside the service road behind the eighth tee. When he attempted to close down a 5 iron and hit the ball out of the bushes, he came up short of the green. I two-putted to win the hole with a birdie and was back to two up.

The eighth hole at Midlothian at the time was a long, two-hundred-plus par-3, which I don't think I ever birdied in all the years I caddied at the club. Rarely did I even make the green, guarded as it was by a long thin bunker in front and two shallow ones on each side.

"I'm pressing you, O'Shea," Drew declared as he walked toward the 8th tee. Now I had to halve or win one of the last two holes to win the front side and the press.

"Don't play for the green," Cornell advised after I told him I always hit a 4 wood.

He gave me the 4 iron and told me to aim for the right bunker. I knew I didn't have enough club to reach the sand. The fairway was bordered on the right by a creek that gave the hole its name, Brookside, though, in truth, the narrow, dry creek rarely came into play.

"You've got a shot into the green," Cornell said, pointing to the opening to the right side of the fairway. "The flag is cut in the back; there's plenty of room to play with." I hit the 4 iron where he suggested and it rolled safely to a stop fifty yards short and to the far right side. It wasn't even close to the green.

"Never up, never in," Drew called out, listening to Cornell and me going on about my strategy for the hole. He pulled out his 4 wood and hit a high draw that flew over the top of the front bunker, landed, and held the green. He was two down, but he could easily win the hole. Walking up the fairway, I saw that Drew had a twenty-footer for a birdie.

"I'll have to give him this one," I told Cornell.

"Don't talk that way," Cornell snapped. "You've got a great short game. Play the ball like Jim Barnes."

"Who's he?" I asked, laughing. Cornell had named another golfer I had never heard of.

"You don't know the first thing about this game," Cornell

said. "I'm talking about 'Long Jim' Barnes. He got his nickname from being tall and for his distance off the tee. He won the PGA a couple of times, the British Open, and the U.S. Open. He also had a great short game. Let me show you how he'd play this approach shot of yours."

When we reached my ball, Cornell slipped my bag off his shoulder and pulled out the 9 iron.

"What you want to do, lad, is hit an abbreviated shot," he explained, demonstrating. "Keep your hands straight and don't break your wrists. You'll get a high trajectory with this nine; it has about forty-five degrees of loft. You'll get very little spin." He looked at the green, then handed me the club and added, "I'll walk this distance off to give you time to practice."

With that, he went striding to the pin, counting his paces. When he reached the flag staff, he turned and came directly back to my ball, still counting.

"You're looking at sixty-one yards." He moved the bag away to give me room. "Turn your feet toward the target," he instructed. "Remember, you won't manage any roll, so fly it to the flag. The ball will check. Hit it now, straightaway."

Drew was pacing on the green and waiting for me to play. Cornell was right. It threw McClain off his game when I took so much time.

I took another few swings, with Cornell reminding me to use just my arms. I opened my stance and played the shot without breaking my wrists. The ball sailed high, then dropped down short of the flag and checked up. Cornell grabbed the thick divot and replaced it and we headed for the green. From twenty yards away I saw that I had stymied Drew.

Today, we think of a player being stymied only by a rock or a tree, but until 1951, when the USGA changed the rule, a ball on a green couldn't be marked or moved and a player had to play around his opponent's ball. I had Drew stymied. My ball was blocking his line.

"You're away," I said, smiling, as I stepped onto the putting surface. I took my blade putter from Cornell as Fugener walked up and pulled the bamboo flag pole.

Drew swore at being stymied, then tried to make his twenty-footer. To miss my ball, however, he needed to putt two feet wide of the cup, leaving himself another putt for par. I drilled my three-footer—as Cornell would say, the putt to make when it mattered—into the back of the cup, halving the hole and winning the front side.

8

WE BOTH HAD PARS ON NINE, AND AS WE WALKED OVER TO TEN
tee Cornell took me aside and ratcheted up his instructions.

"Match-play golf is not just about working the ball," he said.
"It's about working your opponent. You've got to get McClain
thinking about other things besides golf. Work on him. There
was this pro last year out in California who hired a guy to stand
up on the green and jingle change in his pocket whenever his
opponent putted."

"That's unfair."

"Well, the other pros got back at him. They went out and
hired their own heckler who blew his nose with a honk whenever this guy putted. What you've got to learn is how to needle
your buddy—in a nice, gentlemanly way, of course." He glanced
over at me, smiling, and added, "McClain's been on you all the
front side. Let's give our chap a little back and have some fun.
Here's what Mangrum would do. He'd stand on the tee just in
the front corner of the player's vision and when the guy started

his backswing, Mangrum would shift his legs. That simple movement would catch the player's eye and throw off his swing. Try it."

And I did.

Teeing off, McClain cut across the ball and hit a slice into the long rough on the right side of the fairway.

"What the hell are you doing, O'Shea?"

"Nothing," I said, heading to the fairway.

"You moved."

"I was standing ten feet away from you," I said and kept walking. Beside me, Cornell lowered his head to keep Drew from seeing his grin.

I won the tenth and then Drew pulled himself together. He stopped talking to us and charged from shot to shot. The faster he played, the slower I played. On fourteen he got back at me.

Fourteen at the time was the shortest par-4 on the course, a little over three hundred yards. There was no fairway water on the hole as there is today; instead, it was a tight dogleg to the right with a large back-to-front sloping green. If you hit a high ball, you could cut the corner, go over the trees, and with a little luck drive the green, but you needed to get the ball up fast off the tee. Drew could play that shot; I had done it, but rarely.

I still had the honors on fourteen and I teed up on the left edge of the markers to play my fade, and keep my ball left of the long, thin fairway bunker that was two hundred out from the tee, nestled in a long funnel of trees.

"Don't cut it too close, Tommy. Remember what you did a couple of weeks ago?" McClain said it nicely, as if he were just trying to be helpful, but we both knew what he was doing.

I remembered immediately how I had cut the ball too close to the big elm and it had clipped a branch. The ball had dropped straight down into the rough and it had taken me three to reach the green. That thought was still in my mind as I swung and I overcompensated; hit a quick duck hook that barely made it to the bottom of the hill, where the ball dived into the rough.

"Gee, you shouldn't listen to me," Drew said, grinning. He teed up and hit a fabulous drive over the tops of the trees. It would be on the green or close to it, I realized, walking off the tee. I didn't say a word to Drew, didn't even congratulate him on his drive.

Cornell also kept quiet until we were within yards of my drive, and then he started to talk immediately, as if he were in the middle of a lecture.

"You've got to keep yourself loose, Tommy. Don't think about beating him; think that you're just playing a game for fun. Talk to yourself. Talk to the ball. Use your caddie-yard crap-shooting jargon. Say, 'C'mon, be Little Joe from Kokomo,' or, 'Baby needs new shoes.' Roll those dice. Play that shot with the same sort of loosey-goosey rhythm you have down behind the handball court when you're shooting dice. You get that mind-set and you've got a Maginot Line McClain can't dent with all his needling."

"How the hell do I do that?" I wanted to know.

Cornell didn't say anything for a moment. We had reached my ball and the lie wasn't as bad as I had expected. I knew I could play a 4 wood and get it out and perhaps even reach the green, which was two hundred yards away. Drew's ball was visible in the middle of the fairway; he had a soft wedge to the flag cut on the top back edge of the sloping green.

"What you need to do on this shot, and every shot you play, is stop thinking." Cornell sounded annoyed with me. "Don't think of where Drew's ball is; don't think of the match. If you think of anything, think of the last great shot you made, or of something warm and sweet in your memory. Keep so you're not thinking of hitting out of this rough, but just that you're making another easy swing with a four wood, or that you're only banging balls out on the range."

He pulled the bag away so that I could play, adding, "Hit the ball the way you do when you sneak out here at dusk and play a few holes. Let it all hang out, as you Americans say."

I did what Cornell told me. I didn't press the wood. I didn't care if I reached the green or not, and the ball came out as sweet as soft butter. I played for my fade and the ball reached the front left edge of the green and spun up to the flag, curling to a stop six feet below the cup.

"Nice" was all Cornell said, swinging my bag onto his shoulder as he went striding off, walking back out onto the fairway and toward the green. I was feeling great. There was nothing in the world quite as sweet as a golf shot well hit.

"Nice" I exclaimed, laughing. "Sheeit! That's a beauty."

"Don't broadcast it, Tommy," Cornell said, never breaking stride. "McClain knows your game, but when you're playing off this course, playing where no one knows you, don't draw attention to your great swings. Like I said, golf is all mental, and if you act like all your swings are as good as this one, then they'll begin to believe that you're better than they are."

Before Cornell and I reached Drew's ball, he had played his shot. It came up short, didn't even make the slope of the green, and rolled back down the hill. Drew was rushing every shot, as if he just wanted the match to be over. I had him four down going into fifteen. As he got more frustrated, I got calmer. I was swinging the club better, making putts. Golf had never seemed so easy.

Drew three-putted number fifteen, losing another hole. We played the final three holes mostly in silence. He was too upset with himself even to care about whether he won or lost. On the medal side, I finished with a seventy-four, three over par; Drew ballooned to an eighty-two. It was the worst round he had ever played against me, the worst round he had played at Midlothian since he was thirteen years old.

We walked off the eighteenth green together, and I wanted to ride him more about the round, but something told me to keep quiet. I knew that he wouldn't be as accepting as I always was on those losing Mondays. He pulled out his wallet as we walked to the clubhouse and counted out my winnings. He didn't even bother to swear at me as he handed over his money; that's how furious he was.

"You know what Hagen always said," I said, trying to be friendly but not being able to walk away without sticking it to him.

"Don't forget to stop and smell the roses," Cornell said, coming up behind me.

I handed Cornell my putter and slipped the money into my pocket, figuring that later I'd split my winnings with him. We both knew that he was the one who'd won the match for me.

"We'll see if Hagen is still singing his song after he plays against me," Drew snapped.

"Who says you're playing with Hagen?" I asked.

"I'm the club champ, right?" Drew started to walk away, heading to the men's locker room, and then added, "And my old man's invited him to play. It's a done deal." He smiled sarcastically at me. "That's okay, Tommy. You can caddie for me."

Cornell and I stood at the top of the eighteenth green as Drew turned away and walked into the men's locker room, letting the screen door slam behind him.

"One of the most disagreeable sights in the world is watching a wealthy person without manners," Cornell commented.

"He's just upset that he lost to me. That hardly ever happens," I said, defending him.

"Let me tell you, Tommy," Cornell replied, still looking after Drew. "McClain's daddy may be able to set up this match, but your buddy is no match for the Haig."

"Who is?"

Cornell looked my way as he started to walk off the course. "You are."

9

HARRISON'S FIRST WEEKS AT THE COUNTRY CLUB TELL THE STORY of the summer. Soon everyone had something to say, it seemed, about how he had improved their game. They came to see his presence on the golf course as almost magical.

The truth was, he did help some of our leading hackers. The Professor sent him out with the most miserable of them, and they returned all aglow, having shot their best round that year; hell, their best round ever. I don't know how he did it. He wasn't telling them anything more than what Red told them in his lessons or what was in the instructional books or golf magazines.

For example, with old man Alexander, who always collapsed his left arm on the backswing and popped up drives, getting no distance at all, Cornell had him widen his stance and stay that way all through the swing. With good players, like Alex Peterson, who had won the men's club championship in 1942 and played to an 8 handicap, Cornell got him hitting knockdown shots on tight holes by having him shift his weight and play the ball back in his stance.

It was as simple as that. Any seasoned caddie would have known what to tell these players; Cornell's secret was that he got the members believing in what he had to say. They liked him, and if he didn't show up for a few days, everyone would start wondering where he was.

"Who is this guy? It's all I hear about when I'm waiting on tables," Clare told me shortly after Cornell's arrival. "Harrison said this. Harrison did that."

It was late evening and I was on the course, playing a few holes, when I spotted Clare walking across the course, headed home from work. That summer her family had moved into the new development built on the old Purdue farm just beyond our place. She was walking across thirteen to 147th Street as I was teeing off.

I told her what little I knew, leaving out how he had helped me beat Drew. I told her how he had come to Midlothian to caddie in the exhibition and that he knew Walter Hagen.

"Who's Walter Hagen?" she asked.

I had to laugh. Here she worked at the country club where Hagen had won his first Open, and where everyone talked golf constantly, and she didn't know or care about the game.

Clare took off her shoes and walked with me barefoot down the fairway, still in her black-and-white waitress dress that looked like a Catholic-school uniform. She was holding her hair up with one hand so that her neck could catch the cool breeze of evening. Just looking at her, I got a lump in my throat.

I told her how Hagen had played at Midlothian in 1914, when he was a kid of twenty-one. The story was that he had shocked everyone by changing his clothes in the clubhouse locker room.

"What's shocking about that?" she asked.

"Back then, golf pros were thought of as no better than cad-dies. They made a living from golf and were not considered gentlemen and therefore not allowed into the members' locker room. Newspapers referred to a pro only by his last name, and amateurs like Chick Evans were listed as Mr. Evans."

By then we'd reached my drive and I pulled out a 3 wood and drew the ball around the elbow of the dogleg. It bounced for-ward another ten yards on the smooth fairway grass, leaving me a short iron to the green. I was hoping Clare would be impressed, but of course she had no idea what a well-played golf shot looked like. Listening to my Hagen story, what interested her was not that he'd won the Open in 1914 but how he had behaved.

"I wonder how he found the courage to break the club rules," she commented.

"From playing golf," I said, joking, but not entirely. Hagen had been a poor kid who proved himself on the golf course. Clare gave me one of her looks, as if I knew nothing about life.

We kept walking, the irons in my bag clicking softly together, down the middle of the long par-5 fairway and toward my golf ball beyond the corner of the dogleg. It was lovely and quiet out there on the back side of the empty course. The air was rich with the warm smell of newly mowed grass. As the sunlight faded, the trees streaked the fairway with long shadows, and Clare didn't seem to be in any rush to leave.

"He really likes you," she said, not looking at me.

I knew who she meant but I asked her anyway.

"That Harrison Cornell, the new caddie."

"Who said?" I grinned back at her.

"He did."

"You talked to Cornell?"

"I talk to you, don't I? You're a caddie, aren't you?"

We reached my ball and she held my bag while I pulled a club. The corners of her wide mouth sloped down, almost into a pout. How could she resist me, I kept thinking, when she looked at me like I was the cutest guy in the room, or in this case in the middle of the thirteenth fairway.

"Stick it in there stiff," she said, making fun of the golf lingo she heard all day from the members.

I pulled the 9 iron from the bag and told her, "Watch this." Now I was determined to impress Clare. The thirteenth green was elevated slightly and bunkered in front with two small, old-fashioned traps. The green, too, was small and soft because of the shade of the trees.

I stepped behind the ball and swung the short iron, getting the feel of it, deciding how I wanted to play it. I reminded myself of what Cornell had said about preparing myself, calming down, and making all the decisions about where the ball would go before stepping up to hit.

Today everyone knows how mental the game is. Today, it seems, there isn't a pro on the PGA tour that hasn't hired a psychologist to straighten out his thinking; but back then, I was taking a flier on advice from a guy who had walked into Midlothian from out of nowhere.

I closed the face down, played it back in my stance, and hit a low trap shot that landed on the front edge of the green, checked up, and spun forward, short and to the left of the flag cut in the far right side. It was a pretty shot that thrilled me, the way it danced onto the putting surface and came to rest. Clare didn't say a word.

I went back to the bag, pulled the pitching wedge, and dropped another ball onto the fairway. This time I played it forward in my stance and took a full swing; a thick wedge of divot flew up as the ball went high and deep into the green. It landed on the back edge, inches from the frog hair, but had enough spin to come down the slope and below the flag.

"Okay?" I asked, smiling at Clare.

"Okay, what?" She stared at me with a sassy look on her pretty face and instead of answering I walked over and kissed her on the mouth. Surprised, she let go of the bag and it fell with a crash of clubs at our feet.

Then recovering, she pushed me away, her face flushed, and said, "I've got to go."

I reached for my bag and swung it onto my shoulder, as if what she did mattered not at all to me.

"See you," I said. I shouldn't have kissed her. And having done it, I now felt like a fool.

I replaced the divot and started to the green and she walked the other way, heading for the edge of the fairway.

"Bye," she called out. "I'll see you tomorrow." She was trying to be nice, I knew, and I managed to wave my putter in a gesture of goodbye. I still couldn't look at her, but out of the corner of my eye I saw that she had reached the right-side rough. As I walked to the green, I knew that she would slip through a cluster of young trees and long grass, then step off the course and into her other life, one that had nothing to do with the country club.

I dropped my bag at the edge of the green and stepped over to pull the flag and finish out the hole. My two balls were uphill, dead straight in putts, less than ten feet from the cup. I missed them both.

10

THAT LAST SUMMER OF MY CADDYING LIFE, I GOT TO THE CLUB before seven in the morning on weekdays as well as weekends. I had been doing that every summer since I was twelve, when I first crossed the county road, slipped under the metal fence of the golf course, and started looping.

I had farm chores in the morning, but now my kid brothers were old enough to do some of the work, and Dad took care of milking the Holsteins, a job that I helped with over the winter months, when I couldn't escape to the club.

I always walked across the course to the clubhouse by myself. When you come from a big family, it's nice to have time alone, especially that summer, when I had my whole life ahead of me and no idea of what I was going to do with it.

There was the farm, of course. If I'd gone to work with my dad, we would have bought more land and increased our herd. Dad kept suggesting it, saying that he wasn't getting younger. And holding on to the farm was getting harder for him. Around us, one place after another was being sold off for housing developments, as more and more Chicagoans moved out of the city now that the war was over and the GI Bill was helping vets buy homes in new subdivisions.

Another possibility was joining the army. A dozen guys in my high-school class had already enlisted. Even though the war was over, they wanted some of the reflected glory. Also, it was hard for kids like us to find jobs, what with GIs coming home and looking for work. And there was college, but college cost money. When I worried out loud at home about what I would do with my life, Mom always said, "Well, you have the farm, Tommy."

But I didn't want the farm. I had different dreams of glory, and I knew that looping at the club wasn't going to make them happen. If I was ever going to pay for college and medical school, I had to get a real job.

And yet I stayed at Midlothian. The club exerted a force on me. I knew the members. I knew the life. And, I guess, most of all, I knew I was well liked there. Midlothian was my home and I was never happier than when I was walking across the empty course in the early hours of the morning with the grass gleaming and glistening in the dew. Going to work, I always felt as if I was walking on water.

That's how I felt the morning after kissing Clare. I was headed to the ninth fairway, enjoying my time alone, when I spotted someone on the practice range. It was Harrison, I saw, hitting woods out to the far end. He didn't see me at first and I watched him tee up another ball and set himself to swing.

When you hang around a golf course as long as I had, you don't need a college degree to know if a guy is good. And Cornell was very good. I could see it in his silky swing, the way he generated power at impact. But in the quiet morning, the sound of his club hitting the balls wasn't quite right. From where I stood, I heard more of a *swoosh* than a *whaaak,* and when I stepped clear of the trees to get a better view, I saw why. He was hitting golf balls with a hickory-shafted club.

I'd seen old hickory clubs before, tossed aside in the pro shop and left to gather dust in the back. By the summer of 1946, steel-shafted clubs had been in use for more than twenty years, ever since they were legalized by the United States Golf Association in 1924, and by England's Royal and Ancient Golf Society in 1929. A few professionals used hickory into the thirties, but I had never seen a member of the club, or even Red, our pro, try to hit a ball with one. I guess we all thought they were too old-fashioned and too hard to play.

As I walked up and stood near Cornell he teed up another ball. He was hitting a persimmon-head wood, the size of a hybrid utility wood you see so many players use today. It was a beautiful little club with mother-of-pearl embellishment in the fifteen-degree loft face. Cornell took a wide stance and swung slowly, from the inside out, using more of his arms than his body and rolling his hands open on the backswing instead of keeping them square to the target. On his downswing he rolled his hands back toward the target, as though he had a screwdriver in his fingers and was turning it counterclockwise. The soft, flexible wooden-shafted spoon swooshed through the air and the ball came off the clubface with a slight draw, landing beyond the service road two-twenty from the tee, about the distance I hit my 4 wood.

Harrison looked over at me and smiled, then gestured for me to try.

"Good morning," I said, but shook my head no.

"Good morning to you, Tommy. What time is it?" As he asked, he glanced at the rising sun. "Seven?"

"A little after. Have you been out here long?"

"An hour or so, I should think."

"What's with the clubs?"

"I played with hickories in Scotland," he said. "I found these in the pro shop." He held the wood lovingly in his hands, wiping the small face clean of wet grass, then added, "This is a Baffy. I haven't hit one like this in a few years." With that, he set it aside and picked up another hickory wood, saying, "Wilson made these back in the twenties. It takes practice to learn the flex." He teed up again.

"How much loft on that driver?" I asked.

"It's about eight degrees, I should think." As he spoke he set himself to play, and I noticed that he had moved his left hand over the top of the shaft to give himself a more powerful grip. Still, when he swung it was with a slow, easy cadence, and the hickory shaft flexed at the top, then whipped around his body as he swung. The ball cleared the service road and scooted off.

"Not much carry," I said.

"Oh, you can get distance with a hickory club," Harrison answered. "Bobby Jones said he once saw Charlie Hall drive a ball that carried 360 yards at the fourteenth hole at Oakland Hills in Detroit. Jones himself had a 340-yard drive at Inverness.

"When you played on those courses you'd use the driver against the wind, or if the fairway was wide. And you didn't carry a lot of clubs. Francis Ouimet beat Vardon and Ray for the U.S. Open in 1913 with seven clubs in the bag. Old-timers didn't fancy steel shafts when they came into the game. They said a real golfer didn't need a bag full of clubs with all sorts of lofts. A lot of truth in that. Give me this Wilson here, or any driving brassie made by Wright and Ditson, and you can have your newfangled clubs."

As I leaned over to pick up one of the wood-shafted clubs, I saw that Cornell had worked on all of them. The corrosion was gone and the club heads were clean. I could read the cleek mark stamped into the chrome plate on the back of each club.

"How did you fix these?" I asked.

"A few years ago, when I was in Scotland, I learned how to make and repair golf clubs. An old Scottish club maker taught me how to plane hickory shafts, shape heads from wooden blocks, wind leather around the grips. Those were the skills you needed to learn if you wanted to call yourself a professional."

"Were you a professional then?" I asked, seizing the chance to learn more about him.

"Hardly. When I was growing up in Nassau, playing golf for money was considered unseemly. Everyone just wanted to play well for the good of the sport."

He teed up another ball and swung the wood. The hickory shaft whistled in the air. Then, just before he drove, he stepped back and sighted the club, looked down the long forty-two-inch shaft, and straightened it with his hands. "That's the one trouble with hickory," he remarked. "They're like women—supple, beautiful, but they don't keep their shape. This one has softened over the years because it was left in a damp storage bin." He set the club aside and picked up another. Then he stepped up, addressed the ball, glancing once, then twice, down the length of the range, and swung. The ball snapped off the tee and easily carried over the service road.

"Nice," I said, surprised by the length of that drive.

Cornell held up the club. "This one has a G shaft, the best there is. Wood shafts came in four grades, rated G, O, L, and F. Only the top players got G shafts, and the best of them went to Scottish pros, in Great Britain and here in the States. A shaft like this has the same flex range as steel and the same torque. The trouble is, you can't find many G-grade hickory shafts."

He walked over to me and, pointing to the club, said, "See

here? When you flex the shaft it has a natural spring to it. What's important with hickory is the location of that spring in the shaft. If it's too far up, under the hands, you lose your power. The spring has to be six to nine inches below the leather wrapping to generate power."

He stepped back to his pile of practice balls and moved another into position. Then he changed the subject abruptly: "I had a conversation with your Clare yesterday."

"She's not my Clare," I answered immediately, thinking of how she had walked away from me in the middle of the fairway.

Cornell smiled and, glancing at me, asked, "May I call her your friend then?"

I jammed my hands into my back pockets. "She told me," I said.

"I guess I shouldn't call it a conversation," Cornell admitted. "Your friend isn't a great talker."

I smiled, knowing just how Clare had handled Harrison. She wouldn't have told him much; she didn't tell anyone much. She was so secretive that she wouldn't even give people her phone number.

Cornell hit another long drive.

"Clare's not a big golf fan."

Cornell took another easy practice swing, and then another, not looking at me, but I knew he was listening.

So I kept talking. I said that she definitely wasn't my girlfriend; we'd never gone out again after that senior-prom date and I hadn't seen much of her since she went away to college. I said that I didn't think she was Drew's girlfriend either, but that I hadn't asked.

Cornell stopped swinging the old club and stood there with his legs crossed, leaning gently against the long, wooden-shafted driver. As he listened he took a battered pack of cigarettes from his pants pocket, shook out one, and lit it.

When I finished talking, Cornell only nodded, as if he was still contemplating everything. He blew smoke out of his nostrils and asked, "Do you know what Bobby Jones said about playing with hickory?"

The change of topic confused me, and I shook my head, frowning, annoyed with him for not paying attention to what I had been telling him.

He moved a ball out of the small pile and continued: "Bobby Jones said the secret of a good swing was to grip the club lightly, especially with the right hand. That would keep him from tensing up. His shoulders and arms were relaxed, he said, and that allowed him to make that famous slow, smooth, long backswing and then to freewheel the club through the ball without swinging faster or harder.

"The same is true about handling women," Cornell added. He stepped up to the ball, waggled once, and swung easily. His ball carried over the service road, landed two-twenty yards down the range, and worked right to left, running another twenty yards on the hard, dry ground.

"You are saying, what?" I asked, still annoyed.

"Don't squeeze them. You need to stay relaxed and swing freely. If you squeeze the club, that won't happen."

He picked up the empty shag bag and said, "Come along and help me pick up these balls. Then we'll go up to the putting green and I'll show you a few things you're doing wrong with your putting." He nodded down the range. "I want to tell you a story. One with a happy ending, for a change."

He smiled, but I could tell that he was serious. I could hear it in his voice. When we reached the first balls, Cornell started to pick them up as he talked.

"Do you know who Joe Kirkwood is?" he asked, and before I could shake my head no, he told me.

"Kirkwood was the first great player to come out of Australia. The best we ever had from Down Under. This was back in the twenties; he came to the States when he was a lad and met up with Hagen, and then he went on to England and the world, traveling with Hagen, playing matches, and putting on trick-shot exhibitions, which was his real skill.

"Anyway, when he came back to Sydney after his early travels he returned to the Manly Course to put on a show for the members. When he was younger, he spent five years there as a shop boy learning how to play and make golf clubs.

"He was hitting wedges all sorts of ways in this show for the members, making the ball dance and hop, and this girl runs out of the gallery—she was ten or eleven years old—and she spreads a dainty lace handkerchief over one of Joe's big wedge divots. She folds the four corners of the handkerchief around the divot as everyone watches and then she picks up the divot and walks back into the crowd. Everyone is laughing at the sight of her and Joe looks befuddled and he shakes his head, not knowing what to make of what just happened.

"Now time passes. It's seven or eight years later and by then Joe Kirkwood is world-famous. He has traveled the world with Hagen, playing exhibitions, doing his tricks, and he's back home in Sydney when he gets a phone call from a young woman who introduces herself as the daughter of the former greens keeper at the Manly Course. She says that she read in the papers that he was home and asks Joe if he might stop by her house, if he has time in his busy schedule, for she had something to show him.

"He agrees to meet her in a week's time at her home overlooking Manly Beach.

"She meets him at the door but now seems mortified at having phoned him in the first place. But she's a beautiful woman, with bright blue eyes and a wonderful mouth, so he goes in.

"They sit in her little living room and have tea and talk about his life, talk about her late father, who Kirkwood once worked for, about Sydney, about all his traveling, and then finally she bursts out, 'Joe, I do have something to show you.'

"She leads him out the back door of the tiny cottage and onto the porch, which is a greenhouse full of flowers in bloom. She waves at the back lawn of the cottage and says, 'There it is.'

"Now Joe looks out at the lawn and asks, 'There what is?'

"She laughs and says, as she waves again at the lovely lawn, 'It's your divot. I made your divot into this lawn for you.'

"She was that little girl who had taken the divot away in her handkerchief and planted it in her family's lawn. Over the years she nurtured and cared for it, and cared for the whole lawn as well. Now it was lush and trim, without one blade of grass that didn't stand straight as a bristle. She had grown that lawn as a sign. It was a monument of devotion. It was hallowed ground. It was an act of love.

"And Joe stood there on the back porch of that little house and he looked down at this beautiful woman and she just waited, as only a woman can wait. And then he bent down and gathered her into his arms, and kissed this young woman who had stepped from the gallery so many years before to pick up that divot as a way of keeping him close while she grew up. That's what love is, Tommy. It's holding something close to your heart, nurturing it without squeezing it, and having the patience to wait your turn, for love will find you when it's your time. And they were married—Joe and that young woman—on the lawn she had created from his long-ago divot.

"Now let's go up so you can work on your putting and quit

feeling sorry for yourself. Remember what I said—all that mat-
ters in golf, as well as in life, is making those three-footers. If
you had half a brain you'd understand that Clare Farrell has
made her putt and moved on to the next tee."

11

WEDNESDAY WAS LADIES' DAY, AND THE MEMBERS' WIVES PLAYED early in the day so that they could take as long as they wanted to get around eighteen. Caddying for a foursome of women, playing so slowly that eighteen holes took forever, was the toughest loop a caddy could have, and the Professor usually didn't stick me with it. So when little Jimmy Kilcourse came running down to the handball court, where half a dozen of us were shooting craps on the back-side court, I was surprised to hear that he wanted me. "Tell the Professor I'm not feeling good," I said. "Tell him I won't be going out today."

I had the dice and I had already rolled five straight passes. Instead of counting my winnings, I just stuffed the dollar bills into my pants pockets and kept playing. The first thing a caddie learns is that when the dice are hot, you never let them get cold.

Then the kid was back again to say, and this time he was

quoting the Professor directly, "Get your ass up to the caddie shack." He grinned as he delivered the message.

I rolled snake eyes and called it quits.

"Doc Driscoll wants you to caddie for his kid," the Professor explained when I reached his office. He handed me the card. "She's teeing off the back side; the front's jammed up."

"Who's playing with her?"

"I don't know. When Vicars called down for you, he only mentioned the girl. He said to find you."

"Val's not allowed on the course without a member. She's too young."

"That was last year. She's seventeen now and listed as a junior member with all rights and privileges." He lifted the new green membership book with the Midlothian logo stamped on the front. "Get moving. Vicars called twenty minutes ago. I didn't know you were shooting craps."

"I wasn't. I was watching."

"Yeah, tell that to your Father Whatshisname the next time he hears your confession."

Crossing the top of the parking lot, I spotted Valerie standing outside the pro shop. The tee was teeming with women and caddies.

"What's up, Driscoll?" I asked Val.

"We have to go off ten, Mr. Denison says, because of them." Valerie nodded toward the crowd on the tee.

"Who's we?" I glanced at Val, but it was Cornell who grabbed my attention. He was carrying for Mrs. DeMets and Mrs. Irwin, the best women players at Midlothian and among the better tippers. It was the kind of loop I should have gotten, not Cornell, and I swore under my breath, seeing him striding down the first fairway.

"You and me," Valerie answered, moving to her golf bag, which I recognized at once as her mother's.

I swung the light bag onto my shoulder and set off in the direction of the tenth tee, still glancing over at Cornell and his players. He was walking between them, talking and gesturing, and I knew that he was telling them his favorite stories about golf in the Bahamas, stories about the Duke and Duchess. The women, I guessed, had asked for Cornell to loop for them just to hear more stories about the English royals.

"Daddy said you would help me learn the game," said Valerie, not even noticing that I was distracted. "He said Mommy thought you were the very best caddie at Midlothian."

As we headed for the back nine, I tried to refocus my attention. Valerie was wearing brown golf shoes, bobby sox, and a long brown pleated skirt with a white short-sleeved blouse. Her hair looked wet from a morning shower or early swim in the pool. Unlike the older women players, she wore no makeup or jewelry on the course. She looked like what she was, a member's kid; lots of them played, but they usually carried their own bags. No real caddie would loop for a kid unless a parent was also playing, and there I was with Valerie Driscoll, walking past the clubhouse for everyone to see. It made me feel like a new kid, a Class-B caddie.

"Let's see how good you are," I declared, trying to turn the day into a playing lesson, at least in my own mind.

We walked quickly to the tenth tee, matching strides as we went by the open front terrace, past the dining room where they were still serving breakfast to tables of mothers with their children.

"There's Clare," Valerie announced.

Looking over, I saw Clare carrying a tray of breakfast dishes to a far table. She either hadn't heard Valerie or was pretending not to.

"Clare is so nice," Valerie went on. "Is she your girlfriend, Tommy?" We had arrived at the empty tee.

"What is this . . . twenty questions?" I swung her mother's Wilson bag off my shoulder and pulled out a Hagen American Lady driver and handed it to her. "You know who he is?" I asked, pointing to the name on the club.

Valerie was kneeling by the bag, pulling out balls, tees, a glove. "Who who is?" she asked.

I tapped the wood. "Walter Hagen."

Valerie looked up, waiting expectantly for me to continue. Her expression was open and innocent and eager. Her lips were parted and the lower one seemed permanently puffed up, as if bruised.

"What?" she asked, seeing me staring at her.

I shook my head, having completely forgotten what I was asking, and looked up toward the fairway. Val stood, but she didn't move away from me. I could smell her shampoo. I handed her the American Lady, which I knew her father had given her mother the last summer of her life, when she was living her final days in an iron lung. It had been his gesture of hope that his wife would recover from polio and play golf again.

Valerie took the driver, being careful that our fingers did not touch. Seeing Walter Hagen's flowing signature on the top, she said, "Daddy told me he's coming to play at Midlothian next month. Did you know that?" Before I could reply, she added, "Sure you'd know. Are you caddying for him?"

I shook my head and shrugged. For all my tough talk about looping for Hagen, I wasn't sure that I'd be the one to grab his bag.

"What about that man everyone talks about? The caddie who cures slices and hooks." She kept talking as she stepped between the markers and teed up.

"Valerie, shhhhh," I said, softening my voice.

She paused and glanced around, then mouthed the words of a question: "What's the matter?"

"You're on a golf course," I told her.

"I know," she said, indignant.

"Well, there's a certain decorum . . . you know what I mean?"

She rolled her eyes, then knelt and started tapping the tee into the ground, using her golf ball as a tiny hammer.

"What are you doing now?" I asked.

"The ground's too hard." She kept tapping until she had secured the tee, then she placed the ball carefully on top. When she stood up, she took a long, deep breath. "Okay," she declared, and gripped the driver carefully, moving her fingers around the wrapping as if it were sticky. "Don't look," she told me.

"Don't look? I thought you wanted me to help your game." I was laughing now.

"You make me nervous." Ignoring me, she gave the driver a practice swing—a good one, in synch with the way she turned her slim body, moving off her left side and onto her right, then back again. When I opened my mouth to tell her that, she repeated, "Don't look—and don't say anything."

She tried another swing and I moved the bag away to give her room. Watching Val, I saw her mother in her swing, the long graceful arc, the perfect cadence. There was nothing as perfect, I thought, as a perfect golf swing.

"How's that?" she asked.

"You told me not to watch." I pushed my cap up off my forehead and slouched over the clubs and bag.

"I can feel you looking at me."

"You look great," I told her, and I meant it. "Go ahead and drive. If you don't we'll never get off this tee."

She stopped then and looked at me with the smile of a woman who knows exactly who she is.

"What?" I asked.

"If I were Clare Farrell, you wouldn't rush me around the course."

"Clare Farrell hates golf and she's not out here learning how to play the game. Go ahead. Hit the ball."

"Daddy said to ask for you as a caddie because you would help me and not make fun."

I sighed, and said nicely, "Val, you've got to get serious, okay?"

She nodded.

"And one more thing . . ."

"What?"

"Let's drop all the Clare Farrell talk, okay? Clare Farrell is not my girlfriend."

"She's not?"

"She's not. Never has been. Never will be. And she'd be the first to tell you. Let's play golf. No kid stuff."

"I'm not a kid," she snapped and hit her driver. The ball reached the fairway well over 125 yards away and had enough overspin to go another fifty yards.

"Hey!" I exclaimed. "That's great, little Val."

"Don't call me that.'" She walked over and handed me the driver. She was dead serious. All the cute mannerisms were gone.

"Okay," I said, embarrassed. It was her mother, I now remembered, who always called her "little Val."

We fell into step walking off the tee and headed for where her drive had stopped.

Valerie kept pace with me but didn't say anything. I was afraid she might start crying, remembering how she and her mother would walk across Cottage Row from their home and play a few holes together, just the two of them carrying a couple of clubs on the empty back nine on a summer evening. Often I'd be out there playing, and we would join up.

"It's not Mommy," she said after a few minutes. There were no tears in her voice. Her voice was calm and I could tell that she was trying to make her point.

Like a good caddie, I kept my eyes fixed on where my player's ball had come to rest.

"I don't want you thinking of me as 'little Val,'" she said.

"Hey, I don't—"

She cut me off. "Yes, you do."

We reached the ball and I dropped the bag and looked at her.

She was standing with her head cocked to one side and her arms crossed, looking straight at me, challenging me to disagree. There was a tenacity in her gaze that was new and surprising, even charming. Seeing her glare at me, her mouth tight as a fist, I started laughing.

"Stop it!" she said, though now she was laughing too and she came over and hit me on my left shoulder and told me again to stop making fun of her. She hit me again, and I reached out and seized her wrist.

Her arm was soft and delicate under my fingers. She did not try to pull away, and in that moment, there in the middle of the tenth fairway, in sight of the whole golf course, she looked up and arched herself toward me. I was aware of her body, of her long neck, and the way that her lower lip beckoned.

And I kissed her quickly on the mouth.

That surprised her as much as it surprised me. I thought in one wild moment that if I kissed her I would make her think twice. If I kissed her I'd put her in her place, and she would stop tagging after me. I thought that if I kissed her, it would satisfy my curiosity and I wouldn't have to think about her again. But at the same time, I thought that if I kissed her she would in some way always be mine, in the way that a first kiss is never forgotten.

She stepped back, looking away; shy now.

"I better go," she said, gesturing in the direction of her parents' house.

"Val . . . I shouldn't have."

As she slipped past me she pressed her palm against my chest and looked up. "I'm glad you did," she said, smiling smugly, pleased with herself. "I love kissing Tommy O'Shea." And then she was gone, sprinting away from me. She never looked back, but before she vaulted the low stone wall that separated the houses from the course, she raised her arm and waved, fully expecting that I would still be watching. And I was.

I must have stood there for another five minutes, trying to sort it all out. But I couldn't figure out why I'd acted as I had.

At that moment, of the two of us, Valerie had the clearer understanding of what had transpired. All I could think of was the consequences, of the gossip that would sweep through the clubhouse if any of the women had seen me brazenly kissing Valerie Driscoll in the middle of the fairway on the tenth hole.

It wasn't so strange—after all, she was seventeen and I was only a year older. But she was a member's child, and the daughter of a dead mother. I had gone beyond the pale, and if anyone paid for it, it would be me.

12

THERE ARE NO SECRETS AT A COUNTRY CLUB. NO MEMBER'S AFFAIR stays hidden, no caddie's misdemeanor goes unnoticed, no player's cheating is overlooked. Country clubs are closed to the public but open books behind their gates.

But clubs are also families, so failings are understood and accepted, love affairs and bad marriages tolerated. As far as I can tell, from years of observing country-club life, it is only business arrangements betrayed and fortunes lost that drive fatal wedges between members, families, and friends. All else is accepted with an understanding sigh, much like a bad break on the golf course—a good drive, for example, that rolls unfortunately into a fairway divot.

But like most everything at a country club, that acceptance and understanding is reserved for members. For the hired help in the clubhouse and caddie yard, judgment was swift and consequences were often harsh. So I knew that Dr. Driscoll would find me. I just didn't know that he would find me so fast.

. . .

I walked in from ten with Valerie's clubs and stacked them away at the back of the pro shop. Then I walked out the rear door, heading for the caddie yard, and ran directly into Dr. Driscoll.

Wearing a blue blazer and school tie, he had obviously just come from work. Spotting me, he stopped abruptly on the narrow path, blocking my escape. The Doc was a few inches shorter than I was, but everything else about him was massive. He had a full head of thick black hair that he combed straight back, and as long as I knew him, he wore a solid, black mustache. He looked like a young Hemingway, I always thought, though that summer of 1946 he must have just turned fifty. With his big hands and square, blunt shoulders, he looked more like a steelworker than a doctor. He was too young to be a widower, all the women said. I'm sure, too, they were already whispering about who would be perfect as the next Mrs. Driscoll.

"Oh, Tommy, I was hoping I might see you," he said.

I bet you were, I thought, and almost blurted out an apology for what had just happened.

"You know Walter Hagen is coming next month to the club," he said next, surprising me.

"Drew told me he was playing with Hagen in the exhibition," I replied quickly, deciding to find out if McClain's boast had been a lie and also to show off that I knew what was going on at the club.

"Well, yes, he is," Driscoll said quickly, and then added, "It was his father's idea, and young Drew is the club champion. Red, of course, will play with Hagen. We'll fill out the foursome."

He was carrying his golf shoes, and he shifted them from one hand to the other. "We want the best for Hagen," he went on, picking his words as if about to share a secret. "This is going to be a special exhibition. He's presenting the clubs he used in the Open in fourteen to the WGA. They're going to the golf association's museum. But what's most important about the exhibition is that Hagen is going to use those same clubs and play the round with them." He smiled. "There will be a lot of newspaper people here, maybe some film people, too. It will be a historic event, I should think. It will be best ball and the Western Golf Association is offering a prize of one thousand dollars to the winning team."

"That's great, Doctor." I almost said that Cornell had been hitting hickory clubs early in the morning, but then decided that members didn't need to know everything.

"Now, Tommy, if you don't mind. I—we, the members—would like you to be available to caddie for Mr. Hagen. No one is more knowledgeable about the course than you, and I'm told he is very generous with his caddies." He smiled warmly.

"It would be an honor, sir, and thank you for asking. I'll loop for nothing."

Driscoll kept smiling. "Well, I don't think that will be necessary. But thank you for being so agreeable."

He patted me on the shoulder and started to the locker room. As he stepped by me, I could smell his aftershave lotion. It was a smell that all my life I associated with rich people, and even when I was somewhat successful later in life, I could never bring myself to wear cologne.

"See if you can do some research on Hagen before he arrives, Tommy," Driscoll said as he continued up the path. "Maybe talk to that new caddie . . . what's his name, Cornell? I'm told he knows something about Hagen."

"Yes, sir," I said. "I'll talk to him."

"You'll need to be able to give Hagen distances, help him

with his club selection. It was a shorter course the last time he played here, in 1939—par seventy-one, I think, and it played to only six thousand three hundred and fifty-five yards."

"Yes, sir. And now it's par seventy-one and over three hundred yards longer," I answered quickly. I wanted Driscoll to see that I knew everything about Midlothian and that in another month there wouldn't be much about Walter Hagen and how he played golf with hickory shafts that I wouldn't know.

"Good, boy. That's the spirit." Then, as if suddenly reminded of another point, he stopped and said, "Oh, there's one more thing, Tommy." He came back to where I was standing in the shade and tightened his mouth, as if he had bad news.

"It's about Valerie," he began slowly, choosing his words, but not taking his eyes off me.

My heart dropped.

"She's going through a difficult time, you understand, what with her mother. . . ." His voice faded, and he blinked rapidly, as if keeping back tears. "I thought of sending her to relatives in Michigan this summer, but she wanted to be home, and the truth is, I wanted to have her with me. But with my practice and all, I can't be at home most days. I know she hangs around at the club a lot. I don't want to see her get into any trouble." He stopped abruptly.

"Yes, sir," I responded quickly, hoping to appease his uneasiness.

"We all have to be careful with her. She suffered a great loss and naturally she's looking for a kind soul, a warm shoulder to cry on, and, we might say, a safe harbor." He stopped speaking and stared hard at me, searching my face for some sign of comprehension. I kept nodding, agreeing, and he said, summing up, "Valerie is very fond of you, Tommy. I'd say she has a crush on you, and who could blame her. Her mother thought the world of you."

He stopped speaking, and before he could start again, I said, "I understand, Doctor. Don't worry. Nothing will happen to Val at the country club. I'll see to that. She'll be okay." I said it with full confidence, to convince myself as much as him that I would take care of Val.

"Thank you, Tommy." He smiled. "You know, she wants to take up golf more seriously now. If you could give her some lessons and encouragement. . . ."

"Val's a good kid, Doc. I'll help her with her game."

"I knew I could count on you." He gave me a tight smile, nodded goodbye, and then rushed off to the locker room as if he was late for his game or just needed to be by himself for a while.

I stood alone for several minutes, walloped by emotions and everything that was suddenly happening around me. I couldn't figure out if Driscoll had been told about me kissing his daughter or not. Maybe he just picked up her interest in me from dinnertime conversations. I didn't know what girls told their fathers. All I knew was that Dr. Driscoll and I had just made some kind of deal, there on the shady path, and I was not at all sure what it was.

13

THE PROFESSOR SENT ME OUT CARRYING DOUBLE FOR TWO doctors shortly after noon, and when I got back to the caddie shack just after five, Cornell was there. He was sitting out in the yard, leaning back against a tree, smoking a cigarette, and watching a few kids pitching pennies in the dirt.

I got paid by the Professor and walked over to where Cornell was sitting, sank down on the ground beside him, and told him what Driscoll had said, how Walter Hagen was going to play his exhibition round of golf at Midlothian with the hickory clubs he had used when he won the U.S. Open. I told Cornell that the members had asked me to caddie for Hagen. I wanted it settled right away that he knew I was Hagen's caddie.

As he listened to what I had to say, Cornell took out another cigarette and lit it, and then he stated bluntly, "You can't caddie for Hagen without knowing how he plays with hickory."

"I know that," I said. "Doc Driscoll said I should ask you. He said you'd know because you caddied for Hagen in the Bahamas."

"What kind of balls are they playing?"

I shrugged. "I don't know. No one said anything about golf balls."

Cornell smiled and shook his head. "Grand. 'Bout what I thought." He held up his fingers and counted off. "There have been three types of balls in golf: the feather ball used from the very beginning until the 1850s; then Gutta-percha, the gutty ball, until around the turn of the century. Since 1900 we have had the rubber-core ball; that's what we have today, and that's what has changed the game of golf. The ball ran more than a gutty. In fact, the golf ball was changed twice in the early 1930's by the USGA to reduce its distance." Then he said, "They'll use the rubber-core ball. That was the ball they had when he won the Open."

Cornell pulled himself up then, glanced around the caddie yard, and walked over and picked up a fallen tree branch that was just about five feet long. He stripped the smaller branches and leaves from it and then placed his cigarette on the top of a flat rock and turned to me where I was still sitting up against the tree.

"We'll start with the evolution of the hickory swing," he began at once, lecturing. "Otherwise, it's like coming in at the middle of a movie. You won't know what's going on."

His first demonstration, he said, would be the St. Andrews swing. When I said that I'd never heard of it, he shook his head as if I were beyond hope. The truth was that it amused me to continually astonish him with my ignorance of golf history.

Without replying, he said, "Heads up."

He grabbed the branch with both hands, as if it were a baseball bat, and, with a wide stance, swung long and flat with his whole body. He swayed away from the ball on his backswing, then forward on his downswing, the stick whooshing in the wind as he slashed at the imaginary ball.

"Half the members swing like that," I declared, grinning and watching him.

Not responding to what I had said, he continued, "In those early years of golf, that's how the game was played, with a long, loose swing. The ball went all over the place. Then, around the turn of the century, along came Mr. Harry Vardon."

"Now, Vardon is an interesting chap," Cornell continued. "He learned golf on his own in Jersey, on one of those Channel Islands between France and England. He never had a golf lesson, never copied anyone's swing. Nevertheless, he changed golf more than any other player, partly because he came up with the over-lapping grip." He joined his hands together on the branch.

"The Vardon grip." I held up my hands, demonstrating how I held a golf club.

The caddies who had been pitching pennies quit and ambled over to watch as Cornell went on with his demonstration. With the new audience, his voice picked up. I smiled at the way he became more animated with the kids around him, listening to what he had to say. He pushed his panama up off his forehead. It was another one of the theatrical gestures I had seen him use when he was the center of attention. It was almost as if he were onstage and not just talking to a bunch of kids at the end of a long summer day.

"That's right, the double-V grip." He refocused on me, but responded to the attention from the caddies encircling us: "With the forefinger and thumb of each hand forming a double V on the shaft of the club. You know, it was Vardon who showed your Chick Evans that grip, back in Paris in 1911. Evans, like most everyone else, gripped the club as if it were a baseball bat. Vardon got Evans to move his left thumb to the side of the shaft.

"But what Vardon really did for the game of golf was to stop the slashing. The swing he developed centered the player's body over the ball, giving him more control. When Vardon arrived in America in 1900, everyone was stunned at how slowly and gracefully he swung the club. Every movement worked together, without tension or stress, and without banging at the ball he still out drove them all. In many ways, the old bloke had a modern swing, but he would swing flat for a low running draw and upright for a high carry shot."

He stopped and, with his make-believe club, demonstrated the swing, then said, "Next, you had your own Bobby Jones. He had a narrow stance, a full hip turn, and a long, flat backswing that let him loop the club into a sweeping, steep downswing plane. Like this." Cornell swung the stick once; then, demonstrating again, he stopped on his backswing and said, "See how at the top he lifts his hands into what we might call a 'modern' position for his downswing.

"All the players from those wooden-shaft days swung more or less the same way, a slow swing that accelerates. All but one player." He paused and then asked me, "Who would that be, Mr. Number One Caddie?"

"Sir Walter Hagen," I said, using the Haig's famous nickname.

Cornell's eyes swept the crowd of caddies. He looked astonished that I knew the answer, and the kids began to laugh at his show of surprise.

"That's right, Mr. Number One Caddie," he announced, grinning. "The great Sir Walter. He widened his stance because he had learned to swing a golf club after he had learned to play baseball. When he came along, those early players were swinging the club well around their bodies in the backswing, then up and slightly over, and down to the ball. The club moved on a steeper angle during the downswing than it did on the backswing.

"Hagen took a different approach. He started his downswing with his hips sliding to the left. He brought the club back to the ball on a flatter plane than on his backswing. What this meant was that it increased his chances of returning the club head from inside—rather than from outside—and hitting across the target line at impact. Hagen described his golf swing as clipping the tops off daisies.

"Then there was Gene Sarazen," he continued. "Sarazen used a very strong left-hand grip and struck the ball as if he were wielding an ax. Because of his grip, he had to deliver the club late to stop himself from closing the face. When he was a kid growing up in New York, his swing was long and upright. Later, to get more distance, he changed his grip and swung shorter and flatter, with more winding and unwinding. Here, watch, kids," he said, catching the attention of the other caddies.

"What does it remind you of?" he asked, demonstrating Sarazen's swing.

"The St. Andrews swing," several of them shouted out.

"My God, you blokes are brilliant." He pretended to appear astonished. They were all laughing now at Cornell.

Cornell turned back to me, still sitting with my back against the tree trunk, retrieved his cigarette, and braced the stick against his hip. Taking a drag on his cigarette, he asked next, being serious, "Notice anything else?" Then, without waiting for me to answer, he explained, "All these players had one thing in common. Watch my hands." He took another long, graceful swing with his make-believe club and asked, "What did you notice?"

"You moved your hands back first before the club head," I answered, and without moving I demonstrated what I had seen.

"See that?" Cornell eyes swept the crowd of kids. "That's why Tommy O'Shea is the number-one caddie at Midlothian." He led a round of mock applause for my right answer.

Then, with the cigarette still dangling from his lips, he took his stance again and continued, "All the pros from the wooden-shaft days took their hands back first, before they moved the club head. It was the only way they could create a smooth, fluid start to the swing."

He finished his cigarette and stamped it out, and then tossed the stick back into the weeds and came to sit beside me with our backs to the tree trunk. The audience of kids watched him for a few minutes, saw that he was finished demonstrating the hickory golf swing, and drifted off. The Cornell show was over.

"It was a better game then," he said to me. "You could be creative with hickory."

"Then why are we using steel?"

"There was no more hickory left to log."

"Then use something else."

Cornell shook his head. "They tried. Way back in the seventeenth century club makers were using all sorts of wood—hazel and ash, purpleheart, lemonwood, even wood from the danga tree, which traders brought back to England. They kept looking for the perfect wood to make the perfect golf club. It wasn't until the beginning of the eighteenth century that they found it in the hills of Tennessee."

"Hickory," I said.

Cornell nodded. "When American hickory reached Great Britain around 1820, it became the wood of choice for the next hundred years. But it wasn't just any Tennessee hickory. Club makers wanted the center-cut hickory from trees that grew only on hillsides facing north. They wanted trees from where the sun would have hit the hickory in just the right direction so that the tree would grow tall and straight. Like artists in their studios, club makers wanted the perfect light. Finally they ran out of old-growth hickory and then along came steel and the game changed."

"Well, it didn't change that much." I pulled myself together and stood up. It was late. "You still have to make those three-footers," I said.

Cornel stood, too. "True enough." He walked with me to the parking lot, and then he asked, almost offhandedly, "Do you want to learn how to hit hickories?"

I laughed at his suggestion. "No one plays golf with hickory." I stopped walking at the top of the parking lot. I knew that Cornell would head down the club drive to the main entrance and I would cut across the course and go home to the farm.

"What would you say if I told you that if you learned to play with hickory, you could beat Walter Hagen."

"I'd say you were crazy."

With that, Cornell motioned toward the low concrete wall where I had been sitting when he first came down the country-club road. "Sit down a minute," he said, "and hear me out."

"Okay. What?" I said, finding a place to sit on the wall.

"I'll teach you how to hit hickory," he began. "And when you beat Hagen you'll be a local hero. The members will love you for getting their club's name in all the newspapers. Let them know you want to go to college, and they'll create a scholarship fund to pay the way for their famous caddie."

I grinned at him, amused and baffled by his scheme, and said, "There's only two problems, Harrison. One, I can't beat Walter Hagen with my own clubs, let alone hickory. And, two, how's a caddie going to get into that exhibition match?"

"Playing hickory isn't as difficult as it appears—not for a player like yourself who has ability. You forget that golfers have played with wooden shafts for centuries. And don't worry about getting into the match."

"Why should I worry, it will never happen."

Cornell took a long drag on his cigarette as he stared across the empty parking lot. It was as if he was trying to put together in his mind the last loose pieces of his plan. Then he stated, "I'll see to it. You need only to learn how to play with hickory." And he said it with such assurance that, sitting on the low, stone wall, I believed it might just be possible and I would have a way to pay for college. And so it began.

14

THE HICKORY DRIVER FELT LIGHT IN MY HANDS, FEATHERY. I swung it once, then twice, searching for the feel of the club. So much of golf is getting to the point where the club is just the extension of our arms. On any round we are lucky if we can find that feeling on a tee shot or a fairway wood, and it is only then that anyone can call himself a player. And that feeling is ephemeral. We have all read of players like Seve Ballesteros or Ian Baker-Finch, who were once good enough to win major tournaments and then lost their games. It was seven o'clock in the morning the next day and I was standing on the range, wet with dew and listening to Cornell instruct me about playing with hickory.

"What do you think?" Cornell asked, watching me. His blue eyes glistened in the bright early-morning sunlight. He was taking pleasure in the easy way I was swinging the club.

"It's different," I admitted.

"It's the shaft," he said. "The shaft has always been the secret of golf." He tossed me a ball and nodded that I should try and hit it.

I tried. The ball flew sideways off the clubface. It was worse than a shank with a short iron. Before I could finish my wild swing, Cornell tossed me another ball.

I teed up and that time I missed the ball completely. That hadn't happened to me since I was in elementary school. I stepped back and whipped the club in my hand. The soft shaft whistled in the wind.

"Harder than you think," Cornell remarked.

I took another swing, and another, and all Harrison said was, "Slower." It felt as if I were swinging in slow motion.

"Don't squeeze the fingers. The secret is a fluid motion but you can't do that if your hands are tense. If your grip tightens, the muscles of your whole body tighten. Place the left thumb to the right of the center of the shaft and cover it with the palm of your right hand." Cornell leaned forward to adjust my fingers, saying as he did so, "Now the club lies comfortably at the roots of the fingers of your right hand, and your right thumb is to the left of center of the shaft. There, you have it. When you hold the club, grip it a little tighter with your thumbs and forefingers. The knuckles of your left hand should face down the line, and the right-hand knuckles are away from the target."

I nodded, agreeing, but so far Cornell hadn't really taught me anything new.

"The difference is the takeaway, Tommy," he finally said. "You know the one-piece takeaway, with the club, the left hand, arm, shoulder, and knee all working together." He shook his head. "With hickory, move your hands back first, and let the club head follow.

"Drag the club head until your hands reach hip high," he said. "Cock your wrists with your left wrist under the shaft so the clubface is wide open.

"What's important, most important, is keeping the left hand relaxed. No stiff left arm. That will only tense you up. Try it now."

I swung and barely hit the ball. It scooted over the wet grass, sending up a spray of dew.

"Try not to hit from the top; release the club head when it's hip high." He popped another ball over to me. I teed up and took several practice swings, with Cornell telling me to focus only on winding myself up with my arms and then to unwind with my arms, swinging slow and smooth. I caught it squarely that time and felt the sensation of the club head at impact.

The drive carried the service road and landed 240 yards down the range.

The distance surprised me, and I said as much to Cornell.

"Power and distance come from swinging slow and easy, from having the right rhythm at impact. It doesn't come from the speed of your swing. You can't kill the ball with steel, nor can you kill it with hickory."

He moved another ball into position and said, "Let's give it another try and this time forget all your golf instruction and all the golf-magazine articles you've read. Swing away, freewheel the club head, and let's see what we have. Feel the swing, don't manufacture it."

I teed up and did what he'd said. The ball scooted off to the right, again little better than a shank.

"Keep going," Cornell said. His voice had softened, like a priest's in the confessional. "Let your arms and your body generate the power you need and don't force it. Think of what you're doing as having two parts: your address and your swing."

The feel didn't come to me on the next drive, or the one after that, but gradually, as the morning warmed and burned the dew off the grass, I began to learn how to swing the long hickory club.

I thought that I understood what Cornell was saying, but it wasn't intellectual understanding that finally made the difference; it was by the feel of the club. The hickory shaft forced me to slow my swing and, in an odd way, also calmed me down. Gradually the old club became comfortable in my hands and I swung with increasing confidence. It was almost magic.

Perhaps seeing the change, Cornell brought the session to a close.

"That's enough," he announced, picking up the shag bag. "It's getting late. Members will be showing up." We still had to collect the balls that I had scattered down the range. I followed him, and that's when he told me to do myself a favor and keep quiet about our project. "Everyone thinks Red Denison will play, and Drew, maybe Vicars."

"They don't know how to play with hickory clubs."

"That's right." A smile curled his mouth. He was enjoying himself. We had reached the scattered balls. "And the only one who will know how is you."

Then he tossed me the shag bag and added, "But until you learn how to play with hickory, you're still a caddie."

It was after eight when we picked up all the shag balls and walked up to the clubhouse. The sun had taken the dew from the fairways. It was going to be a hot July day, which meant women players in the morning and men in the afternoon.

We went around the ninth and eighteenth greens and across the lawn that swept down from the clubhouse. Cornell was telling me that we had to learn how Hagen had played Midlothian back when he won the Open.

"It was a shorter course," I told Harrison.

"That's all all right. They'll set the course up so we're playing from the short tees, like it was in fourteen."

"How do you know that?"

"I don't. But the members and the WGA will want him to have a good round, not a stiff fight. You and I, well, we want the competition."

"Not me. You."

"You've got to get into the arena, Tommy. Stop hiding behind the barn door. God helps those who help themselves." Cornell kept running off these clichés as if he were joking, but he was making a point about how I should live my life.

Perhaps that is why, when we came up to the scorer's tent by the first tee and Valerie Driscoll came out of the women's locker room, I told Cornell to go ahead, that I'd see him down at the caddie shack. Despite what I'd promised her father, I was putting myself in the arena.

Cornell spotted Valerie and then he looked back at me without saying anything and took the clubs. He didn't register any reaction, and that, of course, meant that he understood exactly what was going on.

I walked up to the terrace where Valerie stood, looking as fresh and bright and shiny as a glass of champagne.

"Hello, Driscoll," I said, pausing on the steps that led to the pro shop.

"Hello, O'Shea," she answered back, smiling at me.

"You're playing?"

She nodded. "With Mrs. Reeves and Kathy Deichmann." She wrinkled her nose in exact imitation of her mother. She leaned forward and looked directly at me, her soft brown eyes filling my face. "Hi," she whispered, then she blushed and glanced away, as if she had embarrassed herself.

"Want a caddie?" I offered.

"Oh, God! Don't you dare."

"Okay." I raised my hands and took one step down toward the pro shop, laughing.

"Are you going to be around tonight?" she asked quickly.

"Sure."

"Daddy is playing later and we're having dinner." Women were coming out of their locker room. She kept watching me, waiting for me to say something. Behind her Mrs. Reeves called out, "Oh, Valerie, there you are. Are you ready to play, dear?"

"I'll hang out there," I said quickly, nodding toward the caddie bench. "At ten."

"Okay," Valerie whispered back, just as Mrs. Reeves came up behind and swept her into a motherly embrace. Seeing me, she said, "Oh, Tommy, was that you hitting balls earlier on the range?"

"Yes, Mrs. Reeves," I said, smiling. "At least I was trying."

"Well, you were wonderful. Harrison was helping you?"

"Sure was." I kept grinning.

"Lucky you! I want him to caddie for me. I desperately need his help."

"He's the best," I answered, stepping away.

"Well, so are you. You should help Valerie. She's just learning."

A blush filled Valerie's bright face.

Mrs. Reeves frowned at Valerie's reaction, then glanced my way.

I waved goodbye and skipped down the steps, as if I had something to do in the pro shop.

Cornell was in back, cleaning the old hickory clubs.

"What were you doing?" he asked as I breezed past him, heading for the back door.

"I've been in the arena," I replied and kept walking.

"Hey, O'Shea!"

I glanced up and saw Billy Boyle, the bartender in the men's bar, leaning out the narrow casement window.

"Com'ere." He gestured at the side entrance of the building. Without waiting to see if I followed his command, he stepped away from the window. I walked into the downstairs men's locker room, which was empty in the early hours of the morning, then up the narrow steps to the Nineteenth Hole, as the second-floor bar was called.

"What's up?" I asked, stepping into the big room.

Boyle was behind the bar, wiping tall beer glasses, stacking them on shelves.

"You want a Coke?" he asked.

I slid onto a stool and waited for him to say more. I knew that he wanted to know something, otherwise he wouldn't have summoned me. Boyle traded information the way other people deal in stocks and bonds.

There were lots of clubhouse stories about Boyle, that he had been Al Capone's driver during Prohibition, that he had served time in Joliet State Prison and been pardoned by a governor who was on the take. Every summer there were new rumors about Boyle and he'd deny them all with a smile and a wink.

Of course, in those days we saw a lot of such characters, men who were on the edge of the law and who drifted into the club for the season and then disappeared with the winter snows, heading south for warm weather and other jobs. All these guys had histories and nicknames and rumors of jail time. Growing up, we believed the stories of their shady past; we romanticized the lives of these itinerant strangers because just having a connection with them made our own lives exciting.

Billy Boyle filled a tall glass with ice and slid it over to me, then went into a cooler beneath the counter and pulled out a Coke.

"Who's your new buddy?" he asked, popping the cap.

I shook my head, knowing just who he meant, and took the Coke bottle from him.

"That guy, Cornell. You two are thick as thieves. What's with him?"

I shrugged as if what he was telling me were totally uninteresting.

Boyle leaned forward. He had a small mouth and tight, tanned skin that looked as if he were spending his days at the pool, though in truth he never seemed to leave the men's bar. His hair was thin and silvery and slicked back with hair oil. He was wearing, as always, a white shirt and black tie and black pants.

"He comes from money," Boyle whispered.

"That's what I hear."

"What else do you hear?" He had his elbow resting on the bar and was leaning forward with one leg propped up on one of the beer kegs beneath the tap. His eyes bulged as he waited for whatever I had to say.

Boyle, I knew, would take whatever I told him and trade up with the information. From someone else he would find out another fact or two about Cornell and begin to patch together the man's story. He collected facts and rumors and notions about people just for the pleasure of being the most knowledgeable bartender at the club. It made him feel important to know something others didn't.

"He's a good friend of Hagen," I said.

"Hagen's coming here," Boyle announced, as if that were news to me.

He stepped over to where he had left his cigarette in a small china ashtray. Taking one long drag, he set the cigarette down carefully and then resumed his position across from me. I filled the glass with what remained from the bottle of Coke.

"How's your girl?"

"Which one?" I blurted out, even though I didn't have two girlfriends. I didn't even have one girlfriend.

Boyle smiled. "That's good. There's safety in numbers." He reached over and slapped the top of my caddie cap. But I knew he was thinking of Clare Farrell.

I finished the Coke and slipped off the barstool without replying. There was no way I'd discuss Clare with Billy Boyle. In that tight country-club world, whatever I said would get back to her before the day was out.

"Thanks for the Coke," I said, stepping toward the door.

"Tommy," Boyle called after me as he lifted the bottle and my glass from the bar with one hand and wiped the bar clean with a towel in the other. He sounded serious.

"Don't get too close to that Cornell guy," he warned.

I stopped walking and waited for Boyle to tell me what he meant.

He walked down to where I was standing and said confidentially, "I see guys like him all the time. Smooth guys. Foreign guys with fancy accents." He shook his head. "What's a guy like him doing here?" he asked rhetorically. "Looking for something. Maybe it's money. The Professor better watch himself. This Cornell, who he let caddie, might be after his job." He nodded knowingly, then stepped away, saying over his shoulder, "You're a good kid, O'Shea. I wouldn't like to see you get messed up with anything."

I nodded, not sure how to respond, waved goodbye, and then skipped down the steps. I was halfway across the parking lot, heading for the caddie shack, before I sorted through what Billy

Boyle had said and admitted to myself that whatever great plans Cornell had outlined for me if I did beat Hagen, I had to realize that he was using me to get back at Walter Hagen for whatever the Haig had done to him down in Bermuda.

15

"I SEE CORNELL'S GOT YOU HITTING HICKORY," THE PROFESSOR said, moving an ashtray onto the wide arm of the wicker chair in his small office. He spoke offhandedly, flicking a thick ash into the tray, and neither of us looked at the other. I was standing in the doorway of the office, drinking a Coke and staring down the sloping bare yard toward the maintenance barn and the concrete handball court.

"I saw you this morning. Spotted you from my bedroom up there on the third floor," the Professor went on. "I was lying awake with the window open and all of a sudden I hear this whooshing noise. I haven't heard that sound in years and I'm lying there thinking I'm dreaming or something and I get up and look out that little porthole window, which is the only kind I got up there, and I see you out on the range with Cornell, whacking away with that old hickory driver. What's that all about?"

I shrugged, trying to think of what to say, wondering how much he knew already, which was probably a lot.

"Cornell thinks I should learn about hickory, you know, since Driscoll wants me to caddie for Hagen in the exhibition." I smiled to show the Professor that I, too, was amused by Cornell.

The Professor nodded as I spoke, as if agreeing to everything I said, as if my explanation made perfect sense.

When I finished, all he said was, "Why would he want that?"

"I don't know," I said, playing innocent in spite of feeling guilty, and then I added as justification, "It's fun hitting balls with hickory."

The caddie master was looking past me, out at the empty yard. When he was thinking seriously, his lips pouted up and he twisted his tight mouth as if he had swallowed something distasteful. He looked down and flicked another ash into the crowded tray. Realizing how full it was, he stood and carried it carefully to the trash can. He banged the ashtray against the side of the can. It made a sharp, tinny sound, like he was shooting off caps. Then, as if he'd given me more than enough time to compose myself, he asked again, "Okay, what's going on?"

He was smiling, showing that he was entertained by my efforts to seem cool and distant. I told the Professor that all I knew was that Hagen was going to play the exhibition match with the same hickory clubs he had used at Midlothian in 1914 and then he was giving them to the WGA museum.

The Professor shook his head as if now he'd heard it all. He didn't quiz me more. He sat down again heavily, and in the stillness of the empty caddie shack on that warm afternoon the sighs and groans of the old wicker matched his own as he settled into the deep seat.

He puffed on the cigarette for a moment, blowing smoke from his mouth and nostrils, and just stared off, contemplating, I guessed, what he wanted to say.

"You need to know about the Haig and Cornell," he finally said.

"Okay." I waited for him.

"It's not something I can tell you."

I took another swig of Coke and looked down at the maintenance barn. Ed and Bill Duehr and their grounds crew were coming to work now in the late evenings. They would be putting out sprinklers after twilight. In the hot days of July they watered fairways and greens almost every night.

I knew that if the Professor didn't tell me now, he would never. Soon the other caddies would start arriving and he'd get busy paying them off, selling them Cokes and hot dogs.

I tried to think of what I might say to trigger him into talking.

"Was it a girl?" I asked.

The Professor's head snapped back. "Who said that?"

I shrugged, as if I, too, were keeping a secret. The truth was that I had no idea why I'd taken that particular guess. It might have been because all the members' wives were always saying such nice things about Cornell.

"He's got a way with women," I answered vaguely.

"It wasn't Cornell the women were after," the caddie master blurted out. "It was Hagen. That's where the trouble started."

I kept nodding as if to suggest that I knew more than I did, and the Professor took that as encouragement to keep talking.

"Nassau was a crazy place, and the Duke of Windsor being there didn't help." He shook his head, then broke off. I heard a few caddies coming down the path; they had finished their loops and were done for the day. The Professor stood up. I had missed my chance.

"I'll ask Cornell about it," I declared, a Hail Mary pass with seconds left in the game.

"I wouldn't do that, Tommy." The Professor drew on his cigarette and eyed me, his blue eyes milky in the haze of smoke. "You don't need to be quizzing Cornell about Gwendolyn Thorne."

16

THAT NIGHT CORNELL AND I WALKED OUT TO ELEVEN, OUT OF
sight of the clubhouse and the members, and played with the
handful of hickory clubs that Harrison had rescued and rehabili-
tated. We had only a few weeks before Hagen was coming to
Midlothian.

When I asked him if I really had enough clubs to beat Hagen,
all Cornell did was remind me that Chick Evans won a U.S.
Amateur and the U.S. Open with only eight clubs. If he had to
drive far, Evans closed the face by turning the top over the ball
and hit a low-flying hook. If he needed height, he'd open the
face and cut across the ball, giving it backspin on the green.

"You've got to play like Chick Evans," Cornell told me.

"I caddied for him once," I said. "He played here a few years
ago."

"Well, now you have to play like him."

And with that, he patted me on the back, and then continued
explaining his plan.

"We're going to build your game on the two greatest golfers who played with hickory: Hagen and Jones."

It wouldn't work, I told him. I couldn't swing like either of them. Trying to make a hickory player out of me in one month would be hopeless.

"Look. This is what I'm talking about." Cornell leaned back on his wood-shafted driver, the hickory bending under his weight, and then he moved and the shaft snapped into shape, and he raised his hand and began to count off his fingers. "Number one, I don't want you to swing like Hagen with his wide stance and lunge. But I *do* want you to learn his approach to the game. Hagen always assumed he was going to get into trouble somewhere on the eighteen holes. He also knew he would get out of it.

"He wasn't a pretty player. He was a scrambler, a recovery artist, and that's why he was such a great match player. He would keep coming back from disaster, from wayward shots, and his ability to recover destroyed the confidence of his opponent.

"Bobby Jones lost twelve and eleven to Hagen in the Battle of the Champions, a Florida event in 1926. Jones said he would rather play a golfer who hit the ball straight down the fairway, got on in regulation, and two-putted for a par. Hagen would miss his drive, miss his second shot, and then win the hole with a long birdie putt. It drove Bobby crazy.

"I've watched you, Tommy; you're a scrambler like Hagen."

I started to object, to tell him I wasn't anything like that on the golf course, but he immediately raised his hand to silence me. "Scrambling is more than how you play golf. It's a way of life. Hagen was a scrambler off the course as well. You keep risking yourself to get what you want. That's what I mean. You're a born scrambler. You don't play safe. But you still need to adjust your swing to play with hickory."

"Like how?"

"Well, we need to change your grip and give you a strong left hand." He held up his club to show me how he wanted me to put my left hand on top of the shaft so that I could see all four of my knuckles at the address. Then he placed the right hand in a weaker position, with the thumb off the left side of the shaft so that it touched only the tip of my right forefinger, and interlocked the little finger of my right hand with the forefinger of the left.

"What else?" I demanded, realizing that I was getting angry at him for thinking that I could just reinvent my game so easily.

"I want you to narrow your stance the way Bobby did and take a longer swing. With a narrower stance and standing closer to the ball, you'll ease the tension in your body. When you aren't stretching your arms and reaching forward, your whole body will relax. Also by lengthening your swing, you'll slow it down."

I listened to Cornell, but, more important, I watched him. I saw how he swung slow and steady to keep the club head from twisting. I also noticed that he cocked his head in the same way as Jones had, so that it was behind the ball as he looked down at it. He turned his chin to the right just before he swung, allowing himself to take a full shoulder turn on his backswing. By the time the club head had moved a foot or two back, he was focused on the ball only with his left eye. He held his eye on it until after impact and then let the club head move him through the ball as he finished his swing. Later, the golf world would see Jack Nicklaus do the same thing.

Now he was hitting a driver, and the ball carried over the top of the ridge and ran another twenty yards on the downslope. It wasn't quite as long a drive as he would have had with a steel-shafted club, or as long as we'd be looking for today, but back in the 1940s it was a fine drive, leaving him a mid-iron to the elevated green.

I stepped over and took the club from Cornell, and he switched back to playing instructor.

"Remember, Tommy, a slower start on the upstroke. It's the only way to hit a hickory. Give it a go."

I teed up and immediately Cornell told me to tee it higher.

"Bobby Jones always teed his ball an inch off the ground. Open your stance on this drive, since you have the out-of-bounds down the right side. A fade stance will give you control; close your stance for getting distance."

I took a few slow practice swings as Cornell kept talking.

"Strike the ball just after the low point of the downswing has been passed—at the start of the upswing. This will give you power as the club head is raised. Remember, a slow back-swing along the ground; let the left arm guide the club, up and down."

I took a few more swings, and each time, Cornell told me to slow down, to drag the club back, to swing flatter and not throw the club head ahead of the hands on the downswing. After each swing he pointed out something else.

"Keep the left arm in the swing, Tommy," Cornell instructed. "Move your left hand on top of the shaft. Keep your left elbow pointing along the line of flight."

My head was spinning with his advice.

I hit the first drive thin and it duck hooked into the long grass without even reaching the fairway. Before it had stopped rolling, Harrison tossed me another ball.

This time, with the anxiety over, I took a long, easy swing and the hickory shaft whistled through the air. The clubface caught the ball square. I could feel the contact of the club with the ball, and when it flew off the clubface the solid impact rushed up through my hands, the length of my arms, and through my body. I knew I had hit a great shot without even following the ball in flight.

I glanced at Cornell. He was smiling and for once he just shut up and stopped lecturing and let both of us enjoy the moment.

I reached down and plucked up the tee, cradling the hickory-shafted driver under my arm, and fell into step with Cornell, who was carrying the other clubs in a small cloth bag. We headed down the fairway after our drives.

"It wasn't the distance," I said, still feeling the sensation in my hands and arms. My sudden affection for the old wood was as thrilling as falling in love.

"It's only one drive," Cornell cautioned, as though he knew what I was thinking. "There's a lot more to golf than one shot."

We reached Cornell's ball, a good twenty yards short of mine. He slipped a club from the bag.

"What are you playing?" I asked. "A seven?"

"You can't think like that. You can't compare clubs, steel and hickory. Each one of your hickory clubs is unique. What's important is the length of the shaft, and where you grip the club, not the number on the head." Cornell had moved his hands half an inch down on the shaft and was playing the ball back in his stance. "When you're carrying only a handful of hickories you don't have the luxury of one club for one kind of shot, another club for another shot. Every shot you play has to be manufactured. Every shot is its own piece of work. I'm playing what was called an approaching cleek."

The names he used for all those old clubs made no sense to me. Nor did how he would play the iron. What I knew was that he had around 140 to the green, which was small and elevated and framed with deep side bunkers. When playing eleven I usually hit a hard eight with enough loft to have the ball stick and hold. I knew that if Cornell hit a long iron into that small target, there was no way he could hold the putting surface.

I was about to remind him, but he was way ahead of me, and said, "I'm hitting a cut fade into the front bank and letting it bounce up." He kept talking as he set up to hit the ball, moving his left foot back and giving himself an open stance. "The secret of hitting any sort of cleek is to turn your body from the knees and keep the feet motionless. The knees control the whole swing, really, and follow the arms and the club. Keep your head down and come down smartly on the ball, hit it firm. Watch."

He didn't even take a full cut but came across the ball, hitting it hard and low and aiming straight for the left-side bunker. The ball never rose, but it did move left to right as if it had eyes, hit between the bunkers, spun onto the green, and rolled across the putting surface toward the pin. It wasn't pretty, but it worked.

"Nice," I said casually. It was a caddie thing never to seem too impressed by what any player did, never to look like you were sucking up to your player. But I was impressed by how he had played the shot. It looked simple, but there was a lot of skill in what he had just done.

Cornell grinned, his eyes sparkling. He took out a cigarette and lit it, and the two of us walked up to my ball twenty yards closer to the hole. I had outhit Cornell, but now I had to figure out how to play the second shot.

Cornell was watching, waiting to see what I'd do next.

"I can't play this shot," I said. "I don't have the right club."

Cornell gestured at my ball and said, "You're looking at a mashie niblick or a regular niblick. With a regular niblick, you'd have to hit hard, and the problem is you can't always control it when the club is forced.

"So you take the mashie niblick and play it this way," Harrison said, demonstrating with the club. "Pull your arms and hands close to your body when you swing, and cut across the ball. The ball will work to the right when it hits the green. Hickory gives you a livelier shaft. Golf with hickory is all about shaft."

He handed me the mashie niblick and stepped away to let me play the iron. I took a few practice swings, trying to match his demonstration swing, and he reminded me again not to rush the iron and to let the mashie niblick do the work.

"Concentrate on your wrists," he told me. "Let them work through the shot."

I wasn't sure what he meant exactly, but I kept my head down, my hands and arms close to my body, and I worked my wrists through the swing without rushing the shot. There wasn't much room for error on the face of the forged iron but I caught the ball cleanly and it came off the face with enough spin to move left to right, to land between the two bunkers guarding the elevated green. The ball bounced up onto the putting surface and spun to a stop within easy birdie range. I had hit the shot as well as Cornell had hit his.

"Nice" was all Cornell said, and he was grinning, getting back at me.

We were striding down the center of the fairway, walking to the green with that great feeling golfers get when they are on in regulation. I can still recall the quality of that moment there on the back nine in the late hours of the day with the sun already set and night gathering in the trees that framed the hole.

After the rush of the day it was quiet and still, except for the sound of Cornell's voice. Now he was telling how Hagen had won his last British Open, in 1929, by switching to a deep-faced driver in order to keep the ball under the wind. "He didn't hit a drive over twenty feet high for two rounds playing in rains and fierce winds. He used the driving mashie and mashie iron, both straight-faced irons, to keep the ball low. Golf is not about having the very best clubs. It's about knowing what to do with them."

As we reached the putting surface, I saw that both of us were safely on, and I had Cornell's ball stymied.

He walked over to the bag of hickories I had left on the fringe and picked one up. "Let me show you how to play this shot."

Normally, I'd have used a wedge, letting the flange skim the surface. The loft would lift the ball, popping it over the one in front.

Cornell didn't play it that way. Instead, he chipped with his mashie niblick. The ball bounced once, then over my ball, and rolled across the green and dropped.

"Simple enough," he said, raising the mashie niblick triumphantly with his two hands. "Joe Kirkwood taught me that trick when he played an exhibition down in Nassau before the war. I'd say lofting a stymie is the prettiest shot in golf."

Standing there in his old shirt and jacket, his thin tie loose at the neck, Harrison looked like a figure out of a black-and-white photograph of some distant Scottish links.

I shook my head, feeling again the weight of this impossible challenge, taking on Walter Hagen.

Cornell stared me down. I noticed that when he got real serious, his eyes darkened and the skin of his face grew taut. "Tommy," he said in a low, hard-edge voice, "Hagen's an old man. He'll be playing from memory."

And then he just looked at me for a long moment before saying, "Remember, God gives us all one skill and it is ours to make the best of it. This is your chance to change your life, to make your name, to be the kid that beat the great Walter Hagen playing with hickory clubs. I can help you, but I can't make you do it. That's your decision."

Cornell stopped talking, though his eyes never left me. He kept watching, waiting for my response.

After a moment I nodded, agreeing. But even as I said okay, I knew from my years of caddying at Midlothian that I was no competition for the golfer everyone called the greatest match player in the game.

17

ABOUT NINE-THIRTY THAT NIGHT I DROVE BACK TO THE CLUB IN my dad's old Chevy and parked at the edge of the crowded lot. I walked up the dark hill to the caddie bench under the maple tree. Beyond the scoring tent, the clubhouse was bright with lights. I heard music and laughter and the voices of young kids.

I stood less than a chip shot from where several members were having after-dinner drinks by candlelight on the open terrace. Clare came out from the bar to serve them, and I recognized her from her silhouette.

I sat down on the narrow wooden caddie bench, thinking that what I was doing was really stupid, that meeting a member's teenage daughter would only get me into trouble. At the same time, I was enjoying the fact that Clare, who wouldn't give me the time of day, was just yards away. What would she think if she knew that I was out there waiting to meet Valerie Driscoll?

"Hi," Valerie said. She had slipped from the shadows and was suddenly at my elbow.

I jumped up from the bench and tipped it over.

"Sorry," she whispered, giggling. She helped me right the bench and then sat beside me.

"Where were you?" I asked. She was wearing perfume and that completely unnerved me.

"Down there." She pointed down the hill. "I was waiting for you. I saw you park your car. You walked right by me and you didn't even see me, so . . ."

"So you thought, 'I'll just have some fun with O'Shea.' "

She shrugged. "Sort of." Her face was in shadows, but from the tone of her voice I knew she was smiling at me.

I leaned closer and whispered, "Does your dad know you're here with me?"

"My dad thinks I'm still thirteen," she said.

"Well . . ."

"I'm only a year younger than you." Her voice rose. "Girls at my school date college boys and you treat me like I was a kid or something."

"If I treated you 'like a kid or something,' we wouldn't be sitting here together on the caddie bench." I reached over and took her hand. She covered my fingers with her other hand.

I leaned closer and kissed her, and when I broke from her lips I asked, "Where did you learn to kiss like that?"

"College boys," she said and kissed me again.

From the terrace, we heard Doc Driscoll call her name.

"Oh, no! Already!" She jumped up from the bench.

I came up behind her and pulled her back into my arms.

She turned around and kissed me, pressing the length of her body against mine.

"I've got to go. Daddy's looking for me."

"Well, I don't want daddy to find you," I whispered, and then

I remembered what I had promised—that I would make sure that nothing happened to his daughter—and I let her go.

"You're wonderful," I blurted out.

"You're wonderful."

Doc Driscoll called her name again.

Valerie stepped away and then as swiftly stepped back and kissed me hastily, whispering, "Good night."

She ran around the first tee and up to the terrace.

"Oh, there you are," Doc Driscoll declared, seeing his daughter emerge from the golf course. Valerie ran up the steps and into his arms.

I watched them embrace. She was as tall as the Doc, I saw. She tucked her arm into her father's and then, arm and arm, they turned and walked through the arch of the clubhouse and disappeared from sight.

I crossed the tee to the water fountain for a drink before heading home. There I found Harrison Cornell sitting by the scoring board. I wouldn't have seen him except for the red spark of his cigarette. That glow in the dark was the perfect metaphor for him, and one of the lasting memories I have of the man.

"Hello, Harrison," I said, as cool as I could be, and then I took a long drink, letting the cold well water wash across my face, clearing my mind and calming me down.

"Enjoying the night air?" Cornell asked.

"You might say." I walked over to him.

"Enjoying Valerie Driscoll?"

"Screw you," I said.

"Better me than that member's daughter." He leaned forward, dragging on his cigarette.

"See ya," I said, pissed now.

"Wait. Don't be such an ass." There was an angry tone in his voice that I hadn't heard before. "Sit down, for chrissake."

"What?" I was in no mood to listen to another lecture from Cornell. "Who are you now, Father Grisham Garrick?" I asked, naming the pastor of our parish.

"Sit down, Tommy," he said nicely.

I could just make out his profile in the reflection from the clubhouse lights, and when he took a drag on his cigarette his face was visible briefly.

I eased down on the other chair used by players when they were adding up their scores. Cornell was a few feet away from me, leaning back in his chair.

We heard music from the ballroom and the voices of the members; we heard the sounds of glasses clinking and the occasional screen door opening as members stepped off the veranda to smoke a cigarette or cigar on the front lawn.

Under the scoring tent, we were in another world.

Cornell took another drag of his cigarette and I caught a glimpse of his profile. He was looking straight at the dark, empty golf course.

"You have to be careful, Tommy. A chap like you doesn't know a lot about women. It's not your fault. You're young and you haven't been anywhere or done much. You're a good kid, but you're playing on the edge; that's another way you remind me of the Haig."

"Well, he did okay."

"Did he?"

"That's what everyone says," I answered, defending myself, defending Hagen.

"That's what everyone here says. But along the way he wrecked a lot of lives."

He finished the cigarette and tossed it away. A small flash

arced through the night and disappeared. Cornell didn't light another one. Instead, he said, "Let me tell you a story.

"I was in the war, you know. I guess the Professor has told you a thing or two about what happened to me. I got shot down over Germany, ended up being a POW, and then when the Nazis were retreating, a few of us managed to escape.

"When I got back to England, I was in bad shape, suffering from amnesia. I couldn't remember anything before my Hurricane was shot down. So I was in England, safe and sound but, seemingly, crazy.

"They put me away in a loony bin up in Scotland, near a village called Lossiemouth. It wasn't a real institution, just the estate of one of the royals, a family named Hester-Smythe. A lovely old place and full of wrecked souls from the war.

"I was there for a couple of years trying to pull myself together. I thought of myself as perfectly sane; it was everyone around me who was daft. The thing was, I couldn't remember who I was. Battle fatigue is what they called it. I could remember the war, but I couldn't remember who I was.

"When I arrived in Scotland, all I knew was that I had been shot down. And I remembered my time in Germany. Nothing else. I didn't even know my bloody name! The sisters would say, 'Harrison, would you like a bit of tea?' And I'd have no idea they were talking to me.

"In the fair weather they put us outside to sit in the sunlight. There was a terrace; we could look out over fields of heather, stare down at the formal gardens, and I'd say the sight and scent of those flowering trees and bushes, why, they had more to do with healing me than the shock treatments and drugs and God knows what else they did to me at that place.

"But what finally brought me back to myself was golf. I didn't recall that I was a player. I didn't know that I came from one of the old families in Nassau, or that I had a wife. It was an odd feeling, as if most of my life had dropped off the edge of a cliff.

"In the spring of forty-three the sisters let us leave the porch—those of us who could walk. We were harmless, or at least wouldn't kill ourselves, and we would drift out like dead men into the formal garden. They left us well enough alone as long as we kept to the paths and didn't pick the flowers.

"God, most of those blokes were so crazy that they'd talk to the flowers as if they were the burning bush.

"By summer and the warm weather we wandered farther afield and away from the big house as we grew stronger. The simple exercise of walking down the long drive to the iron gates brought some life back to us.

"And then one day I left the drive and tramped off into a meadow beyond the gardens. I was walking through long grass to an outcropping of glacier rock when I stumbled into a pot bunker, grown over and lost in the deep heather. I pulled myself up and glanced around and recognized at once, lost in the over-growth, the rudiments of a golf course. There were abandoned bunkers and greens, lost tee boxes and hazards. I had stumbled upon the private nine-hole course of Sir Richard Hester-Smythe, which, because of the war, had slipped from sight and care.

"Finding those few holes frightened me. I was still suffering nightmares and panic attacks and would wake up at night scream-ing and sobbing with fear. My dreams, you see, were all about golf. I was running across fairways, running through bunkers. I was terrified and fleeing but I didn't know from what or whom. For months after I arrived in Scotland, I thought all of them were after me. I was never sure who *they* were, but every night, when the lights were dimmed in the ballroom converted into our quarters, I'd curl up under the bed and fall asleep on the hard bare floor clutching a butter knife I had stolen from the mess because *they* were after me. Whoever they were!

"When I stumbled upon the abandoned course, it all started to come back to me—not the war years, not my life as a POW, but Nassau, the lovely world of the tropical island, the heat and humidity, going out to sea to fish; palm trees swaying in the lingering light of day; dancing in the cool night air; music and champagne and making love under the stars. All of those memories trapped away in the deep recesses of my subconscious tumbled out. The images and memories were endless and disjointed, all those nightmares of my life.

"After that, and for many days, they had to lock me away, drug me into deep sleep, wrap me up in a straitjacket and leave me in the darkness to weep away my fears. Gradually, I began to sort it all out. As if I were arranging files in an old wooden cabinet, I sorted the pages of my past.

"And slowly my history came back to me. And when the doctors and good sisters realized that I was sane enough to go out by myself, I went back to that private course of Hester-Smythe. It was there that I found Mike; he was what you might call the handyman. He was over seventy when we met, living out his years waiting for his lord and master to return from the war.

"He wasn't up to caring for the course, but he kept himself busy repairing old hickory shafts and making new ones. It was Mike who taught me the trade. I persuaded the sisters at the loony bin to let me and my fellow patients work on the nine holes as a form of therapy, and we got out the mowing equipment and cut back the fairways, fixed the greens, trimmed the rough, and made smart new tee boxes. Gradually over the summer months, those days when the sun set after eleven in the evening, we would even play golf with the hickories Mike had restored. In that simple way we brought the golf course back to life and did the same thing for ourselves."

Harrison stopped talking. I was aware again of the music from the ballroom, the deep male voices and the high-pitched laughter of the women. It all seemed so far away from where we sat together in the dark, under the scoring tent.

We sat in silence, he for his reasons and I because I was stunned at this flood of new information. The truth was that I didn't know much about the war, what soldiers had lived through. What I knew—what we all knew at home during those war years—was what we saw in the newsreels at the movies. We were winning battles in Europe and Asia and our brave soldiers were killing Germans and Japs. No one talked about young men ending up in loony bins.

In the dark I heard Cornell fumble in his suit coat pocket for a cigarette. I waited expectantly, and after he lit up he picked up his story, as if a movie intermission were over.

"At Lossiemouth I was a bit of a puzzle to the doctors, although I think they rather appreciated me. Being in Scotland, you know, they appreciated a crazy man who loved golf.

"We would have these sessions, a half dozen of us sitting around in our night clothes talking about what was troubling us. They all had a good laugh when I would tell of being chased across a golf course in my nightmares. Who would have thought it?

"Of course, the dreams weren't really about golf, the docs kept telling me. Golf was the door I had to walk through to find the truth of my troubles—that's the way those chaps talked.

"Another dream I had was one where I was running frantically through an empty clubhouse like this one, a beautiful building with room after room empty of furniture, the bare floors gleaming in the moonlight, the doors thrown open to the warm night breeze. I'm calling a name. I can't recall the name once I'm awake, but it's a woman I'm calling for, and I'm seeking her in the dream.

"I'd wake in a sweat with my whole body shaking and my heart pounding against my chest.

"These were my nights at the Hester-Smythe sanatorium. My days were different. My days kept me alive.

"I'd walk over to the course and help Mike with the nine holes. Every day we made some improvements. The greens were in pretty bad shape and it took most of the summer to get them into condition. What we had to do was just cut down the over-growth. The golf course was hidden beneath the long grass, the acres of wild flowers. It took time because we didn't have all this equipment you have today, but we had plenty of help, all my loony brothers. It became a labor of love, the very best of restora-tion, I should say.

"When we weren't working on the course, Mike would give me lessons with his hickory clubs. He could see straightaway that I had a talent for the game, though I couldn't tell him how or why. It was old Mike who taught me to play with hickory.

"It was no easy task. No two hickory clubs are alike; each shaft has its own feel, and when you break one shaft and replace it, then you have to relearn how to play with the new club. The pros in those days didn't want to break the shaft of their favorite club by hitting it too much, so they often had a second set of practice clubs.

"Mike had steel-shafted clubs in his shack, but he wouldn't use them. He had been a caddie and a club maker, and he knew the great players from before the war, English champs like J. H. Taylor and James Braid, Sandy Herd, even the great Harry Vardon. Mike wasn't interested in anything modern. For him, wooden shafts were the way to play the game."

Cornell took another drag on his cigarette. Like the flash of a camera, it lit up for a moment, and I saw how tired and sad he looked.

"We had lots of bad weather," he said, starting up again. "At that northern edge of Scotland, there were many days of blowing, raw wind, even in summer, and we'd sit in his workshop and Mike would tell me stories about the great players.

"There was the time Archie Compton missed a five-footer and a kid in the gallery says to his friend, 'I could have made that putt.' Compton hears that and he grabs the kid by the neck and drags him out onto the green and gives the lad his putter and tells him to prove it.

"Shaking in his boots, the boy takes Compton's putter, and with the pro hovering over him and the green surrounded by a gallery, the boy goes ahead and holes the five-footer."

Cornell chuckled, telling the story, and then he said, "Of course, Mike had lots of stories about Hagen, his first trip to Great Britain and the Opens he won. I didn't remember who Hagen was at first; I didn't even know the famous story from when Hagen went to England back in 1920. They wouldn't let him change his clothes inside the clubhouse at Deal because it was a gentleman's club, and Hagen was a professional.

"So Hagen parked his fancy Austin Daimler in front of the clubhouse, changed his clothes in the car, and had his chauffeur meet him at the edge of the eighteenth green with his Savile Row polo coat when he finished a round.

"Hagen was a hero to Mike. He couldn't believe there'd be a commoner who would come across the pond and not kowtow to the upper crust. Hagen thought he was just as good as the next chap—better, even—because he played the game so well. Mike liked that because, being Scottish, he thought he was better than most Englishmen anyway.

"And the irony was that I was loving the tales he told of how

Hagen stuck it to the Brits, having no idea at the time what my own lineage was, or that less than three years before, down in Nassau, this same Walter Hagen had wrecked my marriage, ruined my life, and sent me off to the wars, where I nearly got killed. Instead, I find myself sitting in a tiny shanty in the rainy cold north of Scotland listening to this old codger's glory tales about the great Walter Hagen, America's first touring professional.

"How do you think I felt when I got my memory fully back, Tommy; when I remembered what Hagen had done to me? You're the bloke who wants to be a doctor." As he spoke, his voice sounded more amused than angry.

I shook my head, too amazed to answer. Perhaps thinking better of having confided in me, Cornell stood and began to pull himself together. He was ready to leave, with the rest of his life still a mystery to me and his story of Scotland and Nassau left dangling in the moist night air.

"Tommy, you have your auto. Would you be kind enough to drive me into town so I can catch the train to Blue Island?"

"Sure. I'll drive you," I offered. "You're living in Blue Island?"

"I found myself a room. It's not the Ritz, but . . ." I heard the smile in his voice as we headed down the path to the parking lot.

When we got into my Chevy, he spoke up even before I had a chance to turn on the engine. "I didn't mean to go on like that. Boring you with stories. I would be obliged if you wouldn't say anything about me and the loony bin."

"Yes, of course," I said, eager to agree.

"I won't say anything to Dr. Driscoll about you and his daughter."

"Hey!"

Cornell raised his hand to halt me. "It's not for me to tell you what to do, Tommy. But take it from someone who has had his life destroyed by pleasure-seeking men: you need to be more careful how you deal with women."

"I know," I said, cutting him off. "I shouldn't be emotionally promiscuous."

"That's right! A lovely way to phrase it."

"What if I told you," I said, "that I didn't know what I was doing when it came to women?" With that, I reached over and turned the ignition key.

"I would say," Harrison answered, smiling, "welcome to manhood."

18

THE TRUTH WAS, I DIDN'T NEED HARRISON TO TELL ME THAT I shouldn't get involved with Valerie Driscoll. It wasn't money. It wasn't that we were too young. It was who our parents were and what our dads did for a living.

Back in the 1940s, work and society were locked up in class and ethnicity. People cared whether you were blue collar or white collar, Irish or Italian. My cousin from the South Side of Chicago had been banished from the family because she married a Polish guy she'd met on the el going to work in the Loop. He was Catholic, just like her, but that didn't matter: nationality trumped religion. Jews weren't allowed to join Midlothian Country Club, and in clubs on the wealthy North Side of Chicago, Catholics were the ones who were banned. Blacks couldn't join any club, nor could they caddie. Girls couldn't either, not that any of them even thought to ask.

I was thinking about that on the following Monday morning when I walked across the course, heading to the clubhouse. It was Caddie Day, but I wasn't playing. I was meeting the pro, Red Denison. There was a pro-members tournament that day over at Flossmoor, and I was going with him to caddie in his foursome.

I went up the rise behind fourteen green and headed to the fifteenth hole. At that time there was a small refreshment stand by the fifteenth tee that was staffed on busy weekends. It was also a shelter for players caught out on the course in a sudden rainstorm.

That Monday morning, it should've been empty—but there was Clare, sitting alone on the big double-sided wooden bench. She was dressed in her black waitress uniform with white shoes and a white apron, and she was crying.

Before I could say a word, she told me to leave her alone. She tried to dry her tears with the backs of her hands, but that did no good, so she gave up and buried her face in her arms and sobbed.

I sat down and put my arms around her. She kept crying, but she let me hold her. The sun had just cleared the trees beyond the first fairway and already the air was warming. I felt the heat on my face. It would be another hot July day.

After a few minutes she stopped sobbing and briefly fell asleep against my shoulder, breathing in deep, steady, exhausted breaths. The weight of her whole body lay against me. I couldn't move, nor did I want to. We were alone on the back nine. I saw Bill Duehr cutting the greens on the front side. It would be another hour before he reached the fourteenth green and spotted us in the shelter. That was good; it gave me time to find out why she was alone on the golf course on a Monday morning. I knew that waitresses sometimes stayed overnight when they worked late, sleeping in the tiny staff bedrooms on the third floor. But Sunday had been just another ordinary night; there wouldn't have been any reason for her to sleep at the club.

Her head was nestled against my shoulder, her face flush against my chest. Afraid of waking her, I moved just enough to look down and see the state she was in. There were grass stains on her dress, a film of sand on her ankles, and smudges of dirt on her white waitress shoes.

Her blouse, too, was soiled with grass and missing a button. In the caddie yard there were always stories, embellished by the telling and retelling, of how a caddie crossing the course on a summer weekend evening stumbled upon members who weren't married to each other making love in the dark behind a bunker or in the recesses of a green.

At that speculation my body stiffened and Clare stirred and woke. Immediately she began to pull herself together, mumbling that she needed to get home.

"Are you okay?" I asked.

"Yes," she answered, standing and moving out of the shelter.

"What happened?"

"None of your business. It has nothing to do with you." Then she broke into a run to get away from my questioning, or to get away from whatever had happened the night before that had nothing to do with me. She ran down thirteen fairway toward the back edge of the golf course and her home.

I stepped back into the shelter. It had no walls, just a bench and a table for a small grill and an empty ice chest for soft drinks and beer. I spotted something glinting on the cement floor. It was Clare's silver cross and chain. I picked them up and slipped them into my pocket, then glanced around to see what else she had left behind in her haste to get away from me. I circled the stand and searched the grass around the tee; I got down on my

hands and knees and looked under the bench. That's when I saw
the wallet. I reached in and pulled it out, and when I flipped it
open I saw a black-and-white picture of Drew McClain grinning at me from his Illinois driver's license.

After that, I sat on the bench for a long time trying to guess
what might have happened, my imagination going crazy with
the possibilities. Finally, I couldn't stand being there any longer
and I got up and walked to the clubhouse at the crest of the hill.
It was late and I knew that Red would be waiting.

"There you are!" Red exclaimed when I walked into the pro
shop. "What happened? Oversleep?" He was dressed to play, and
without waiting for me to explain myself he said, "McClain
called this morning. He can't make it, so Doc Driscoll is taking
his place. The Doc wants you to caddie for him." Red headed to
the stairway to the second-floor men's locker room, giving me
instructions as he walked off: "Grab Doc's bag and take it out to
the circle; he'll swing by within the half hour and pick you up.
And lock up the shop when you leave."

I glanced at the wall clock. It wasn't yet eight and already my
day was a mess. As I pulled the Doc's bag from the rack, I kept
hoping that Valerie hadn't said anything about our secret meeting
on the caddy bench. But even if she hadn't spilled anything, I
knew that Driscoll hadn't asked for me just because I was the
number-one caddie at the club. On top of all that, I had McClain's
lost wallet, slipped inside my pocket like a warm piece of shit.

Carrying Driscoll's bag, I walked around to the front of the
clubhouse and the bag-drop area. As I arrived, Red swung his
big blue Buick out of the parking lot. He hit the horn and waved
and I waved back. Beside him, in the passenger seat, sat Harrison
Cornell. He tipped his panama to me and smiled.

Of course, Red would want Cornell on his bag. Everyone, even the pro, had decided that Harrison was the best caddie at Midlothian. Whatever Cornell thought about me as a golfer, he'd also cost me.

Leaning Driscoll's bag against the rack, I pulled Drew's wallet from my pocket and flipped it open, counting out ninety dollars in singles and fives. It was more money than I had made in a week of looping.

Tucked in with the money was a folded slip of stationery with the club's MCC monogram.

I saw that it was from Clare, written in her Catholic school Palmer script:

"Sweetie—I'm out of here at Cinderella Time! Meet you by the tenth tee? Want to play a little night golf?????? C"

I refolded the note carefully and replaced everything exactly as I'd found it, closed the wallet, and slipped it back into my pocket as Doc Driscoll's Cadillac came over the rise of the country-club drive. He swung into the circle and, seeing me, drove down to the bag drop. Then I spotted Val sitting beside her father, beaming at me through the windshield.

"Hi!" she exclaimed, jumping out of the car as soon as it stopped. "Daddy said I could come and watch. You sit in front." She was wearing shorts and golf shoes and a short-sleeved white blouse. Her long arms were bare and tanned.

As she stepped around me, she clandestinely squeezed the fingers of my left hand. Her father got out of the car and said, "Bring the clubs back here, Tommy, and we'll put them in the trunk. My daughter needs lots of room; she's all legs and arms. It's like transporting a giraffe."

As she slipped her long, slender self into the backseat, she blew me a kiss.

"Val tells me you gave her a lesson the other day," Doc

Driscoll said, heading down the country-club road to 147th street.

"Well, it wasn't much of a lesson," I answered. A rush of fear filled me, coloring my face. I moved in the seat, fidgeting. Valerie was leaning forward, her face braced against her crossed arms on the back of the big front seat. All I could see in the rearview mirror were her bright brown eyes as she glanced from her father to me, then back again to her father.

"Well, anything you can do to help her learn the game would be most appreciated. Right, Val?"

"Most appreciated." Valerie tapped the back of my neck with her elbow.

We drove through the stone pillars of the country-club gates, but before turning left onto 147th Street, Doc Driscoll stopped the car and said, "Listen, you two. . . ."

"Yes, Daddy," Valerie whispered.

"Have fun." He spoke softly. "You should have fun. You both are young kids. You might not believe it, but I was once as young as you are now, and so was your mother, Val, when we first met." He looked at me with a regretful smile. "I don't want my daughter to grow up, Tommy, and someday perhaps you'll appreciate that feeling. However, I know there's no way I can stop her. I could, of course, send her off to the nuns, but I don't think any respectable convent would take this one." His eyes sparkling as he glanced at Valerie.

Then he turned to me and continued, measuring out his words: "Tommy, I think you're a fine young man, and if I didn't I wouldn't be having this conversation. I want you both to know I'm making you responsible for the two of you. Right?"

I nodded slowly, pinned as I was in the corner of the seat.

"Valerie is going back to school in the fall and a year from now she'll be off to college. But there's no reason why you shouldn't have a nice summer." He stared at me again. "Don't do anything to ruin things."

"Yes, sir," I said.

With that, he shifted into first and pulled out onto 147th Street, turning toward Cicero Avenue. The day was only beginning and I was already drenched in sweat.

19

"I'LL GO WITH TOMMY, DAD, OKAY?" VALERIE ASKED WHEN WE arrived back at Midlothian after four that afternoon. Without waiting for her father's reply, she jumped from the backseat and stepped around to where I was pulling his bag from the trunk. "Okay?" she asked me, whispering.

Doc Driscoll looked at his watch, then said carefully, "All right. But see that she's home by six, Tommy."

"Yes, sir." I swung his bag up onto my shoulder. Valerie kissed her father on the cheek and the two of us walked up the path to the pro shop. When Val heard the car drive away, she reached over and laced her fingers in mine, then bounced against me, and when I glanced down, she stood on tiptoe and kissed me on the mouth.

"Val, we can't go around kissing in public," I said.

"Daddy said it was okay."

"Daddy said we could go out," I answered, "but we don't want members talking about us."

"Can't we take a drive somewhere? Go get a Coke?"

"I have to practice my hickories."

"What do you mean?" She fell into step with me on the path and we went into the pro shop through the back entrance. I was going to leave her father's clubs to be cleaned by Vicars the next day, but then thought better of sticking him with the job. Also, the pro shop was dark and quiet and it was nice to be alone with Val, who immediately jumped up on the workbench, dangling her long legs and looking at me with what I thought of as her Lauren Bacall look.

Then I started to laugh, because she never could look truly sulky like Bacall. Val was too sweet and cheery, looking at me expectantly as if she had been waiting all day for me just to walk by.

I plopped my caddie cap on her head, then went to the sink and filled a pail with hot water, poured in cleaning detergent, and came back to the bench and started to clean the club heads, one at a time.

"What do you mean, practice hickories? What are they?"

"Okay," I said, "but you can't tell anyone, not even *Daddy*."

As I told her the plan that Cornell had concocted, I realized that this was our first grown-up exchange. And sharing the secret made me feel immensely better. I moved over and stood between her legs as she sat perched on the workbench. She wrapped her arms around my neck and hooked her legs around my back, her lovely face inches from my own.

I'm not sure that she understood all the implications of what I outlined, but when I finished, all she said was, "Can I help?"

Of course she could, I realized at that moment. She could ask her father to see that I was in that foursome, playing with Walter Hagen. Her father would never deny his daughter anything.

I shook my head. "I just wanted you to know."

"Thank you." She kissed me sweetly and I swept her off the workbench and carried her up to the front of the pro shop. She was soft and light in my arms and she was giggling now as we horsed around.

I set her down at the front door of the pro shop and kissed her again, filling my mouth with her lips. She kissed back, pressing her body against mine until I moved her away.

"You better go," I told her, "before something happens."

She sighed and kissed me again.

"I could kiss you forever," she said, and to keep her from doing that I opened the front door and stepped out into the warm late afternoon and locked the door behind us.

"I'll walk you home," I suggested and immediately she took my hand. I tried to pull away but she wouldn't let go.

"Hey, do you want to get hit over the head with a mashie niblick?" I warned.

"What's that?"

"A seven iron. Hickory clubs didn't have numbers in the old days. They were given names like baffies, brassies, cleeks, mashies, mid-irons, and spades."

"Oh, no! Golf is hard enough, now I have to learn all those names. It's like being in school!"

We were walking around the clubhouse terrace toward the Driscoll house at the end of Cottage Row Drive. Valerie's home was the last one, across the narrow drive from the tenth green. They were called cottages but they were really big houses, bigger than my farmhouse, bigger than the homes of my friends. All the cottages had formal gardens and landscaping, all were Tudor, Shingle, and Classical Revival, and all had been built before the turn of the century, at the same time as the country club.

"There's Drew," Valerie said, pointing down the slope.

"Where's he been? I haven't seen him around the club for days."

Standing on the range beyond the ninth fairway was Mc-Clain, hitting woods out to the empty practice field. He didn't have a shag boy.

"Let's go say hello," Valerie suggested.

"No; but I need to speak to him. Can you go home by yourself?" I asked.

"You're not going to walk your girlfriend home?"

"I've really got to talk to him."

"Fine!" She dropped my hand abruptly. "Go see him then. Bye!"

"Val!"

She had already started to walk off.

"You're behaving like a kid," I said, thinking that would get her goat.

But Valerie was past that. She had her man and no longer had to defend herself. So she kept walking, head up, shoulders square, past the open, empty terrace, the putting green, and the dining room. Never once did she look back or break her stride. I waved goodbye, though she couldn't see me, then I walked down to where Drew McClain was banging out balls.

He didn't look up until I was within twenty yards, and when he did, he glanced across the fairway and saw Valerie, by then a shadowy figure, disappearing in the distance.

"Who's your new girlfriend, O'Shea?" he asked, teeing up another ball.

I didn't bother answering. I stood opposite him and waited till he hit another drive, and then I asked him why the late-afternoon practice.

"Hagen's coming to town."

"He's an old man," I said. "You can beat an old man."

"Yeah, sure, if the old man wasn't Hagen." He teed up again, regripped, and glanced down the length of the range, as if teeing off the first hole.

"How's Clare?" I asked.

"How should I know? You're the one sniffing after her, or you were before you started sniffing after that high-school kid." He laughed, then stepped up and swung, hitting a beautiful soaring drive that drifted 260 yards down the range.

I didn't answer.

"Right, Tommy?" He glanced over at me, impatient that I wasn't reacting to him.

"What happened last night?" I asked.

He took a practice swing, saying nothing, just adjusting and readjusting his grip on the wood. He shook his head as if he didn't know what I was talking about and then moved to hit another ball.

I didn't say anything more until he was about to swing and then I said calmly, "I found Clare this morning in the shelter on fifteen. She was crying her eyes out."

Drew hit a quick duck hook that ended up in the trees. As he swore, I started walking home. When I was a dozen yards beyond him, I stopped and called back, "Say, McClain, I think this is yours." I sailed his wallet back to him. It skidded across the grass and stopped at his feet. When he reached down to grab it, I added, "I found it on fifteen, where I found Clare."

When he looked at me, I caught the apprehension in his eyes, and I knew he was wondering how much I knew and what I might do. And before he could start lying to me, I told him, "Leave her alone."

With that, I turned and headed home to the farm.

20

LATE THE NEXT AFTERNOON, WHEN I FINISHED UP A SECOND round, I went into the pro shop looking for the hickories. Red was working at the desk up front and he smiled as he watched me gather up the old clubs. "You're not actually going to try to play with those relics, are you, Tommy?" he asked.

I hesitated at the back door. Caddies weren't allowed to play golf on the course, but I had been looping long enough at Mid-lothian that everyone just let it pass. "Back side," I said. "Ten, eleven, and twelve."

"What's going on, anyway?" Red asked, ambling over to where I stood. He was my height, with a ruddy complexion that had inspired his nickname.

"Cornell is teaching me how to play with these," I said.

"Why?" Red asked, watching me.

"I told him I was interested in hickories," I said, squirming and glancing off.

Red stepped a little closer and leaned against the workbench.

"What's going on with you and Cornell?" he asked softly, but there was enough edge to his question that I knew I couldn't lie to him. In a caddie's world, the club pro is the final authority.

I didn't lie to Red as much as tell him another story, a version of what Cornell had told me about learning how to play with hickories from a Scottish groundskeeper. I didn't mention the loony bin. I told him that Cornell's story had made me curious about what it was like to play with wooden shafts, and he had offered to teach me.

Red kept staring at me, smiling wryly as if amused by my explanation, and then he said, "What is that bullshit, Tommy?" He gestured with his fingers, motioning that I should come forward with the truth, to spill the beans and tell him what we were really planning, and so I did.

He listened to my explanation of how Cornell wanted me to play Hagen. Cornell had assured me that the members would be so thrilled that they'd step forward and help pay my way through college. It had all sounded possible when I listened to Cornell in those early morning practice sessions and down in the caddie shack on rainy afternoons. Now, repeating Cornell's scheme to Red Denison, I saw the holes in the story and all the flaws of the plan, but I kept talking, kept trying to make it sound as if it all made sense.

When I finished, Red asked, "How does Harrison Cornell think he's going to get you into this exhibition with Hagen?"

I shook my head. "He said he could do it. He says that he knew Hagen down in Nassau and he would 'work it out'; that's what he told me." I shrugged.

Denison nodded. "Well, Drew McClain is practicing with hickory. Drew's old man wants his son to play with Hagen. I'll play, and maybe the club will ask Chick Evans since he knows how to play with wooden shafts. For good players like you and Drew, there's not that much difference between steel and hickory, but you need to get comfortable with the hickory. Old man McClain is friends with the pro at Beverly and he got Drew a set of old hickories. He's practicing with them at Beverly."

"Cornell is helping me learn," I said.

For a moment, Red stared down at the clubs in my hand and then he commented flatly, "There's no way you can beat the Haig playing with those relics." He gestured at my fistful of clubs.

"I've been practicing every night."

Red shook his head. "There's no way you can beat Walter Hagen, Tommy. He's the greatest match-player golfer of all times."

"He's fifty-four years old," I said, repeating what Cornell had told me.

"He could be a hundred and fifty-four and you couldn't beat him." He then nodded, as if he had just made a decision. "If Cornell is getting you in the game, I don't want you making a fool of yourself. You can't do it with those clubs. To play against Hagen you need what they called pro shafts, the clubs that were made by Scottish club makers especially for professional golfers."

With that he walked to the back of the shop and unlocked the storage door. He flipped on the single light bulb inside, disappeared for a moment, then stepped out again, carrying a set of hickory clubs in an old canvas golf bag.

"These belonged to Jack Patterson. He was the pro here at Midlothian for years beginning in the twenties. I got the job when he retired. For some reason, maybe because he had long since shifted to steel-shafted clubs, these were left behind when Jack retired. They'll need some work, but Cornell should know how to repair them."

"How do you know they're Patterson's?"

Red set down the small canvas bag and pulled up one of the irons. "All these pro shaft clubs were made especially for club pros in the U.S. by Scottish club makers. This set was made by Tom Stewart Jr. in St. Andrews, and Patterson's name, as well as Midlothian, was stamped on each club. See?"

"Handmade," I said.

"Handmade by the best club maker in the world." Red pushed the golf bag into my arms and added, "You won't find hickory clubs better than these. They are as good as Hagen's own. You'll need to do some work on them, replace the pins and clean the heads, but they're good enough to play with, and my guess is no one has hit a ball with these woods and irons since Patterson put them away."

"I'm going out and play a few holes and give them a try, okay?" I said. "Do you want me to bring them back tomorrow?"

Red Denison shook his head; gesturing at the hickories, he said, "They're yours to use, Tommy. This is all I can do for you. You and Cornell will have to figure out the rest."

"Thanks, Red." I set aside the few old hickory clubs I had been using, swung Patterson's canvas bag onto my shoulder, and headed for the rear door.

"Tommy," Red called after me. "Keep it between us—where you got those clubs. I don't want Mr. McClain coming to me when you beat Drew and asking why I didn't give them to his son."

I grinned then and asked if he thought I could beat Drew McClain.

"You can beat Drew, Tommy. You can beat me on any given day, and you can beat any member at Midlothian, but you can't beat Walter Hagen."

I took off my caddie cap, ran my fingers through my hair, reset the cap in a small theatrical movement that was reminiscent of Cornell, and said with full confidence and a lot of arrogance, "Watch me, Red; watch this kid do a number on the great Haig."

The first hole on the back nine was deserted and I was tempted to tee off on ten, but I didn't need a member noticing the hickory clubs I was using and asking about them. So I walked down the tenth rough, then crossed the bridge over the creek and up to eleven tee.

"Hi!" Valerie called out. She was standing in the entrance of the small wooden rain shelter set back in the trees and to the right of the men's tee. She stood with her bare legs crossed and her left arm stretched out, bracing herself against the frame. She was wearing sneakers and shorts and a white blouse. She smiled the moment I appeared, inviting me with her eyes to join her in the shelter.

"What are you doing here?" I asked, setting down the bag of clubs.

"Waiting for you," she answered. "I've been watching you, O'Shea. I know how you always like to play the back nine late in the day." She sounded smug, as if she had me all figured out.

I walked over to the shelter. She had a way of smiling that was both derisive and demure. The truth was, she knew exactly how cute she looked.

"Well," she said haughtily, "what took you so—"

I pressed her against the bare wall of the shelter and kissed her lips and eyes and the nape of her neck. She surged against me, running her hands into my hair. She could not keep her mouth from mine.

I slid down to the bench and she came with me, sliding easily onto my lap.

"I came to play golf," I whispered.

"Forget your silly golf; I want you to play with me."

"We can come here later tonight," I suggested. "This could be our hideaway."

"I can't; I'm having dinner at the club with Daddy. Why don't you come too?" While she waited for my reply, she kissed my neck and then curled against me.

"I'm not dressed for dinner."

"It's Tuesday night, Tommy. No one dresses."

"No one looks like a caddie."

"What's wrong with looking like a caddie?" she asked.

"You wouldn't understand." I lifted her off my lap and stood, retrieving my golf cap and moving to the tee.

She kept talking, saying that if I wanted to go home first and change clothes, that was okay, as the reservation wasn't until seven thirty.

I didn't answer. I swung Patterson's driver several times, trying to concentrate, thinking again of what Cornell had told me about pacing my swing. The shaft was stiffer than the hickory I had been using. It felt like my own steel-shafted driver. Valerie kept talking until I stepped up to the ball and then she fell silent waiting for me to tee off. I took one deep breath and then another, focused on the ball instead of the fact that she was standing only a few feet away, and then I remembered what Cornell had said about thinking about the caddie yard and shooting craps. "Okay," I whispered to myself, "let's roll Little Joe from Kokomo."

I swung slow and easy, catching the ball in the center of the club's small sweet spot, and it carried the ridge and worked to the left in a gentle draw. It would hit hard, I knew, and run down the slope. A tee shot of at least 250 leaving me about 120 to the green.

"Nice drive, Tommy," Val exclaimed, applauding.

I picked up my tee and reached for the bag, but Valerie already had it swung up on her shoulder.

"I'll caddie," she said, smiling.

"I don't need you carrying my clubs."

"I want to. I'm not embarrassed to be a member *and* a caddie." She took the driver from me, slipped it into the canvas bag, and went striding down the fairway as if she were the real thing.

"Val," I said, grinning, and started after her.

She wouldn't slow down. She charged ahead until she reached my ball, set the bag to the right of it, and tilted it forward as a seasoned caddie would do, so that I would have easy access to the clubs.

"What do you think, kid?" I asked, playing along with her caddie routine. "What would you hit?"

She glanced at the green, which in the late afternoon was not yet in shadows. It looked serene and lovely in the distance, small and elevated and framed by bunkers and a cluster of surrounding trees.

"I'd hit an easy five iron and work it left to right, spin it up to the flag, which is set back, as you see, on the right edge," she answered confidently. Then she grinned. "But if I were you, I'd get out my brassie and hit the hell out of it." She laughed then, amusing herself by repeating the old golf joke.

I gently slipped my hand behind her head and kissed her softly on the lips. She let go of the clubs and the bag fell to the fairway turf. We kissed until she broke away and shook her head. There were still players and caddies on the course, she said. We saw them in the distance and the grounds crew out in their pickup truck, moving from fairway to fairway, turning on the sprinklers for the evening.

"You started it," I told her.

"You kissed me first."

"Only because that joke make you irresistible," I answered, not looking at her but sorting through the hickory irons. I pulled out the mashie niblick and glanced at the lie. The ball was sitting up.

I took a few practice swings, again being reassured by the familiar stiffness of the shaft. Red had been right. These clubs were the real thing.

Val asked, "If I'm so irresistible, why won't you come to dinner with me?"

"I'm a caddie. I don't belong inside the clubhouse." I stepped up to the ball and picked a spot to the left side of the green where I would aim. I wanted to hit the mashie into the high plateau and let the ball work to the right, where the pin was cut on the far right side. Coming in high, the ball would check up for me and hold.

"I'm not ashamed to kiss a caddie. Why are you ashamed to eat dinner with a member?" Valerie answered back.

"I'll have dinner with you and your father anywhere. I'll come to your house. I'll take you out on a date. But sitting in the clubhouse with all the members would make me feel strange, that's all. Now be quiet; I have to concentrate on what I'm doing."

I moved into position, waggled twice to settle myself over the ball, and on the third waggle I took a full swing and hit down and through, taking a patch of turf with the thirty-five-degree loft of the mashie niblick.

The flight of the fairway shot silenced us both and we watched the ball carry high into the evening sky. When it was in the air I knew that I had enough club, and I watched with pleasure as the ball drew toward the flag as if it were being pulled by a string. It landed just short of the pin, took one high hop, spun to a stop, and disappeared from sight.

"Wow," Val whispered, genuinely impressed by the iron. "That was great, Tommy." She stepped over to me, slipped her arm into mine, and smiled up at me. "How did you learn to hit those hickories like that?"

"Cornell taught me," I said and leaned to kiss her again.

"Stop that!" She moved away. "I'll kiss you *only* if you come to dinner at the club tonight."

Without replying, I replaced the divot, slipped the club back into the bag, and pulled the blade putter as we walked side by side up the rise to the eleventh green.

"I'll think about it," I said, already refocusing my attention on my birdie putt. The ball had run beyond the pin, leaving me an eight-footer coming back.

"Are you afraid Clare Farrell will see us together?" Valerie asked. "Maybe she'd be waiting on our table." Her brown eyes were burning.

"Now, that would be amusing." I knelt behind the ball and studied the break. There was a pool of water to my right, the water hole of the par-3 number twelve, and I knew that the Bermuda grass would grow in that direction.

"Not for me," Valerie answered. "You still like her, don't you?"

"Yes, I like her," I said, not looking over at Val but stepping up to the putt and trying to remember Cornell's preputt routine, and added, "but Clare's not my girlfriend."

"Well, I'm not, either." With that, she dropped the canvas bag of clubs, turned around, and ran off the green and down the length of the fairway. She ran past the tee, across the narrow bridge, and into the trees that divided number-eleven tee and the tenth hole.

"Give me a break!" I called after her as she disappeared from sight, although she was too far away to hear me; and only then, frustrated by what had happened, did I return to the putt, and I hit it too hard. The ball never took the break and ran two feet past the pin. Without even taking the bamboo flagstaff out of the cup, I went around and putted for my par, and missed that one coming back.

For a moment I just stood there staring at the ball. Then I bent over, picked it up, grabbed the new clubs Red had given me, and walked back to the clubhouse. I was finished practicing with the hickories. I glanced around once, hoping that I'd see Valerie, that she might be returning to me to say she understood and was sorry. But the fairways were empty, the tees deserted. Valerie was gone.

21

I dropped patterson's hickory clubs in the back of the shop and walked down to the caddie shack. Cornell was there, eating a dinner of hot dogs and a Coke, and I told him about the set of hickories that Red Denison had given me and why we had to keep quiet about that.

"It's a complete set, woods and irons, and Red said all the shafts are pro. I played number eleven with them just now. It's like hitting with steel, but they need to be fixed. Some of the heads are loose and they need to be cleaned up."

Cornell smiled and said, "That's great news, Tommy. Nothing is as good as pro shafts from the twenties."

"And there's more," I added. "Drew McClain has been playing with hickory over at Beverly Country Club."

Cornell smiled wryly. "So, that's where the lad has been." He shook his head and added, "Good."

"Good? How am I going to get into the match if Drew's already playing with hickory clubs?"

He waved off my concern and said, "Let's go work on those hickories."

As we crossed the parking lot, headed for the pro shop, Doc Driscoll drove by with Valerie in the front seat. He slowed, tapped the horn, and waved, but Valerie never once looked my way. Her blond hair sparkled in a flash of fading sunlight as they sped by. The car hadn't yet disappeared when Cornel asked, "How's your new girlfriend?"

"Not my girlfriend."

"A quick romance, was it?"

"No romance at all," I told him; then, to my surprise, I felt suddenly sick at heart, realizing that I was right—Valerie and I were over, all the romance in my life was gone.

"What happened with Valerie?" he asked. He spoke softly, with no edge to his voice, no suggestion that he was going to make a joke of my situation.

"Nothing," I said, but he wasn't buying it. He just glanced at me as we kept walking across the lot, so I told him that she was angry because I wouldn't go to dinner at the clubhouse. As I explained, I got agitated all over again, realizing that all of my neuroses were as obvious to him as they were to me.

When I finished, Cornell's first question surprised me. "Don't you think you're worth enough?"

"I'm a caddie, Harrison. You want me to go into that dining room with all those members?"

"Tommy, everyone in life is someone's caddie. Those members you think are so fancy are no different. I've been on both sides of the window, looking out as well as looking in. You know, the view is a lot better from the outside."

We walked into the shop through the back door as Red was closing up. When he saw us, he nodded, knowing that we had come to work on Patterson's clubs. He told me to lock up when we left, and then he stepped closer and, lowering his voice, told us, "Don't say anything about Patterson's clubs and fixing them for the match. McClain's not going to be happy if he finds out I gave you these hickories. Got it?"

"No problem, Red," Cornell said. "Mum's the word."

"See that it is, Harrison," Red answered, watching him.

"It's okay, Red," I added quickly, seeing the way Denison was staring at him. I realized Red didn't like Cornell, didn't trust him, and I thought then that it might just be because Cornell had been so successful at improving the golf games of members.

Red nodded to me and without saying goodbye walked out of the pro shop, leaving us alone in the back of the shop.

"Testy, isn't he," Cornell commented, picking up the canvas bag of Patterson's clubs and moving them to the workbench.

"Red's okay. He's taking a risk helping us. We can count on him."

Cornell smiled. "He's not the country-club type like I am, right?" he commented, and then he moved off the topic: "Let's get to work." He pulled Patterson's clubs out of the bag and arranged them in order by the workbench. He began by knocking a steel rivet out of the hosel of the jigger, explaining to me what he was doing as he worked. "Hickory shafts were attached to iron hosels by force-fitting assembly and cross pinning. What Scottish club makers did was take a tapered hickory shaft, then hand file it so it would fit snugly into the hosel. Watch and see that the shaft is always installed so that the wood grain is at right angles to the face of the club when looking down from the butt end. That's the strongest side of the shaft."

Cornell stopped talking and turned on the bench grinder. "Watch this! We've got to get the rust off this jigger." He gently pressed the face of the iron head into the revolving wire wheel, checking it constantly as he removed the rust. "The secret is to not damage the patina," he explained.

When the rust was removed from the face and back and hosel of the club head, he held it up to the light smiling. "Almost like new."

"So, how hard is it to repair these clubs?" I asked, gesturing at the jigger that Cornell had cleaned up.

"First off, all of these clubs of Patterson's that you've been using were handmade, not assembled by factory workers who wouldn't know a golf club from a shovel. Bobby Jones's club maker said he might go through three or four hundred shafts before finding the right one to make a club for Bobby. Pros— especially in Great Britain—made their living by making and repairing clubs. That's why it took so long for the game to shift to steel shafts—those home pros were afraid of losing their liveli- hood."

"Hagen made clubs in Florida," I reminded Cornell.

"Indeed he did, and it was a failure. Florida was so humid, the hickory swelled up. A head might fit fine at the factory, but when it was shipped out west, say to Arizona, the wood dried out and the heads rattled off the shafts. That was almost the end of his club-making business.

"All right, let's get you to work on getting rid of the rust. Grab that niblick and clean the face the way you saw me do it."

We worked on the clubs until after nine, with Cornell doing most of the job. He reset and repinned all the hosels to the shafts and straightened out the warped ones, using a Sterno can to heat the hickory. We reset the lead backweights with Mortitle putty, hammered them into place, then both of us took pieces of wool cloth and spruced up all the shafts with Murphy's Oil Soap,

Gillespie's Old Furniture Refinisher, and tung oil. Cornell re-wrapped several of the leather grips and we finished by varnish-ing the woods and setting them aside to dry. It was only then that Cornell said, "Let's call it a night."

It was late for Cornell to catch a train out of Midlothian, so we walked across the dark golf course and I picked up our car and drove him home to Blue Island. Not until we were headed up Western Avenue did Cornell ask me for the first time that night about Valerie, going back to her inviting me to have din-ner at the country club.

"My guess is she'd rather go have a hamburger with you than dinner with those old farts in the clubhouse. But she asked you there for a reason, Tommy."

He was slumped down in the passenger's seat with his win-dow open, smoking another cigarette. My window was open too, and a warm evening breeze fanned us both as I drove.

"She wants to show those members that she's somebody now, that she can date the cutest kid at the country club." He smiled and took another drag.

"I'm not going to sit around with a bunch of members, that's all." The truth was that I had never eaten in restaurants or fancy dining rooms. I couldn't remember ever having gone out for dinner with my family. There were so many of us that it was just too expensive, even for special occasions. The few times I had suggested to Mom that we go out on Mother's Day, she just shook her head and said her cooking was better than anything we could eat at a restaurant.

I couldn't explain any of this to Cornell. He had grown up rich, hung around at country clubs, and gone to war overseas. He had eaten in restaurants I had never heard of, places that were written up in expensive magazines like *Town & Country* and

Vogue. I'd never ordered food from a waiter; if I tried, I wouldn't know what to tip him. If Cornell knew the truth, he'd have been embarrassed for me.

When we reached Blue Island, I slowed down on the tight residential streets. Cornell was directing me, telling me which way to turn. He finally told me to stop in front of a small frame house, indistinguishable from any other on the street.

"It's owned by a young widow," he explained. "She lost her husband in the Pacific." He nodded at the dark house. "She has the star on her front door," meaning the gold emblem that the armed services delivered to the families of the slain. Then he whacked my shoulder. "And you think you have troubles, going to dinner at your country club with the prettiest girl at Midlothian."

With that, he got out of the car and walked around the front, the headlights picking him out as if he'd been caught in a searchlight escaping from his POW camp. I had seen plenty of those scenes in war movies.

Cornell came to the driver's side and stopped at my open window. I smelled cigarette smoke on his breath as he leaned down and said softly, "Women are like hickory, Tommy. No two are alike. They don't react the same way to the same smile, let alone the same quick remark you might toss off. Valerie is not Clare. Maybe you need to think more about the girls, what makes them tick, and less about yourself. Until you start to understand them, they'll do nothing but drive you crazy."

No one had ever talked to me about girls before. Not my father. Certainly not the priests or nuns in school. If anything, we had been told to leave girls alone, until after we were married. What I knew about women I had picked up from books and movies. Mostly they just confused me; as Cornell was saying, I seemed never to know what they wanted.

"See you in the morning, Tommy," he said, tapping me on the shoulder. "We'll play a few holes on the front side, work on your game."

"See you at seven."

Cornell slipped away between cars parked on the street and went up the concrete walk to the front porch. As he went, he lit another cigarette. I saw its small red glow like a tiny red light of warning in the distance.

22

I SHIFTED MY DAD'S CHEVY INTO FIRST AND MADE A TURN AT THE corner, heading southwest toward Midlothian. It was after ten and the streets were deserted; even without speeding, I could be back at the country club by eleven o'clock easily. While it wasn't a weekend, and there were no parties, I knew that the clubhouse would be open and I could use the public phone outside the men's room to call Val.

It was risky in that age before cell phones and private lines to call so late at night. All I could do was hope that she would beat her father to the phone, and she did.

"Hello?" Her voice sounded sweet and faraway.

"Val?"

"Tommy. What's the matter?"

"Nothing. I just thought I'd . . . call." My plan didn't extend beyond getting her on the phone. "Would you like to go out or something?"

"Now? It's eleven o'clock almost. Where are you?"

"At the club. I'm using the telephone by the men's room."

"Have you seen Daddy?"

"You mean here?" I glanced around. From where I stood I saw only a sliver of the main room of the clubhouse. It was deserted, although I heard voices and laughter from the lounge at the far end of the building.

"He's playing cards," she said. "We had dinner and I came home and he's playing cards."

"Oh, in the men's bar." Once a month, year round, it was the site of a members' poker game.

"Do you want to come over?" she asked next.

"Is that okay?" I asked, surprised.

"Why not? I can have boys over to my house whenever I want."

"Okay," I said, not wanting to further the annoyance I heard in her voice. "I'm on my way."

"Hurry," she whispered and hung up.

I stepped back from the wall phone and took a deep breath. Valerie wanted me to hurry. Then I stepped out from under the staircase and ran right into Doc Driscoll, heading for the men's room.

"Tommy," he declared. "Are you working tonight?"

"No, sir." I edged away, gesturing toward the telephone. "I just stopped by to make a call." He smiled and nodded but didn't rush off. He was dressed for golf, wearing a blue polo shirt, gray linen slacks, and brown tasseled loafers.

He looked as if he wanted to say something. Then he just nodded again. "Good night, Tommy." He turned away and opened the door to the men's room.

"Doc, I was just talking to Val. I was going over to see her, if that's okay with you." My voice trailed off.

He halted. "Well, Tommy, it's awfully late. I'm in the middle of our game." He glanced at his watch, and then asked, "Did Val say it was all right?"

"Yes, sir," I said, and then realized that she might have been told not to have anyone over, and if so I was getting her in trouble.

Doc Driscoll smiled, seeing my discomfort. "I think a visit at this hour is not a very good idea, don't you agree? Thank you for asking me, Tommy. As I said the other day, I'm depending on you. And you're really coming through." He smiled good-bye and went into the men's room, leaving me standing in the narrow hallway under the stairs.

I waited until the door closed, then spun around and headed to the front-office exit. I'd told Doc Driscoll the truth—but now I had to face Val. I couldn't just phone her again from the hallway and have her father walk out and find me. I figured I'd just drive by the house, explain what had happened, and tell her that I couldn't stay. But I needed to hurry.

I ran past the deserted pool and down the drive to the Chevy. Spinning the car's wheels on the gravel, I headed for the Driscoll home at the far end of the country-club drive.

Cottage Row was narrow, bordered by the golf course on the left and summer homes on the right. Both sides were tree lined, with low stone fences and thick shrubbery, so the road was dark and shadowy.

Just past the clubhouse and before reaching the entrance to Cottage Row Drive there was a small wooded area that years before had been used as a short nine-hole course for members learning the game. Now a few acres had been turned into a tree nursery for the golf course itself.

I flipped on the high beams as I passed the clubhouse and that was when I saw her. She bolted from the nursery on the right side of the road and ran across the narrow drive, headed straight to the tenth fairway. She was naked, with her clothes clutched in her arms. I could see her fair skin creamy in the bright head-lights, her flaming red hair long and loose and tumbling forward to hide her face.

I hit the brakes and the car skidded to a stop, burning the tires on the tarmac. I pulled on the hand brake, then jumped from the car and ran to the stone wall, to the spot where Clare had slipped through a gap and disappeared into the dark. There was no moon, no starry night. Clare could have been standing twenty yards away and I wouldn't have seen her.

She would head for home, I knew, and she could walk that route with her eyes closed. And I didn't think she'd have gone far—she would have stopped to put on her clothes.

I had braced one arm against the stone wall, preparing to jump it, when I heard someone behind me.

"Let her go," Drew said. The hard, angry edge of his voice cut through the warm air. I turned and saw him coming toward me, spotlighted in the high beams of the Chevy. As he walked, he tucked his shirt into his pants. "What the hell are you doing out here, O'Shea? I'll teach you not to sneak around after us."

He didn't stop walking until he reached me and then he shot out both his hands, hitting my shoulders and knocking me against the wall. I hit it with the backs of my knees and stumbled, and he seized the moment, swinging wildly, whacking my nose and left cheekbone. I tasted blood in my mouth even before I swung back with a hard left to his mouth and a right to his midsection, knocking the wind out of him and doubling him over. But he dived back at me and sent me sprawling. I tumbled over in the dirt, rolling down into the shallow ditch beside the drive, and before I could find my footing he was on top of me, kicking my ribs again and again, telling me to keep my fucking face out of his fucking business, to leave him and Clare Farrell alone, and to get my black Irish ass off the country-club grounds.

I didn't fight back; I couldn't. I didn't move, and soon he stopped swearing and kicking me. He was breathing hard and deeply. I smelled liquor on his breath as he bent down to see if I was breathing, and then just as abruptly as he had attacked me he was gone, not over the wall to go after Clare, but heading up the drive in the direction of the clubhouse.

It took me three tries to pull myself up onto my knees in the ditch. I rested for a moment and then managed to get to my feet. I couldn't walk, but I stumbled over against the Chevy. My whole left side hurt, and my nose was bleeding. The motor was still running, the headlights still shining down the narrow drive.

I pulled out my handkerchief and leaned my head back against the roof of the car and waited for my nose to stop bleeding. When I finally had enough strength to fold myself into the driver's seat, it still took an effort to overcome the pain and shift the gear into first and let out the clutch. Giving the Chevy just enough gas to keep it moving, I crept down the road to the Driscolls' house at the dead end of the drive.

All the first-floor lights were on, and Val was standing in the doorway as I brought the car to a jerky stop at the bottom of their property.

"What took so long?" she called.

As I shoved the door open, the interior light went on and she saw my bloody face.

"Tommy! Oh, God."

She didn't wait for a reply. She took charge. She helped me from the car and half carried me up the walk, into the house, and then to the white and enormous kitchen. With the competency of a nurse, she cleaned my face with warm water, wrapped ice in a thick towel, and had me press it against the side of my face to stop the swelling.

She phoned her father and told him that I had been attacked on the Row. When she asked him if she should call the police, I waved at her, signaling not to do anything. She asked her father to come right home and hung up the phone.

She didn't panic. She didn't cry. She was calmer than I was and more assured. I wanted to thank her but my lips were puffed up. I could barely move my mouth.

She went somewhere to find a hand mirror and held it up so that I could see just how bad I looked. "God, O'Shea, you look like you just fought Rocky Graziano," she said. She kissed the bruise on my left cheek, where Drew had clipped me with his first punch. When she stepped away, there was blood on her lips.

23

Doc driscoll didn't say anything to me while he examined my face; he just asked Val if it had been her idea to use the ice. She said that it had and he smiled and opened his bag and took out a half dozen small containers.

"You're going to look like hell for a while, Tommy. Whoever it was did a thorough job on that face of yours."

While he applied antiseptics and bandages to my face he asked where else I had been hurt. I could barely speak, but I gestured to my shirt, which was muddy and ripped.

"Val, why don't you leave us alone for a few minutes."

"No; I want to help Tommy," she said. "I've seen boys with their shirts off, Daddy."

Leaning over and patching my face, Doc Driscoll's eyes caught mine. I saw that he wasn't enjoying this exchange.

"Were you kicked in the ribs, Tommy?" he asked.

I nodded, and Driscoll stepped away, put the bandages on the table, and said, "Well, this is going to hurt, taking off your shirt. Nurse Val, are you ready to help our patient?"

She stepped around and stood in front of me, pressing her legs against mine. I felt her softness and smelled the warmth of her body.

Her father was giving her instructions, telling her to hold my arms straight above my head. But when she took my hands and raised them, I winced and whimpered in pain. She dropped my hands.

"Val, you said you wanted to help," her father said.

I looked at Val and tried to manage my puffy face into a half smile.

We tried again and this time I squeezed my eyes shut and held my breath as I raised my arms over my head. Doc Driscoll pulled off my shirt, soaked with sweat and blood, then examined my ribs.

"Well, they're badly bruised and a couple might be broken. I'll bandage them for tonight. Tomorrow we'll get some X-rays." He cleaned up the cuts with antiseptic while I held my arm up, my fingers clutching my hair. "Now, do you want to tell me what happened? When we have you fixed up, I'm calling the police."

"No, I don't want the cops," I mumbled.

"You know who it was?"

I nodded and glanced at Valerie.

Doc Driscoll looked at his daughter, who was leaning against the white kitchen cabinets. Her arms were crossed. She shook her head at his unspoken question.

"Okay, Val, but what Tommy tells us stays with us. You don't tell your girlfriends, understand? Is it okay if she stays, Tommy?"

I nodded, and then I explained, as briefly as I could, how I had seen a girl on the drive and what Drew McClain had done to me. It was not a long story, but when I finished, both of them were stunned and silent. I didn't tell them who the girl was, and they didn't ask. Maybe they didn't have to.

"Was he drunk?" Doc Driscoll asked.

"He had been drinking."

Driscoll nodded, as if that made everything more understandable. Then he shook his head and said, "Well, I can see why you don't want the police." He glanced at his daughter. "Val, not a word."

"I won't say anything," she whispered.

"We'll talk about this in the morning," The doc finished taping my ribs, then shook out two tablets from a small container and asked me if I was allergic to anything. I told him no, and Val gave me a glass of water.

When I had taken the pain pills he said, "I'll call your parents and tell them you're okay, and it is better if you stay here with us tonight. I'll arrange to have your car delivered back to your home. Tomorrow I'll take you to the office for X-rays. Val, why don't you see if the spare room is made up and get Tommy some towels. And, Tommy, I'll get you a pair of pajamas to sleep in. In the morning, Grace is in early. She'll wash these clothes of yours."

"I'll do it," Valerie said quickly. She shrugged and smiled shyly. "I don't mind."

"Well, that's a first. Valerie Driscoll doing laundry. Will wonders never cease." He winked at me and then snapped shut his leather bag and headed to the swinging doors into the rest of the house. "Good night, you two. Don't stay up late. Tommy, those pain pills will start to take effect within the hour. You'll want to be in bed when that happens, so you can fall asleep."

. . .

The spare room, as Doc Driscoll called it, was as large as our living room at the farmhouse, with a four-poster, a fireplace, a sitting area with high-back winged armchairs, and even its own radio. It looked like a whole house to me, or a room in a fancy hotel, though I had never stayed in any kind of hotel in my life.

Valerie had opened the windows and there was a breeze off the golf course when I came out of the bathroom in pajamas. This would be a great story to tell around the caddie yard, I thought, but I knew that I couldn't say anything to anyone.

It might have been the bright moonlight streaming in that woke me. Perhaps it was Val. I'm not sure. When I opened my eyes she was with me, curled against my body. She had one arm across my chest, her head buried against my shoulder.

"Val," I whispered. "Your dad?"

"He's asleep. It would take an earthquake to wake him." She nuzzled closer.

I kissed her soft hair, swept up again in the rich, sweet scent of her, but when I moved my other arm to embrace her, pain shot up my side. I moaned and felt tears in my eyes.

"Don't," she ordered, and stirred under the soft light blanket. This time she slipped her bare leg over mine so that the length of her body was pressed against me. She was wearing only a thin cotton summer nightgown.

My whole body felt electric. I was having trouble breathing. I couldn't tell whether I was reacting to the pain pills or to the nearly naked Valerie curled against me; I had never before been in bed with a girl. While it didn't seem to trouble Valerie, I was listening intensely for any sounds in the hallway, terrified that Doc Driscoll would come down the hall to check on his patient.

"I'm sorry you got hurt, Tommy, but it's so wonderful having you in my very own house." She pressed her lips against my neck. "I've never seen you with your shirt off," she said next, and then, surprisingly, she asked, "Do you think they were, you know, doing it?"

"I don't know and I don't care."

"You care. Don't tell me you don't care about Clare." She pulled herself up on her elbows so that she could look at my face.

"Who said it was Clare?"

"Oh, come on." Then, controlling her annoyance, she leaned down and kissed me lightly. When I winced, she asked, "I'm sorry, does that hurt?"

"That's okay, I like it when you make me suffer."

She giggled and burrowed closer, saying with a sigh, "This is so neat."

The warm length of her body again pressed against me. I slipped my left arm under her, wrapped it around her slim waist, and reached up and cupped her small breast. She moaned when my fingers touched her nipple. "Oh, God," she whispered. Seizing my head, she smothered me with kisses as she moved her body on top of me.

"Don't," I pleaded. "You're hurting me."

"No, no, oh, no . . ." She slid off me, apologizing.

"It's okay," I said, when I found my voice and the pain in my ribs had ceased. I kissed her and she slowly and carefully kissed me back. "We can't," I said. "I promised your dad."

"It's a sin for you, isn't it," she said. "You're Catholic."

"I can see you've been reading the Baltimore Catechism," I said.

"What's a Baltimore Catechism?"

"Never mind. That was supposed to be a joke."

"Does Clare know the Catechism?"

"Will you stop it with Clare?"

"Not until you tell me you don't like her."

"Valerie, you're being a little girl."

"I'm being a girl, that's all."

"Okay," I said, sighing. "I once liked Clare Farrell, but I was never her boyfriend, and she is not my girlfriend. Okay?"

"What happens when I go back east to school?"

"I'll write you letters, that's what will happen."

"And you won't date her?"

"She's Drew's girlfriend."

"That's who was with Drew tonight, wasn't it?"

In my beaten-up state, her need to know was stronger than my ability to resist.

"Don't tell your dad," I said.

"I won't. I won't tell anyone. I don't care what Clare Farrell does, as long as she leaves you alone."

"She leaves me alone, all right."

"But in the fall when Drew goes back to Yale."

"Clare will be back at Smith, back east."

"And where will you be?" she asked, her tone changing.

"I don't know."

"Aren't you going to college?"

"It depends."

"On what?"

"On whether I can afford it. College costs a lot of money." That was something she'd never have to think about, but I didn't say so.

"You have to go to college, Tommy. Everyone goes to college."

"Not everyone. In fact, hardly anyone *I* know."

"Do you want me to ask my dad if he knows anyone . . . ?"

"No." My sharp rebuttal silenced her and I added quickly, "Thank you, Val, but this is my problem, not your dad's."

She nodded.

"I'm a caddie, Valerie, but I'm not a caddie for life. Walter Hagen started as a caddie and now everyone at Midlothian is welcoming him back as a champion. The whole world knows him. Val, everyone is a caddie, in one way or the other." Sometimes, listening to Harrison Cornell came in handy.

Valerie nodded, but I wasn't sure that she understood. In fact, I wasn't sure myself what it meant.

Now I could no longer concentrate on what I was saying.

"I have to go to sleep, Val."

She whispered okay and slipped from under the covers.

"Good night, darling," she whispered.

I closed my eyes and when I woke again the bedroom was filled with bright sunshine. Val was gone, but on the pillow beside me was a note, written in looping girlish script: *"Good morning, Rocky. I love you."*

24

"YOUR RIBS ARE BRUISED BUT NOT BROKEN," DR. DRISCOLL SAID, "so take it easy for a few days." We were at his office and he took my shirt off the hanger and helped me slip it over my head, adding, "I'll need to put new bandages on next week. Come back then."

Driscoll wrote out a prescription and handed it to me. "Have this filled at the drugstore in town. It will help with the pain." He smiled up at me and then gestured that I should sit down across from him.

I obeyed and kept watching him. He had more to say and was mulling over how to say it.

"Tommy, it seems as if you and Val are turning into quite a couple. When she's with you, she acts more grown-up, less like a child. Of course, as her father, I don't necessarily enjoy that."

I started to speak but he raised his hand to stop me. "I'm just making an observation. I'm happy to see Val engaged in life instead of sulking away in her bedroom because of her mother.

This has been a very difficult time for our family, and I'm glad you've been able to help her realize that she has a life to live and new people to meet."

He swung away from me in his chair. "On the other hand, I hope nothing happened last night." His voice was lowered and level.

"No, sir."

"I know what it's like to be a teenage boy. I also know how beautiful my daughter is."

"I promised you, Doctor."

"I know." He raised his hand to silence me and leaned forward. "Still, she did go to your bedroom." When I started to protest, he said, "I saw her slipping out of the guest room this morning."

"I was asleep."

"Well, I'm sure she was able to solve that problem." He paused for a moment.

"I have a little parental control over my daughter—less than I wish—for the next few years of her life, and then she goes on to make her own decisions and choices. What I know very well, because of my experience and training, is that teenagers often behave impulsively. They make rash decisions that even a few years later they would never consider," he continued. "As teenagers, they don't understand the consequences of their behavior. I could say the same for you, Tommy, but you seem much more mature than most boys your age. You're the oldest child, am I correct?"

I nodded. "There's seven of us, five boys and two girls."

Doc Driscoll smiled. "Well, that explains it. You've had to grow up a little faster, being the oldest. Valerie, as you know, is an only child and has had the luxury of coming of age slowly, of having the opportunity to hold on to her childhood.

"Now, I suspect some of this might be of special interest to you. You want to be a doctor, I understand."

"How did you know?" I had not said anything to Valerie.

"Oh, word gets around. There aren't many secrets at the club." He picked up his fountain pen and twisted it in his fingers. "I'm sure by the end of today almost everyone will know about your altercation last night with Drew McClain."

"I won't tell anyone, Doc."

"No; but I did. We can't have members' sons attacking people. And it happened on club property. If you had been seriously hurt, the membership would have been responsible. I had to let the president know."

"That's Drew's dad!"

"That's right."

I sank back into the chair, realizing what Doc Driscoll had done. I was just a caddie. McClain would get rid of me to make sure that his son didn't get into trouble.

I looked away, saying nothing. If Driscoll didn't understand what would happen, there wasn't anything I could say that would make him the wiser. He lived in a world where, I guessed, gentlemen all behaved with a certain degree of honor. I read all about that in books.

I stuffed the tail of my shirt into my pants and thanked him again for taking care of me. He walked me out of his office, to where Valerie was waiting. I saw from the look on her face how anxious she was.

Doc Driscoll told her to take me to the farm and to call him when she got home. He reminded her that Grace, the housekeeper, would be there, which might have been as much a warning to me as it was information for her.

It wasn't until we were driving into the country-club grounds that it struck me. Doc Driscoll hadn't told Mr. McClain because he was worried about a lawsuit. *He* was the one who wanted me out of there. He wanted me away from Val. And the simple way of making it happen was to let McClain Senior do the job for him.

"Drop me at the club, Val. Please?"

"Don't you want to come back to my house? I could make you lunch. Daddy said you're not to caddie."

"I've got things to do."

"I want you to come home with me." She banged the steering wheel with her small fist.

"I'll call you." Stalling, I reached over and touched her thigh. The car swerved.

"Why can't you come now?"

"I've got to talk to Cornell and tell him what happened to me. I can't play against Hagen."

Valerie drove over the bridge and slowed her car, approaching the clubhouse. Her lower lip was quivering.

"Val, come on."

"I'm going back to school in another month. I won't see you until Christmas. Don't you want to be with me?"

"We have a month together," I declared, but even as I made that claim I knew it wasn't true. Doc Driscoll wouldn't let me spend time with his daughter.

Valerie swung her car to a stop in front of the bag drop.

"I'll call you," I promised.

Glancing around to see who might be watching, she quickly found my lips and kissed me.

"Bye," she whispered.

"Bye," I whispered back, wondering if it was goodbye for good.

Slowly and carefully I got out of the car, then stood back to watch as she spun around the circle and headed home. She waved back before the car disappeared down the drive.

I turned and walked into the clubhouse through the lower-level men's locker room and up the short flight of stairs to the second floor. From there I could walk through the main locker room and take the steps to the pro shop on the other side of the building. Caddies usually stayed away from the men's locker room unless summoned by a member, but that day, after my run-in with Drew, after everything that had happened, I no longer cared about protocol. I knew now how Doc Driscoll was going to keep me away from his daughter.

At the top of the stairs the men's locker room was to the right, the men's bar to the left, and Boyle spotted me and waved me over. There were a handful of members at one of the tables at the far end of the room, close to the windows that overlooked the course.

I walked to the service counter at the corner and Billy slipped me a cold Coke.

He took one look at me and shook his head. "Who kicked you in the face?"

"A horse," I told him.

He grinned and nodded again with a raised eyebrow, just staring and waiting for the true story. So I told him that I had gotten into a fight with my brothers. That satisfied him. Like almost everyone else at the club, he was concerned only about what happened inside the gates. Lives in the outside world held no real interest.

Boyle leaned across the metal service counter and whispered, "I found out about Cornell." I saw a sparkle in his eyes, the pleasure of knowing something new. All I could think was, I didn't need more bad news.

"I was talking last night to a friend of mine who worked in a hotel down in Nassau. He said Cornell killed his wife a few years back." Boyle glanced around the empty bar as he whispered.

"That can't be. He was in a POW camp in Germany. His plane was shot down in the war," I told Boyle.

"This was at the start of the war, in forty-one. My guy was living there."

Boyle never left the bar or the country club, but he was one of those people who always had buddies who were in the know.

"Her name was Thorne," Boyle continued. "She came from a wealthy family and was killed in Nassau, the week Hagen and Bobby Jones and all those players were playing a Red Cross event. My buddy says the Duke of Windsor—you know, the former king of England—was somehow involved and that's why they hushed it all up, kept it out of the press; they blamed it all on an accident."

I shook my head, trying to puzzle out what he was telling me. "How would they let Cornell in the service if he had killed his wife? It doesn't make sense." My mind was racing, but Boyle's story was enough of a match with what Cornell had told me to suggest that it wasn't another tale fabricated in the caddie yard.

Boyle waved away my protest. "Those people have the money to fix anything. You know how the rich operate." He looked across the room at the table of members to make sure that they hadn't heard him.

I did not know how dukes and rich people operated. Boyle didn't either. What I did know was that by evening, everyone at the club, from members to caddies to the kitchen help, would have heard some version of Boyle's story, embellished it, and whispered it confidentially to someone else. There was no way to stop that rumor about Cornell, even if it wasn't true.

"I got to go," I said, finishing my Coke. "Thanks."

"Watch out for that brother of yours," Boyle cautioned.

I nodded, saying nothing, and waved goodbye and then walked to the locker room. There were only a few men changing clothes and shoes. Early mornings during the week were always slow at the club. In the afternoon, members cut out from work to play eighteen before dark, and at the height of summer they played well into the evening.

I walked down the narrow back steps to the pro shop, feeling again the pain in my bruised ribs, and when I reached the shop, Vicars was there, unpacking new merchandise.

"You've seen Cornell?" I asked, not even waiting for him to ask who had hit me.

"He's out with old man McClain and Drew. They were ready to tee off when I got here this morning. They should have made the turn by now."

I stood for a moment at the screen door of the shop and looked out at the first tee. A threesome was standing together by the scoring tent, waiting to play. I thought about going up to the tent, because from there I could see most of the course and would be able to spot Cornell and the McClains on the back side. But the members were there and they would see my bruises and want to know what had happened.

Instead, I went out the back door of the shop, crossed the empty parking lot, and walked down the slope to the caddie yard, where a dozen kids were pitching pennies at a crude line drawn in the dirt. A few other kids were down at the bottom of the hill, playing handball on the court with an old tennis ball. My guess was that there was also a crap game in progress out of sight on the other side of the concrete slab. I thought about going down there to try to make some money; once I got fired I would need it. But I knew that my ribs couldn't handle the rolling and reaching for dice.

Instead, I went into the shack and up to the mesh wiring and asked the Professor if I could use his phone. I wanted to call home and tell Mom that I was okay.

Leamer picked up the black phone and stretched the cord so that it would reach the small opening. Then he lowered his voice and asked about the fight with Drew McClain.

"What fight?" I asked, keeping my voice low. There were a few caddies sitting on benches in the shack, playing cards and reading comic books.

"The fight last night. Don't hold out on me, O'Shea."

He told me then that Doc Driscoll had called earlier to tell him to make sure I didn't caddie for a few days. The doc sure knew how to spread the word while seeming to care only about my well-being, I thought.

I could have cleared up the mess quickly if I had told the Professor about seeing Clare Farrell run naked across Cottage Row Drive. I could maybe save my job, but only by naming names, and that I wouldn't do.

I waved off the Professor's concern, telling him that it was no big deal. Drew and I had had words, I said, that was all. We were still friends and golfing buddies. I smiled, trying to make it seem like a misunderstanding between teenagers, and dialed the farmhouse. My kid sister, Mary Margaret, answered and I told her to tell Mom that I was okay and I'd be home soon. She started asking questions, telling me that a doctor had called the house, and I told her again that I was okay and that I was at the club and would be home in a few hours. I hung up before she could start on me again.

All this time, the Professor watched me through the wire mesh. I knew he wasn't buying any of my story. But he let it go. That was the thing about being caddie master: despite being holed up in the shack down at the ass end of the country club, he wouldn't have to wait long to know the whole story. Like mud and waste, gossip always flows downhill, and that's where the caddie shack was located.

"Well, you're not looping today, O'Shea. Doctor's orders." He turned away from the wire and went back to his wicker chair.

"Fine with me," I said dismissively. "I need a few days off." I walked out of the shack and into the warm July sunlight. I went up the slope and sat down gingerly on the low concrete wall above the parking lot. When Cornell finished his round, he'd come that way on his way to the caddie shack.

I didn't have a paperback shoved into my back pocket so I had nothing to read. I just sat there and watched the lot fill up with cars. These were driven mostly by wives, arriving with their kids to spend the day at the pool. Most of them were social members, and, while I recognized them, I had never bothered to know them since they didn't play golf.

There were also several carloads of teenagers coming to spend the summer day at the club. I watched them pile out of the cars, kidding around, none of them needing to make money for their families. They didn't have jobs. They never paid for drinks or food at the snack bar; they just signed their dads' membership numbers and never worried about what anything cost.

I didn't envy those kids. Their world had nothing to do with my family and my life on the farm. Drew and Valerie had pulled me across the invisible line of demarcation that separated our worlds, and look what it had gotten me. I felt poor and used and angry, and it was in that state that Cornell found me.

Instead of remarking on how I looked, Cornell sat beside me on the wall and lit a cigarette. "I just caddied for Mr. McClain and Drew, and what a coincidence that Drew appears to have gotten himself all beat up last night."

I said nothing, thinking all the while about what Boyle had said happened in the Bahamas. I couldn't really believe that Cornell had killed his wife. My guess was that there was another story, yet to be heard, one that was somewhere between Boyle's version and what Cornell had told me so far.

"You want to talk about what happened last night?" Cornell asked.

"You want to tell me how your wife got killed in the Bahamas?" I asked back, staring him down.

Cornell's bright eyes darkened and then flickered and hardened for a moment before he replied softly, in full control of himself, "Well, the cat's out of the bag, it appears."

"It appears," I said, but in truth I had no idea what information I was looking for.

Cornell took another long drag of his cigarette. Like me, he was staring across the parking lot, watching the members arrive, all smiles and waves. Then he said, "Tommy, I need you to be able to play against Hagen."

"If Doc Driscoll has his way, I'll be out on my ass before Hagen even gets here."

"What the hell happened last night?"

"No; you tell me what happened in Nassau. I get to the club this morning and there's a story floating around about how you killed your wife. What gives?"

Harrison nodded and then stood up and looked down at me. "Let's take a walk."

"Why?"

"Because you need to go home. Your mother needs to see you. I'm sure she's worried."

"What happened with your wife?" I asked again, not deceived by his apparent concern for my well-being.

"I'll tell you as we walk. It has everything to do with Walter Hagen and why I need you to be able to play this match."

25

"I WASN'T AS LUCKY AS YOU, TOMMY. I NEVER HAD TO MAKE MY way in the world. I was a rich kid living on this tropical island, privileged and sailing smoothly through life, from party to party.

"Nassau was an island for the rich and the famous. In the late thirties everyone came there. Hollywood stars like Errol Flynn, Greta Garbo, Gloria Swanson—they were all on the island before the war. I remember when I was a kid seeing FDR sail into the harbor on a yacht belonging to Jay Goldsmith, the famous New York City tycoon.

"The Brits came as well. The Duke of Kent and Princess Marina honeymooned in Nassau. Most of the royals came at one time or the other, even before the Duke and Duchess of Windsor were sent there to get them out of the way.

"Regular tourists didn't set foot in the Bahamas. Only the very rich came, arriving from New York by boat to spend the winter in their fancy homes up on Prospect Ridge and out along

Cable Beach. The island didn't even have seaplane service from Miami until right before the war, in thirty-seven. For local families like mine, Nassau was always on holiday. In the mornings, we swam; we went sailing in the afternoons and had fish fries under the palm trees or played golf until it was dark and time for dinner and dancing.

"All of us drank too much. People felt as if they were off duty, so to speak, once they reached the Bahamas; that they could do what they wanted. We wrote our own rules. If we didn't make public fools of ourselves, we could do whatever we wanted, and with whomever we wanted.

"There was a good deal of wife swapping. Colonies have always been that way, of course, especially the islands. There are only so many suitable people, and never quite enough to go around.

"I was twenty-two when I married. Our families expected it—had planned it, actually—but the truth is, I was crazy about Gwendolyn. She was wonderful, worldly, much more so than I was, and wild in the most delightful way." Cornell smiled, remembering.

"We had been married less than a year when the war broke out. Of course, the Bahamas wasn't exactly London. No one was bombing us; for us, 'the war' meant we got to do a lot of playacting, looking for German subs, that sort of thing. All great fun and excitement, especially for me.

"I learned to fly, and took a small plane out on aerial patrols. I did spot a couple of submarines, but they turned out to be American, not German. It was my flight experience that eventually got me into the Canadian Air Force, when I left the Bahamas after the accident.

"When the war started, the Duke and Duchess of Windsor were sent over to the Bahamas. That was big news for us."

"It was all Churchill's idea. He wanted the duchess, Wallis Simpson, out of Europe. The rumors were that she was pro-German, which might seem preposterous, but she was furious at the British government for how they'd treated her and her husband. When Edward abdicated in thirty-six to marry her, the British government got them out of the spotlight by giving the duke a face-saving mission in France. He was supposed to be some kind of liaison between the British and French armies. But while they were in Paris, it was rumored Simpson gave the Germans information about British plans. Churchill was livid; he decided to send Wallis far away from the war, somewhere she couldn't cause trouble. So he assigned the duke to the Bahamas as the royal governor, and the royal couple came to Nassau.

"I learned all this background from my wife, who became very close to Wallis on the island. Because she was young and beautiful and had lived in London, she became a favorite of the duchess. And, of course, the duke played golf, so he and I saw each other often on the links. He spent a lot of time in Nassau; the government offices are there, and so is the club. Everything in the Bahamas really happens in Nassau. It was charming in those days, all pink and white and far from the madding crowd."

"So where did Hagen come in?" I asked, in no mood for one of Cornell's tangents. What I didn't realize then was that, as much as he wanted someone to know his real story, it was still hard for him to tell it. Especially the next part—the part about Hagen and Gwendolyn.

Cornell sighed. "Well, the duke invited a group of professional golfers to the islands for an exhibition match to benefit the Red Cross. They had been touring America, playing and raising money for the war effort—Haig, Jones, Armour, and Sarazen.

"They arrived from Palm Beach on the SS *Berkshire*. A ship's arrival in those days was a source of excitement. New people to meet and talk about; a little diversion for our boring lives. We all went down to the dock to greet them. Later that day, we all took the duke to the club to play a round of golf. We played every day for a week before the exhibition, and every night there was a party to attend. That's when Gwendolyn first met Hagen.

"She was a smart woman—she went to Newnham College back in Cambridge—and she had no patience for afternoon bridge, ladies' luncheons, and drunken dinner parties. She got into trouble, I believe now, simply because she was bored. I was lucky: I had something to do. Searching the seas off Hog Island for U-boats was great fun for me and my mates. And when Hagen and the others came to help out the war effort, I couldn't have been more thrilled. Hagen was my hero.

"The pros were on the island for two weeks. There were practice rounds so that the pros could understand the Bahamas course, not that anyone was taking the match that seriously. It was a charity event; still, wagers were made. The Red Cross was a good cause, and Wallis Simpson made a big show of the event. We were all involved.

"And we all wanted to caddie for the pros. There were so many volunteers, the duchess decided to auction off caddie spots at the Bahamas Club the night before the match. Or maybe it was Gwendolyn's idea. Later, I always wondered.

"I liked the idea of caddying so I could get closer to the Haig. He was so friendly and accessible to all of us island people; we must have seemed simple and innocent to someone like him who had been all over the world.

"In the ballroom that night I bid three hundred dollars to caddie for Hagen, and when I won the spot I turned excitedly to Gwendolyn, only to discover she had slipped away.

"The french doors were wide open and a cool breeze blew

the white curtains into the room. I walked out onto the big terrace thinking she might have needed a breath of air.

"There were people out there, men in white dinner jackets and ladies in gowns, couples kissing in dark corners, a few groups of men chatting together as they smoked cigars in the moonlight. Some of them congratulated me on being the winning bidder, but I kept looking around for Gwendolyn. I wanted to share the news with my wife.

"I leaned against the pillar and lit a cigarette. I was waiting for Gwendolyn to find me, to emerge from the powder room, perhaps, and come searching for me, as any wife might, and I spotted a couple embracing deep in the shelter of the clubhouse. The sight of them made my desire for Gwendolyn even more intense.

"The couple broke apart and came slowly up the slope of the lawn, moving from darkness into shadow like actors in a grainy movie. I recognized the familiar slant of the woman's shoulders and realized with the most sickening feeling that it was Gwendolyn. Beside her there on the lawn, his arm still around her waist, was Walter Hagen.

"You can't imagine the nausea that filled me. I spun away from the pillar, walked, then half ran off the terrace, into the bushes, and in the darkness heaved up all the rum I had been drinking that night. I was sick to my stomach, sick of what I had seen.

"Here I was being cheered in the ballroom of the Bahamas Club, raising the bid again and again for the privilege of carrying Walter Hagen's clubs, and there he was, outside in the darkness, having his way with my wife."

We had been walking fast, which was the only way Cornell ever walked, across the course, and he had been talking all the time, puffing his cigarette, gesturing, spilling out his story. At the fourteenth tee was a rain shelter and I told Cornell I needed to rest. My side was throbbing, my ribs aching. Cornell nodded and sat down beside me, but he was so wrapped up in his story that he wasn't paying much attention to how I felt.

He took out another cigarette and kept on talking. I had a sense then that he might have been waiting all summer to share his story.

"Hagen didn't know me," Cornell said. "I was just another rich kid living on this paradise island, living off my family's money. Hagen couldn't have cared less about me, or any of us, really. He was an entertainer. He came into town and played a round or two and dazzled us. He usually had young Joe Kirkwood traveling with him, and Joe would put on a show of his trick shots. A visit from Hagen was a big event at a country club. Few men had done anything like that before: make money by playing golf. Hagen was the first American."

The course was empty on the back side. The early players hadn't made the turn. I heard a few squirrels and birds in the tall trees that framed the hole. Behind us, on the other side of the metal fence, was the two-lane county road where a car or truck would occasionally pass, leaving a whooshing sound in its quick wake.

Cornell would tell me the whole story now, I knew. I just had to be quiet and let him tell me in the only way he knew how—as if he were playing eighteen holes and reliving what had happened on his round, shot by shot.

"When I finally went back into the ballroom, Gwendolyn came up to me and said she was going home. She asked me to go with her. I was too drunk to drive home alone, she told me.

"I didn't answer her. I didn't even look at her. I was staring at Hagen. He was telling a crowd another story, this one about the

French Open that he won in 1920. It was the only national championship he won that year, but he had won the U.S. Open in nineteen, and would go on to win a major title nearly every year for the next decade.

"Hagen said that at the French Open, which was held in La Boulie, outside Paris, pros weren't treated any better than they had been at Deal for the British Open. He was with George Duncan, who had just won the British Open, and Abe Mitchell, the runner-up. They were told to use the stables to change clothes, to hang their stuff on nails. 'They wanted us to bunk in with the horses,' roared Hagen.

"So Hagen led the three of them into the office of Monsieur Pierre Deschamps, the president of the club, and told him they were withdrawing unless they were allowed in the clubhouse. Deschamps had no choice but to give in.

"'But Monsieur Deschamps would get even with me,' says Hagen. Then he pauses and takes a drink. He was making us wait in anticipation.

"Gwendolyn asked me again to leave with her and I bellowed, 'No!' At the noise, Hagen glanced our way. There we were, interrupting his tale, but he smiled at Gwendolyn as if she were the only woman in the room.

"The others were clustered around Hagen, hanging on his every word. The crowd had grown as the evening lengthened. Men pulled over leather chairs and women perched on the thick arms. A ring of men with drinks and cigars in their hands stood behind the chairs. It was a roundabout stage with Hagen in the center, sitting in a deep, leather armchair. He was drinking gin and tonics and smoking a cigarette in an ivory holder. He flashed his famous, engaging smile at anyone who walked within range.

"Gwendolyn thought she was the chosen one, but so did half a dozen other women on the island that winter, and many of them might have been proven right, if not for what happened to Gwendolyn.

"Hagen went back to his story. He said Deschamps had tea with the three of them after every round of the Open, and made Hagen feel at home at La Boulie. It was an inland course and fit his game, not like one of the British links. So he did well, finished in a tie for first with Eugene LaFitte of France, after four rounds.

"Now, Hagen wanted to leave Paris by noon to do a tour of the battlefields of the First World War, but Deschamps says no. He said Hagen and LaFitte needed to settle the tie by playing thirty-six holes. It couldn't be decided in a single-round play-off. Deschamps was getting back at Hagen for blackmailing him about changing clothes in the clubhouse.

"Hagen took another sip of his drink, another long drag of his cigarette. He was having a grand time, telling his story.

"So the next morning, they had the play-off, Hagen says, and he played the thirty-six holes in two and one-half hours and beat LaFitte by four shots. Hagen pushed LaFitte on every hole. On the twelfth hole, for example, where the tee was two hundred feet up an incline, Hagen had the honors and drove off before LaFitte even reached the top of the rise.

"LaFitte wasn't used to playing fast, and on that hole, rushing to keep up with Hagen, he hurried his shot and drove it into the rough right in front of the tee. That was the beginning of the end of his game, and the match.

"But there was more. That night Hagen had a celebration dinner for his friends, a big banquet at the hotel. He dresses up in white tie and tails and when he walks toward the room where the banquet is being held, he spots Pierre Deschamps at his regular reserved table. Hagen walks over to thank him for his courtesies during the tournament.

"Deschamps looks up, startled, at Hagen approaching him,

and his monocle drops. Monsieur Pierre Deschamps doesn't recognize him and Hagen says, 'The French Open . . . ?' by a way of a reminder.

"Deschamps says, 'Non, Ha-*ghan,* he win the championship.'

"Hagen nods, thanks him, and walks off. Monsieur le Président of La Boulie had not recognized him, the great American golfer, when he was off the course and wearing white tie and tails. To the good monsieur, professional golfers were no better than the hired help."

Cornell stood up abruptly, as if he had wasted too much time sitting there in the cool shade, and asked, "Why do you think Hagen told us that long tale?"

I had no idea, of course, but Cornell didn't pause for my reply. A wide smile spread across his thin face, which now, after nearly two months in the Illinois summer, had lost its paleness and tanned into a rich brown, and he supplied the answer: "What Hagen was telling us—all of us rich kids safely away from the battles of Europe—was that he was better than the lot of us. We were like Monsieur le Président of La Boulie: we didn't recognize him in white tie and tails. We didn't know him at all."

For the first time since he'd started talking, Cornell seemed to really look at me. "When you finally come out of the caddie yard, Tommy, you'll be different. You'll have an itch about you. You won't go back to the farm, nor will you be one of those faithful servants in the clubhouse. No, that's what caddying teaches a kid. Hagen learned that a long time ago, when he was looping at the Country Club of Rochester."

Cornell stared at me for a moment, taking in the way I looked, and then, with concern in his voice, he asked if I was okay. I nodded that I was, and he said, "I better get you home."

"No," I said, grabbing his arm. "Not until you tell me what happened to Gwendolyn."

He smiled ruefully, almost as if I'd caught him stealing.

"I find it hard to talk about," he said, "and that stops me." He sank again onto the bench and shook another cigarette out of his beat-up pack. He wasn't looking at me. Then he said, "But you are entitled to know what happened."

With that, Cornell reached into his pocket and pulled out a silver medal and flipped it to me. I caught it in midair and read the inscription.

> *The Duke & Duchess of Windsor*
> *The Bahamas Club*
> *&*
>
> *Bahamas Red Cross*
> *Congratulates*
> *Walter Charles Hagen*
> *"The Haig"*
> *March 1941*

I handed the medal back to Cornell and he slipped it into his pocket.

"I never told Gwendolyn what I'd seen. I caddied for Hagen in the exhibition, then went flying the next Monday morning. I patrolled the far side of Cat Island searching for U-boats, then came back to Oakes Fields and drove home to our house on Prospect Ridge. I knew Gwendolyn wouldn't be there; she had a golf game that morning. The women always played early, when the weather was cool, but we were meeting for lunch at the club.

"It was our normal routine for me to come home after my flight, shower, change into my golf clothes, then drive over to the club.

"I was still in a rage about Gwendolyn and Hagen, but I decided

I couldn't make a fuss and embarrass the royal governor and the duchess, or maybe I was just too cowardly to do so, too afraid of losing her.

"When I went into the house, the staff wasn't there. The whole house was empty. Later I would find that Gwendolyn had given them the day off, even the gardener. I went through the house, calling for Flo and Blanche. No one answered me, but it wasn't really a concern. The servants were my wife's responsibility. I ran up the marble stairwell to the second floor, taking off my tunic, rushing to shower and shave and be on my way to meet her at the club. I hurried into our bedroom at the top of the stairs.

"The bedroom was empty. The outer doors were open to the sea. The bed was unmade. I had left the house before dawn, before Gwendolyn was awake. She would have left the room for the staff to deal with, but none of them were there."

Cornell paused and smiled, then asked, "Have you guessed why the staff were given the day off, Tommy?"

I figured that I knew why, but I couldn't bring myself to say it.

"I thought nothing of the bed being unmade," Cornell continued. "I went about getting ready for lunch and then a game of golf. When I sat down on the edge of the bed to put on my shoes, I kicked a piece of metal." Cornell paused and pulled the silver piece from his pocket again and flipped it with his thumb and finger, then grabbed it out of the air as if he were snatching a golf ball in flight.

"Now, how might something like that happen? How might a special award from the duke and duchess end up under my wife's bed? I asked myself." Cornell looked my way and his eyes widened, and I glimpsed again the sadness deep within them.

"I went a little crazy," Cornell said. "I drove to the club. Gwendolyn was already eating lunch on the terrace with two of her girlfriends, and I went up to the table and tossed the medal into her chicken-mango salad. I was in such a rage that Gwendolyn and the other women were all blurry in my vision, but I do remember how Gwendolyn, using her knife and fork, lifted the silver medal from her plate as if it were an unappetizing slice of meat and set it aside, then stood and walked away from her playing partners—walked away from *me*.

"I followed her through the dining room full of people barraging her with accusations and questions along the way, right in front of all the members. I followed her out into the parking lot where she had parked her small Austin and only then did she turn and deal with me.

"She lambasted me for my behavior in front of her friends, and now how could she show her face on Nassau Street again? She tore into me for embarrassing her, but never answered my question about how Hagen's silver medal had found its way into our bedroom. Then she slammed the car door and drove out of the parking lot, squealing tires on the pavement and leaving me choking in a thick cloud of exhaust fumes. That was the last time I saw her alive."

He stopped speaking. He was still staring down the length of fourteen, from our bench in the shelter, through the tight chute of maple and oak trees, into the wide open landing area a hundred yards away, where the bunker jutted out and the fairway doglegged right.

I was holding my breath, waiting for whatever he might say next, and he picked up his narrative, still speaking calmly, but each word full of the pain that he had gone through in Nassau.

"The roads on the island are tight and twisting and she was speeding, getting away from me. We think a tire must have blown, for she lost control of the car near Oakes Fields where the road straightens out. She was passing a truck and the Austin flipped over."

He stopped again. There were more details, of course, and in time I would discover them myself, but he couldn't continue.

"It's okay," I said, nodding, and touched his shoulder so that he would know I understood. Beneath the fabric of the jacket he insisted on wearing even in the warmest of weather, his arm felt thin and weak.

"So," he concluded, standing now, "I've come to see Mr. Hagen to settle with him about this!" He flipped the silver coin into the air, where it spun in the light, and caught it. I realized that he was so deft at the trick that he had probably practiced it night after night as he sat alone in empty rooms. Then he said, "Tommy, let's go. I want to see you safely home so nothing bad happens to you."

I stood slowly and moaned with pain.

"Easy, lad," Cornell said, seizing my elbow to steady me. "You need to rest, or you'll never be able to beat Hagen."

I had to laugh at the ludicrousness of that idea. There was no way I could match up with Hagen, with my bruised ribs. I was about to tell Cornell as much when he stopped, understanding what I was thinking, and said with complete seriousness, "If I can get through the war and out of that German prison-of-war camp and the loony bin, you can play an eighteen-hole match against an old man like Hagen. You want to go to college, don't you?"

I drew myself up to my full height and took a deep breath. "Look, I can't help you, Cornell. Doc Driscoll will see to that. By the time Hagen gets here, I won't even be working at Midlothian anymore."

He stared as I explained what had happened, his eyes hidden

in the shadow of his panama. But when he raised his head to look me in the face, the pain was gone and his eyes were bright with pleasure. It was a look I had seen before when he was onto something, and even before he spoke, I knew that he had a plan.

26

I TOOK A FEW DAYS OFF FROM CADDYING, ALTHOUGH IN THE EVE-
nings I walked over to thirteen green and worked on my short
game and putting, using Patterson's clubs, which Cornell and I
had repaired. What surprised me most was how much the hickory clubs were like my steel shafts, once I got the feel of them.

During the days I hung around the farmhouse and played with
the little kids on the front lawn, picked early apples from our orchard for Mom, and drove a few times into town to shop. But
mostly I sat on the screened-in porch and read the half dozen new
novels Mrs. Butterfield had sent me from the Midlothian Public
Library. And then on Wednesday afternoon Valerie Driscoll came
to see me, wheeling her father's big Cadillac into our driveway.

She hopped out of the car, walked up to the screen door, and
rang the bell as if she had been coming to the O'Shea home all
her life. In her arms was a bouquet of wildflowers.

"Hi," I said from the deep corner of the porch, and my voice surprised her. She leaned forward and shaded her eyes to see inside.

"Hi!" she said, and the delight in her voice filled me with joy. I came over and opened the screen door. "I didn't see you," she said, her eyes sweeping the porch. Then she quickly kissed me. "Hi," she said again, softly, and handed me the flowers. "These are for you."

"Wow." I took them. "No one has ever given me flowers before." In fact, we had never had flowers from a store in our house.

"You've never been nearly killed before," she said, and then asked, "May I come in?"

"Oh, I'm sorry." I moved aside and she stepped onto the wide front porch. I glanced around, suddenly realizing what a mess everything was, with the kids' toys and my piles of papers and books. I was barefoot, in old pants and a work shirt that I wore when doing chores. I always wore my best clothes when I caddied.

"You've caught me off guard," I said, gesturing around.

"Don't apologize," she told me. "This is your home. I'm the one who should apologize for not telephoning. But I was afraid you'd say no, so I just came."

Then she looked over my shoulder. Following her gaze, I saw my mother standing in the door of the house. As always, she was wearing an apron over her dress, which she had made herself.

"Mom, this is Val . . . Valerie Driscoll, from the club," I said quickly. It was the first time I had ever introduced a girl to my mother.

Valerie stepped forward to shake hands, smiling, chattering greetings.

"Driscoll," my mother repeated, as if thinking out loud. "That's an Irish name."

"It is?" Valerie said, "I don't know much about my family history, I'm afraid."

The kids arrived next, standing behind Mom's skirt, wide-eyed and silent at the sight of Valerie.

"Hello," Val said. She glanced at me again. "How many of them are there?"

I laughed at her surprise at the sight of so many children. Seeing that I wouldn't send them away, they swarmed onto the porch and gathered around me. As they arrived, I introduced them.

"There are seven of us. This is Mary Margaret; she's ten."

"Eleven," corrected Mary Margaret, her eyes fixed on the blond stranger.

"And Emmett's nine; and Patrick, eight; and the baby, Eileen." I tapped their heads, introducing them. Seeing them all together, thinking of how they must look to Valerie, all of them with dirty faces from playing in the yard, wearing old clothes passed down from one to the next, I wished that she had called and not surprised me with her visit. I could have cleaned up the kids.

"And the others?"

"My kid brothers, Jimmy and Mike. You know them—they're caddies."

"Jimmy caddied for me once last summer," Valerie said. "He looks like you." Then her eyes swept the lot of us and, laughing, she said, "They *all* look like you!"

"I'm the best-looking, Mom says," Mary Margaret piped up.

Valerie leaned down and smiled into Mary Margaret's face and whispered. "And I agree."

"I'll get a vase for these lovely flowers," Mom said, moving back into the house. As she did, she called to the kids, "Leave Tommy alone now."

None of them moved. They wouldn't move. Their eyes were wide, taking in everything about Valerie, who had appeared in a lovely summer dress, wearing jewelry and lipstick and driving a big fancy car. They couldn't get enough of her.

In a few minutes, once their shyness wore off, they would begin to pepper her with questions. Mom came back with the flowers in a tall glass vase and told Mary Margaret to get us glasses of iced tea, and told the others to leave us be. She set the flowers on the small round table near the porch swing and admired them for a moment, telling Valerie again how lovely they were. I know she was already wondering how much they had cost and why would the girl pay good money to buy flowers in a florist shop when they grew wild along 147th Street.

I sat back and watched with amusement. Later, I knew, I would have a million questions, and Valerie would be immediately dubbed "Tommy's girlfriend."

Mom, too, would have questions, though she would pose them as comments, saying how nice it was that Valerie Driscoll—never just "Val"—had driven over just to bring me expensive flowers when she could've just spent the day in the country-club pool.

"Okay," I told the kids, "all of you—out of here."

They could hear in my voice that I meant it, and slowly, as if they were emerging from hypnosis, they began to drift off to play games in the yard or disappear into their rooms and read books. Secretly, of course, they'd find ways to keep staring at Valerie. And who could blame them. She looked lovely in her bright yellow dress, smelling of lilac. I couldn't take my eyes off her either, and my mom, I knew, could see my reaction.

"They're adorable," Valerie whispered when the porch cleared. "You're so lucky."

"Most days I wouldn't call it lucky."

Even though they were gone we could still hear them playing and arguing.

"That's one reason I like golf," I said. "I like the peace and quiet."

"Even in the caddie house?"

"Yep, even in the caddie shack. Not house." I smiled, amused that she didn't know the most basic caddie terms. I told her then about how I walked across the course in the stillness of the early morning when there was no one out playing. I told her how I went through the groves of elm and oak and listened to the birds and the rustle of rabbits, imagining that the place belonged to me. And as I walked, I would promise myself that if I ever made any money I'd build my own golf course, not just for myself but for others to play. I'd design it as if I were an artist painting an oil.

Valerie was sitting in one of the wooden porch chairs, and when I finished going on about the golf course, she got up and came over and sat beside me, kicking off her sandals and curling up on the swing.

"That's so neat," she said.

"What?"

She shrugged. "Oh, that you think those thoughts. That you have those feelings and ideas. I don't know." She shrugged again and blushed a little.

" 'Thank you for the flowers," I said, nodding at them.

"You're welcome; but they're just my excuse to come over. I missed you."

I leaned forward and kissed her quickly. Behind me, from the doorway, I heard Mary Margaret say, "Mom wants to know if she'd like to stay for lunch."

"You mean Valerie?" I said.

"Mom wants to know if Valerie would like to stay for lunch," Mary Margaret said again, sighing.

Watching me, Valerie whispered. "Is that okay?"

"I would love it," I said.

"Okay then." Valerie smiled and then added, "But only if you'll come to dinner at my house on Saturday night."

"I don't know about that."

"Why? Don't you miss me, too?"

"Yes, of course I do. But I doubt your dad misses me. He's probably glad I'm not around."

"See, that's where you're wrong," Val said triumphantly. "When I asked daddy if I could take the car and come see you, he told me to find out if you thought you'd be back caddying soon. He said everyone is asking for you."

"He did?"

"Why wouldn't he be concerned about you? That big exhibition with Hagen is in a couple of weeks or so. Aren't you playing in it?"

I shook my head. "I don't know. I don't know anything." I didn't say what I thought—that her father wanted me out of Midlothian and away from her. Instead I said, "It's a deal. I'll come for dinner." Without turning around, and knowing that my kid sister was still in the doorway watching us, I told Mary Margaret to have Mom to set another plate at the kitchen table, that Valerie was staying for lunch. And then I said to Valerie, "Brace yourself."

27

"Hɪ!" ᴠᴀʟᴇʀɪᴇ sᴡᴜɴɢ ᴛʜᴇ ꜰʀᴏɴᴛ ᴅᴏᴏʀ ᴡɪᴅᴇ ᴏᴘᴇɴ ᴡɪᴛʜ ᴀ flourish. "So nice of you to come." She leaned sassily against the frame, wearing a light blue dress, a ribbon in her hair, and earrings that sparkled in the light.

"You didn't have to get all dressed up," she whispered as I stepped carefully into the foyer. The lamps were ablaze in every room. At home, my dad was always going around the house shutting off lights, muttering about the electric bills.

"You're dressed up," I whispered back.

"That's a girl thing," she said. "You can take off your tie, if you want. Daddy never wears a tie at dinner. And your jacket. You can roll up your sleeves and be comfortable." With that, she leaned closer and kissed me quickly on the lips, then spun away and closed the front door, leaving a trail of perfume in her wake.

"Oh, Tommy. Good. You're just in time," Doc Driscoll said, appearing at the wide living-room entrance. He had a section of

the Sunday *Tribune* in one hand and was holding a drink and a
cigarette in the other.

"I have to go help Grace put dinner on the table," Val said.
Slipping behind me, she poked me in the back, nudging me forward.

I followed Doc Driscoll into the front room. I didn't remember the house from when I had spent my emergency night in
their spare bedroom. I hadn't been in any condition to notice
anything. Now I saw that the living room was enormous, stretching the depth of the house. There were deep sofas and wing
chairs clustered around a stone fireplace. Beyond them were a
grand piano, leather chairs, and a wall of books. I had never seen
so many books in anyone's home before. The back wall was all
glass, with sliding doors that were opened so that a warm breeze
blew in. Lights were lit deep in the garden, displaying flower
beds in bloom.

"Sit down, Tommy," Driscoll said, waving me to one of the
armchairs. "Would you like a Coke?" He moved to a small por-
table cabinet stacked with bottles. "I need to freshen this gin and
tonic," he said. "Oh, Tommy, I had a seventy-nine today; birdied seven, nine, and twelve. I would have been lower if I had
gotten a few breaks. I missed an easy five-footer on number two
for a birdie, and missed par on eighteen when the ball just lipped
out."

He proceeded to tell me about his round, hole by hole. With
his handicap, he had made money that afternoon, playing
five-dollar Nassau with his foursome of doctors.

I had caddied for Doc Driscoll hundreds of times over the
years when he played early in the morning, sometimes going
again with him and Mrs. Driscoll for a round of mixed four-
somes later in the day. I knew his game and knew that today he'd
been lucky.

He came back with my Coke in a tall glass filled with ice and handed it to me, asking, "How are those ribs? Holding up?" He dropped down into a wide leather chair and lit a cigarette. The *Tribune* was in a pile on a leather footstool. A standing lamp was on the other side of the chair and the bright reading light shone down on his face, making him look old. His eyes were glassy and I knew that he had spent the afternoon hours at the club playing gin rummy in the men's bar. The summer before, he would have been on the golf course with Valerie's mother.

I was sitting forward in the wing chair, holding my cold Coke with both hands, too tense to relax. I kept hoping Val would hurry back to the living room. I was afraid of what Doc Driscoll would say to me, now that he had me in his house again.

He snapped out of it and looked at me. "We were talking about you today, Tommy. You know, with Hagen coming in a few weeks."

"Saturday morning, right? Twelve o'clock tee time?"

Driscoll gestured with his cigarette hand. "Twelve or one. Hagen is famously late, I'm told. Seems he runs his own show. Of course, the WGA will be here and they'll have something to say about all of our plans. No, we were talking about you in regards to who will play with the Haig."

I had a sudden fear that Valerie had said something to her father, that Cornell's grand scheme was common knowledge in the clubhouse.

Driscoll went on. "I know I had mentioned to you about caddying for Haig; everyone agrees you're the best kid we have at the club, and you've been caddying, what, five years or more?"

"I started the summer I turned twelve, sir," I said. "It's been seven years all together."

"I remember you back when our bags were almost as big as you." He chuckled then and shook his head at the memory.

"Well, the members have a lot of nice things to say about you, Tommy, but the feeling is that this Harrison Cornell might be the best caddie for Hagen. They know each other from the Bahamas. It should make some news, that's what Doug McClain believes. The *Tribune* and the other Chicago papers will be sending reporters to write the story of Hagen's last round of golf with hickory clubs. Of course, everyone wants you to caddie in the foursome."

"Who's playing?" I asked, realizing that Driscoll and the other members didn't know our plans for the match against Hagen.

Driscoll shook his head. "That hasn't been decided. I'm told Hagen will have his say. Perhaps Drew, since he's the club champ, and Red. Cornell will be the Haig's caddie," Driscoll insisted. "The membership thinks that would be best, since Cornell told us he caddied for Hagen down in Nassau."

"Sounds reasonable," I said, and wondered then if any of the members had heard Billy Boyle's story of what had happened in Nassau.

"Now, I hear there's this rumor going around—Billy Boyle was telling me—that Cornell was in some trouble in Nassau. We checked into it with the Western Golf Association; they never heard anything of the kind. You know how Billy likes gossip." He waved away Boyle's story, and I wondered how shocked Driscoll and the other members would be if they knew the real story about Hagen and Cornell.

"I'll make sure we get a photograph of you with Hagen, and an autograph. How 'bout that?" Driscoll said next, as if he was still worried about my reaction to not looping for Hagen. Driscoll leaned forward, smiling, waiting for me to agree that this was best for everyone. That was always the disposition of country-club life, smooth sailing with no awkward, embarrassing scenes.

I nodded and smiled.

"Good." Driscoll pulled himself out of the leather chair and went to the bar for more gin.

"There was a long meeting of the House Committee today," he said next, putting some liquor in his drink.

"They had to fire a waitress," he said, keeping his back to me. "It seems one of Ed Duehr's men saw her running across the golf course stark naked; the girl you saw the other night. That's totally unacceptable for a private club like ours. We can't have girls like her working at this club. The wives won't allow it. Oh, you might know her, Tommy. Her name is Clare Farrell."

Then Valerie appeared in the doorway and announced, "Daddy and Tommy. Dinner is served."

28

After dinner, Valerie walked out with me to Dad's chevy. The course was shrouded in darkness on the other side of Cottage Row Drive.

I took out my car keys, but Val motioned that I should follow her and kept walking. Wordlessly, she led me to the low stone wall that bordered the club property. Finding a flat stone, she swung her legs up so that she was sitting on the wall facing the tenth fairway. It was only then that she said, "It wasn't Daddy's idea."

"What wasn't?" I asked.

"You know what I'm talking about."

"They're not kicking McClain out of the club, are they?"

"He wasn't running naked across the golf course."

"No, he was too busy beating the hell out of me."

When she didn't answer, I said next, "I've got to go. Thank you for dinner and everything." As I turned, Val's voice rose.

"Tommy, this doesn't have anything to do with us. Don't be mad at me."

"I'm not mad at you." I stepped up behind her and wrapped my arms around her shoulders and she leaned back, turning her head so that her face was nestled in the nape of my neck.

She took a deep breath and said, "I'm sorry, Tommy."

"It's not your fault."

"Then why are you blaming me?"

"I'm not."

"You're blaming Daddy and that means you're blaming me." She pulled out of my embrace.

I had had enough of that. I turned away and started tramping through the long grass back to my car. I had reached it, and had my hand on the door, when I heard her sobbing. She had pulled her legs up under her and made herself into a tight ball, her head buried in her knees.

"Dammit." I turned around and stomped back to the wall and pulled her into my arms and let her cry. We were hidden in the darkness, and even if her father was at one of the upstairs windows, trying to see what his daughter was up to with the kid from the caddie yard, he could not have seen us there. I half expected to find him standing in the light of the entranceway at any moment, calling out her name, summoning her home like the household pet.

Valerie wiped her tears by drying them against my shirt and sports jacket and then hungrily, in a rage of emotion, began to kiss my lips, my neck, to fill her mouth with my flesh. Then she pulled away, jumped down inside the wall, and seized my hand to pull me after her, onto the dark golf course.

I could see in her eyes what she wanted and I shook my head and whispered, "No."

"Yes, we can. It's what I want, Tommy. I love you. I want to before I go back to that awful school." She seized my hand with hers and pulled harder. I slipped off the wall and embraced her, pressing my body against hers. Half of me wanted to slip down into the dark on the cool grass and make love to her. The other half of me knew that it was crazy and that at any moment Doc Driscoll would appear at the wall, waving a searchlight in our direction.

"Please," she begged, dropping to her knees and pulling me down to the soft ground. I slid off my jacket and tossed it aside and went to her just as we heard Doc Driscoll. He stood in the doorway and was calling her name.

"Damn." I'd never heard Val swear before. Then she called up to her father, saying that she would be right there. She sat up and I helped her to her feet, standing quickly and retrieving my jacket. I slipped it on, tucked in my white shirt, and pulled myself together.

"Where are you?" Driscoll called back, starting down the brick walk. I saw the lighted tip of his cigarette as he stood there scanning the black night.

"We went for a walk, Daddy," Valerie called. There was an edge to her voice as she straightened her dress and headed for the stone wall. Together we stepped through the long grass and onto the country-club road.

"Oh, there you are." Driscoll sounded relieved. "I was afraid you might get lost out there," he said, laughing, trying to make a joke of his vigilance.

"Tommy would never get lost," Valerie answered, defending me.

"I better get going," I said. "Val, Dr. Driscoll. Thank you for dinner." I couldn't stop jingling my car keys.

Doc Driscoll shook my hand and said good night for the second time in minutes. He walked back up the narrow walk to the open front door, then turned and waited for Valerie. Instead of going to him, she walked with me to the car and, in a show of defiance, kissed me on the lips in view of her father.

I drove down Cottage Row Drive to the dead end, turned around, and drove back, passing the Driscoll house. Valerie was still standing on the sidewalk in front of her home. I waved good night as I slowly went by. She blew me a kiss and ran up the steps and into the house.

Driving to the club, I decided to stop and check in with Boyle, to tell him that no one believed his story about Cornell murdering his wife. There were a half dozen members' cars scattered about the lot and the clubhouse lights were blazing. I knew that Boyle would still be working and would know the story behind Clare's getting fired.

"You've heard?" he said under his breath as I slid onto a bar stool. There were two tables of members playing poker. I saw money as well as chips tossed onto the green felt tables.

I nodded.

Boyle opened a bottle of Pabst and slid it across the bar to me.

"Go ahead." He nodded at the beer. "Besides, it ain't the first beer you've ever had in your life."

"So, what happened?" I asked, taking a long sip.

Boyle perched his leg up under the bar and, softly and confidentially, whispered his story.

There had been a special meeting of the House Committee that afternoon, he reported, pointing at the spot where the members had gathered. Clare had been the only item on the agenda.

"There was a big to-do about her," Billy said, "as if she were the first female to drop her panties on the fairway." He puffed away on a cigarette as he went on with his story.

"McClain kept saying the country club couldn't risk any incidents like that, and she should be fired as an example." Boyle smirked.

"Anyone ask if there was a man with her?"

Boyle shook his head. "Not a one. Oh, they knew well enough Drew was involved, but his name never came up—not with his old man sitting at the head of the table."

"Was Driscoll there?"

"Not at first. He came into the bar from the locker room and wanted a drink. He's not on the House Committee, but Mc-Clain asked him what he thought, told him the whole story. It was one of the groundskeepers who spotted her. He had been watering the back side and was on the service road, heading for the barn, when Farrell, I guess, came running out of the bushes. He didn't know who it was, but someone else came forward and tattled."

Boyle blew out a thick cloud of smoke. I could tell that he knew who had identified Clare to the committee. Now he wanted to tell me. He was waiting, wanting me to ask him, but I didn't have to. Suddenly I knew who had told the members.

"Cornell, right?" I said.

"Your good buddy." Boyle shook his cigarette hand at me. "I warned you about that fella, didn't I?" He kept nodding as he slipped the cigarette between his thin lips, looking immensely pleased with himself.

29

I DROVE MY DAD'S CAR BACK TO THE CLUB IN THE MORNING, wanting to catch the Professor at the clubhouse before he went down to the shack. I found him in the employees' dining room, having breakfast.

The look on his face when he spotted me told me that he knew why I was there.

"What's going on?" I slipped into the chair opposite him at the small table.

"I had nothing to do with it, Tommy." He waved his fork.

"Does Cornell think I'm a complete goddamn fool?"

Sandy came into the dining room and slid a plate of eggs and bacon in front of me.

"Have something to eat," he said, "and watch your goddamn language or I'll throw you out of my goddamn dining room." He grinned and left us.

"I don't know what Harrison Cornell is thinking or planning," the Professor said softly. "I had nothing to do with anything that has happened here."

"You talked about what happened that night," I said, digging into the free breakfast.

"Everyone talked about it, Tommy, just not to you. You know if it wasn't your darlin' Clare Farrell, you'd be spreading the story yourself."

"Why did Cornell go blabbing about it to members?"

"Who said he did?"

"Billy Boyle." Then I told him about having had dinner with Driscoll and how the members wanted Cornell on Hagen's bag, not me.

The Professor poured himself another cup of coffee, pushed his chair away from the table, and, leaning back, lit a Lucky Strike. He was smiling.

"What's so funny?"

"I thought you were going to play *against* Hagen, not caddy for him."

"Who told you that?"

"No one told me that. I see what's going on, you and Cornell playing with those hickories."

"What are you trying to tell me?"

The Professor tapped the ash of his cigarette into the remains of the egg yolk.

"C'mon, what's he planning?" I asked.

The Professor planted his elbows on the tabletop. "I don't know. The Duehr brothers didn't see who she was. Ed told me so when I asked him. Cornell *volunteered* that information. Now why would he?"

"I'm going to ask him."

"Be careful, Tommy. The man has a story of his own."

I knew that Cornell was no murderer, but I didn't tell the Professor that. "If he's so dangerous, why did you let him start looping here?"

The Professor didn't respond at once. He took a final drag on his cigarette and snuffed out the butt on his breakfast plate. "He helped me out once. He did it when he didn't need to, and you don't forget that. There are enough bastards in the world who are willing to screw you, so you don't forget the fellas who give you a break." He shrugged. "I owed him."

"I don't owe him," I answered, pushing away my empty plate.

"Don't be so sure. Hagen hasn't arrived yet." He stood, picked up his plate and coffee cup, and returned them to the kitchen. "What are you going to do?"

"Find Cornell."

The Professor did not respond until we walked outside and were beyond where anyone might hear us. He stopped at the breezeway and lit another cigarette.

"Look," he said, "you're a big boy, Tommy. You got to be smart about this. You know how all the members think Cornell is the best caddie they've ever had. It's magic, really. Black magic. He goes out with someone and they shoot the best round of their career."

"So?"

"Look out for yourself. Don't go waving your caddie towel for Clare Farrell. What has she done for you but tell you to take a hike? She went after the member's son, the kid with money. Don't try to get her job back, Tommy."

"She was running away from McClain, for chrissake."

"Yeah, running away buck naked. What do you think the two of them were doing out there—talking to a serpent, eating an apple? Grow up, kid."

He flipped his cigarette into the bushes and headed down to the caddie yard, moving slowly and limping on his bad leg and leaving me to deal with my problem.

I walked around to the front of the clubhouse and looked for Cornell. We had planned to play, so I knew that he would be there, either down on the range or putting. I spotted him on the putting green.

"Where have you been?" he asked, looking up.

"Having breakfast. Talking to the Professor."

Cornell nodded. He was using a blade putter with a hickory shaft, and he said, "I'm going to make sure the greens aren't cut the morning you play. You'll do better when the greens aren't fast."

"What about Clare Farrell?" I asked, disregarding his golf talk. I made a point of not raising my voice, of being calm and collected.

"Ah, Miss Farrell." Harrison smoothly stroked the putt. He didn't look my way.

I waited him out.

With the putter blade he toed another ball into place and settled over it. Then, without looking up, he said, "The truth is, I am sorry Clare has become a victim of circumstances." He stroked the ball, then looked directly at me. "Doc Driscoll came to me a day or so after your mishap with McClain. He had heard from the Duehrs about a naked girl. He put two and two together and asked me if it was Clare Farrell."

"You didn't tell him!"

Harrison shook his head, smiling wryly. "As you've said yourself, there are no secrets at a country club."

"Christ, this is my fault. Instead of going to Val's that night, I should've just gone home and not gotten Driscoll involved."

"Should have, could have, would have. The story of the human race." He cradled the putter under his arm and took a Zippo lighter from his pocket. Watching him, I thought how every day he looked more and more like a member instead of a caddie. He still wore a panama, but it was a new one now, and he had a new dark tie, a white shirt, and light, soft cotton pants. Even the kitchen matches were gone.

He flipped open the lighter and lit his cigarette as he said, "This will all work out for the best."

"I see you managed to get yourself on Hagen's bag."

Cornell waved it off. "I'll be looping for you, Tommy. Don't get yourself all twisted up over that girl. She wasn't a child; she knew what she was doing out there in the dark with the club president's boy." He shook his head. "You want to worry? Worry about yourself playing against Hagen." He walked to the cup and lifted the small metal flag, bouncing his golf ball out of the hole and onto the smooth green, then set himself to putt. The cigarette was still wedged between his lips and he squinted to avoid the drifting smoke.

I followed him and said calmly, "No, you worry about caddying again for Hagen."

I turned around and walked off, back to the car, back to the farm, back to a world that had nothing to do with country-club life. I was done with caddying.

30

THE NEXT MORNING I GOT UP AT FIVE O'CLOCK AND WENT TO work for my dad. He sent me off on our Farmall F-12 tractor with its big steel spiked rear wheels to cultivate the lowland cornfield south of the barn and never asked why I had quit the club. It wasn't his way to quiz me. He'd let me take my time to tell him what had happened. Mom didn't say anything either; but I knew the day wouldn't finish without her wanting to know why I had stopped caddying.

I finished working in the south field a little after eleven and drove back to the barn. It was a hot summer day and I was sweating and exhausted. Dad had offered me a farmer's hat but I had worn my caddie cap instead, and it wasn't enough. The back of my neck was burned and my shirt was soaking wet. Unlike the golf course, the cornfield had no shade.

I drove the tractor into the barnyard, parked under the shade of the big oak, and leaned my head against the narrow steering wheel, closing my eyes and resting for a few minutes. My whole body hurt from wrestling with the big tractor.

I was climbing down, at last, when I spotted Clare. She was standing in the shade of the barn, leaning against the wide door frame in a white blouse and a pair of blue jeans. She didn't move or say anything, just watched me as I came up the rise. When I got close enough, I said "Hi," and walked into the barn, and felt the relief of its dark shadows.

"What are you doing?" she asked, not moving from the doorway.

"What farmers do," I said. I flopped down on a bale of hay near the wall. "I've been cultivating." I was suddenly and surprisingly angry at her for everything that had happened.

She followed me to the bale and sat down, being careful not to sit too close to me. My whole body was wet with sweat.

"I got a telephone call this morning from that caddie guy, your friend." She spoke carefully, as if English were her second language.

"You mean Cornell?"

"You're playing golf against Walter Hagen, or something?"

"Not anymore. I quit working at the club."

She studied me for a minute and then said seriously, "Don't do it because of me."

"Not play Hagen or not quit the club?"

"This isn't your problem. What happened to me is my fault." I heard pain in her voice and I glanced her way. She was staring straight ahead. Her hands were laced together between her legs and she kept anxiously twisting her fingers.

"It's my fault, what happened to you," I said.

She stared at me in puzzlement and I told her the full story of going to Driscoll's house, of seeing her, of Drew McClain beating me up, and of how, instead of going home, I had gone to Valerie's house and talked to Dr. Driscoll. I had never mentioned her name, I told her, but the story had gotten back to the House Committee, and now she was out of a job because I'd gotten help from the wrong man.

"Oh, God!" She jumped up and began to pace. "This is a nightmare." She had her arms wrapped tightly around her, hugging herself as if she were freezing.

She came to where I was sitting, stood over me, and told me to go back to work and not to use her as my excuse.

"What are you talking about?"

She had her finger in my face, leaning over me, her blue eyes flashing.

"Just what I said," she said. "You're running away from this match, Cornell told me."

"I'm not running away from anything," I answered back. "I'm pissed at them for firing you. They had no right."

"They had every right to fire me," Clare answered, still hovering over me. "It was stupid, what I did. But I did it, not you. I don't care if you play Hagen or not, but I won't have you going around claiming you quit Midlothian because I shouldn't have been fired for what I did."

She began to cry then and spun away from me, burying her face in her hands. Then she started to storm off, but I grabbed her from behind, seizing her shoulders to keep her from leaving.

"Let me go," she ordered.

I dropped my hands and saw that I had soiled her white blouse with my sweaty fingers.

She didn't move. I stepped carefully around to keep her from bolting out of the barn. With her palms she wiped the tears from her cheeks, leaving her face streaked with smudgy dark lines.

"You know what your problem is, Tommy," she said calmly, still drying her face, using the short sleeves of her blouse to dry away her tears. "You think like a caddie. You're always there waiting for some member to tell you to carry his bag, or go up on the green and pull the flag, to wash his golf balls, to do whatever little chores he might want you to do."

"It's a job, Clare. And I'm good at it," I defended myself. "Besides, what are you being so uppity about; you're a waitress, for chrissake."

"I *was* a waitress, not anymore. I was working at Midlothian to get what I wanted, a college degree, so I'd never again have to kowtow to members like them."

"Harrison says everyone is a caddie, one way or another."

"He's some authority. If he's so smart, why is he still looping?" Clare shot me a look and stepped around me. Now she really was leaving, but before she stepped into the sunlight, she paused at the barn door and turned around and said calmly, "The night you saw me on the golf course I had had a fight with Drew. I wanted him to take me to the dinner dance they're having when Hagen comes to play. We've been going out all summer and members have seen us together, but he said he couldn't take me. He said it wouldn't be right, taking a Midlothian waitress to a club dance. It's okay, I guess, for him to take me out into the woods and make love to me in the dark, but he can't be seen with me at his country-club dance."

She was crying silently now. Tears washed down her beautiful face and I moved forward to comfort her, but she raised her hand to stop me and kept talking.

"You see, Tommy, I thought I could just waltz myself into their society. Oh, I'm a poor Irish kid, all right, from across the county road. But I'm smart, a scholarship student at Smith College, a college as fancy as Drew's Yale. I foolishly thought I was just as good as the McClains. But no, to them I'm not as good; I'm a mackerel snapper, as Drew's mother is fond of saying. I thought I would be accepted by people like Drew's parents. It was a big mistake on my part, not Drew's. He's not strong enough, I see now, to make a decision on his own. His parents will keep their thumbs on that boy for the rest of his life. Yes, the McClains can keep me from dating their son, but they can't stop me from proving them all wrong. Watch me, Tommy. Watch what I make of myself once I earn my college degree. You'll never see me waiting on people like them again."

She turned and walked into the sunlight and down to the barnyard drive and only then did she hesitate, glance back, and make her final point. Her voice softened and she said nicely, "You're a better person than most of those members, Tommy. Go make something of yourself."

Then, without even a "goodbye" or a "good luck," she walked up the drive to 147th Street. She turned left and never looked back.

Long after she was out of sight, I stood in the barn doorway with my arms crossed, my whole body aching from half a day's work in the farm fields and my mind spinning with everything she had said. I was still standing there when Dad came back from town, driving the truck into the yard and walking over to me. He had seen that I had finished cultivating the corn and asked me what I planned on doing next.

I told him that I was going over to the back nine of Midlothian and hit balls. I told him that I had a match in two weeks with one of the greatest players in the game and didn't have much time left to practice with my hickories.

31

"THERE HE IS," HARRISON ANNOUNCED. HIS VOICE WAS SOFT AND low, as if he was sharing bad news.

I looked up. We were sitting on the wall at the top of the parking lot and I spotted, a quarter mile away, the long black limousine sailing over the country-club bridge. It glided smoothly under the elms and oaks and maples that shaded the private road, then burst into the sunlight of the lot and kept going. The car continued up the slope and into the circle drive and stopped in front of the clubhouse entrance.

The club's board of directors had been waiting and watching for Hagen. As the limousine pulled up, they walked down the clubhouse path and then waited while the livery driver jumped from the front seat and went around to open the rear door. It took several moments before Hagen emerged from the dark backseat into the bright sunlight of that August Saturday morning.

I realized then that I had been holding my breath in antici-pation. When Hagen stepped from the car, he reached out immediately to shake hands with Mr. McClain, Drew's father. He and the other members, including Dr. Driscoll, clustered about the legendary player. Standing with the board of directors were a few other men, dressed in distinctive green jackets and ties. They were, I guessed, from the Western Golf Association, and had come to accept Hagen's gift of his U.S. Open–winning hickory clubs.

Off to the side was another man, this one in a blue blazer and tie. He was tall and thin, and although he was with the WGA directors, he had a different demeanor. He waited for Hagen to come to him, which the big guy soon did, stepping out of his circle of admirers to embrace the mystery man and shake his hand warmly. I realized then that it was Chick Evans, who'd finished second to Hagen in the 1914 Open.

The Haig was dressed flashily in a white linen suit, a pink shirt, a bright blue tie, and white buck shoes. He was hatless, so I saw that his thin, still coal-black hair was slicked back smoothly on his perfectly round head. He looked more portly in person than in the black-and-white photographs I had seen in golf magazines. He looked more like a maître d' than a golf legend.

"So that's him," I said to Harrison.

"That's him, and dressed to a T."

"That's Chick Evans he was hugging," I said, showing off what I knew.

Without answering, Cornell stood up and snapped, "C'mon, let's go to work." Without waiting to see if I was following, he went striding down the slope, crossed the gravel lot, and headed to the clubhouse.

I had no idea what work Cornell meant. The last two weeks I had spent my time playing with hickory, mastering the feel of Jack Patterson's clubs. It was still a mystery how I would get into the foursome, but I had stopped asking Harrison his plan. He had his agenda for the match; I had mine. I was going to show Valerie's father that I wasn't just another poor caddie in the yard; I was going to prove that I could beat the greatest match player of all time, Walter Hagen.

When we reached the clubhouse, Cornell didn't follow Hagen and the members in. Instead, he detoured to the side locker-room door and upstairs to the bar, where Billy Boyle was working. The place was crowded with members, waiting for Hagen to tee off.

At the bar, Boyle moved to meet us and then leaned over to whisper something in Harrison's ear. I saw Cornell slip a folded wad of big bills across the bar to Boyle, who covered the cash as if it were a hole card and slipped it into his black trousers.

Cornell told me to wait there and then disappeared into the locker room itself.

"What the hell is going on?"

"I'm doing your buddy a favor."

"What favor?"

Boyle waved off my question. He went to the far end of the bar, where two new members were waiting to order drinks.

I glanced around the big, comfortable room. All the green felt-topped card tables were crowded. Some of the men were playing gin, but most were having lunch as they waited. If it had been winter and I was working, I would have been running back and forth to the kitchen to fetch sandwich orders. It was easier work than caddying and paid more, but it lacked the importance of partnering with a player, of being out on the course in the middle of a match where, on every move, every shot, there hung the chance to win or lose. There was no other job at a country club, whatever it was or whatever it paid, that matched looping for a good player. No other job could equal the excitement of coming down eighteen fairway late on a Sunday evening with the club champ or the husband/wife Benedict team, or the winners of the Pater-Filius.

Clare was wrong. Caddies were more than bag rats, did more than lug golf clubs around the course. If they were any good at all, they played half a dozen roles on any given round, from cheerleader to coach, father confessor to psychologist. Caddies made a difference in the game, and that was more than Clare could say about a clubhouse waitress delivering drinks or dinners to the veranda.

Cornell came back into the bar and motioned that we were leaving. I followed him down the stairs and into the lower locker room, which on that August afternoon was the coolest place at the club.

I thought we were headed outside and back to the pro shop to pick up bags for the match, but instead Cornell stopped abruptly in the rear of the locker room.

"We'll wait here," he said. He didn't sit down. He took out a cigarette and lit it as he paced between two rows of wooden lockers. I had never seen him so agitated.

"What now?" I asked.

"We wait."

"Wait for what?"

"For Hagen. I left a message in the locker he's going to use."

Cornell reached into his pocket and pulled out the silver medal and began nervously flipping it up and catching it.

At the other end of the room, a door opened and I looked past the rows of lockers and there he was. The Haig came walking down the carpeted aisle toward me.

Hagen did not notice Harrison, who was hidden by the lockers. Seeing me, Hagen looked momentarily puzzled, and then he smiled and reached out his hand to shake mine, saying enthusiastically, "Hello there, sonny. I'm Walter Hagen. I had a note that you were looking for me?" He was being friendly, but he was also on guard, having no idea who I was or what I wanted.

He was still wearing his street clothes, and holding a lit cigarette in an ivory holder.

I glanced over at Cornell, and Hagen followed my look, spotted Harrison, and dropped my hand.

"You!" Hagen exclaimed.

"Hello, Walter," Cornell said and stepped from the shadows.

Hagen stared at Harrison and then whispered, more to himself than to us, "Harrison Cornell."

"Back from the war, Haig," Cornell said. He smiled sadly. "And back from the dead. Sit down, if you don't mind." He gestured to the bench across the aisle and then looked up at me. "Tommy, I'll meet you on the tee. Don't worry about the clubs. I'll get them," he said, dismissing me without warning.

I turned around and headed to the back door. I had never seen Harrison so icy in his manner, so tense.

"I heard you were a POW," I heard Hagen say as I hurried away.

"And I'm sure you heard I was in the loony bin in Scotland," replied Harrison.

When I reached the door and glanced back, Hagen was sitting on the bench and Harrison was pacing in front of him, talking fast. At the door, I hesitated.

"Yes, I did hear you were in a hospital. But you're fine now, I see." Hagen raised his voice, as if he was giving Cornell a compliment.

"Not quite. But I will be, once you make restitution for what you did to me before the war."

"I didn't do anything to you, Harrison," Hagen answered defensively. "I've heard about those stories you were spreading in Nassau after I left the island."

"Well, explain this," Cornell said.

From where I was standing I couldn't see what Cornell was showing Hagen, and then Hagen said, "It was a gift to your wife for being so nice to me on the island."

"Oh, I'm sure she was," Cornell shot back.

I leaned back against the lockers by the back door, trying to control my breathing and afraid that they might hear the pounding of my heart.

Then Cornell said firmly, "This is what you're going to do for me. I want you to go back upstairs and tell the WGA and the club president here—McClain—you'll play with his son, Drew, the club champ, against me and that young kid you just met, Tommy O'Shea. Do that, and I'll keep our secret between us."

I eased out the door and hurried up the path and into the pro shop. Red was at the back of the shop, putting on his spikes. Seeing me, he asked if I knew where Harrison was. I told him that Cornell was talking with Hagen in the locker room.

Red paused and nodded and then said quietly, "Did you know about this quarrel between Hagen and Cornell?"

"A little," I answered vaguely.

Red stood up and kept talking as he went to his bag and pulled out a small USGA rule book and slipped it into the back pocket of his trousers. "Chick Evans mentioned earlier this morning that there had been trouble between them in Nassau before the war."

"How does he know?" I asked.

"Chick said Cornell told him."

Cornell had never told me that he knew Chick Evans.

"Cornell caddied for him a few times this summer up at Edgewater, where Chick's a member." Red Denison smiled wryly and commented, "That's also something Cornell didn't tell you, right?"

He nodded at Hagen's bag of old hickory clubs and asked, "Take them up to the tee for me, would you, Tommy?"

I picked up Hagen's sticks, my mind still whirling. Now I realized that when Cornell was missing from Midlothian, he'd been on the North Side of Chicago caddying for Chick Evans. What was that all about? I wondered.

Carrying Hagen's bag, I went out through the screen door and up the steps to the tee, now crowded with members, a half-dozen reporters, and newsreel camera crews. They were all waiting for Hagen.

Valerie was also there, off by herself.

I walked over to her, slipped Hagen's bag off my shoulder, and said, "Hi."

"Ready?" she asked, looking tense.

"Ready as I'll ever be." I looked around. No one was paying attention to us. I was just a caddie saying hello to a member's daughter.

"Where are your clubs?"

"Cornell said he would get them. They're in the shop."

There was a stirring then on the tee. Hagen had emerged from the clubhouse and he looked around, nodding to all, as he came down the steps. Walking with him was Drew McClain, dressed to play, Drew's father, and Western Golf Association officials as well as Chick Evans.

There was a chorus of *ah*s and a round of applause at the sight of Hagen. And what a sight he was, wearing a checked cap, tie, a long-sleeved white silk shirt with bright red, blue, yellow, and black stripes, white flannel trousers, and a pair of brown hobnailed shoes—a strange outfit, I thought, until I realized that they were the same style clothes as he'd worn in photos of his first Open win at Midlothian.

Hagen walked through the cluster of people who framed the tee, pausing to shake hands, to introduce himself, as if that were needed. He would take off his cap each time he approached a woman, take her hand in his, and cup it with his other hand while he stared intensely at her, smiling all the while, focusing his full attention on her, like a politician running for office.

At the back of the tee, craning to see, was a crowd of caddies and clubhouse help, including the Professor. The only person who was missing was Cornell.

32

BREAKING AWAY FROM THE CROWD, HAGEN MOVED TO THE center of the tee box as if walking onto a stage. There was another round of applause and he smiled back, accepting their acknowledgment of who he was and what he meant to the game. While he waited for the applause to die away, he removed a cigarette from his pocket and took his time fitting it into his ivory holder and then lighting it, drawing the attention of everyone crowding the tee. I thought of what Cornell had told me: how Hagen would dramatize a shot that appeared difficult but that he knew he could make, just to heighten the tension for the gallery.

He slowly paced on the flat green carpet of the tee and addressed the spectators. He began by saying how wonderful it was to return to the scene of his first tournament win, when he'd been a boy, as he put it, of twenty-one.

He'd won, he said, with clubs that golfers today had since abandoned in the backs of their garages and the dark corners of their attics.

"And where are my old sticks now?" he asked rhetorically, glancing around.

Taking my cue, I stepped out of the gallery and walked to the center of the tee.

"Ah, there they are," he announced.

I set down the bag, and when he pulled out the driver, I moved away, giving the tee stage back to him. He took the driver in his hands and held it up close to his face, and my first thought was that his eyesight had faded. But then I realized that he was examining the hickory shaft, checking to see if the wood had split over time. Next, he swung the driver, slowly and rather lovingly, once, then twice. The gallery that had been silently watching him burst into a quick round of applause at the pleasure of the great champion swinging an old hickory club. Once again I scanned the crowd for Cornell. He was still a no-show.

When I looked back, Hagen was leaning on the club with one hand, though he was careful, I noticed, not to put his weight on it. His legs were crossed and he gestured with the cigarette holder in his other hand.

"You know, it was here at Midlothian that I became a true professional. I last played here in thirty-nine at the Silver Jubilee of my win. But what I remember best was that 1914 Open championship and winning over that wonderful man over there, Chick Evans." Hagen gestured at the edge of the crowded gallery, where Evans was standing with the WGA officials. He smiled and waved to Hagen as the members applauded the presence of the famous amateur from Chicago.

Hagen waited for the clapping to die away and then resumed his talk.

"You might have heard the story of how I got deathly ill the night before the opening round at Midlothian. I had come down to Chicago from Rochester on the day coach with my good buddy Dutch Leonard. It was the first time we had been to Chicago, and for boys of twenty-one, the town was a lively place.

"We were staying at the Great Northern, and that night after I had qualified, the two of us went out and had ourselves lobster and oysters for the first time in our lives. Well, they didn't agree with my small-town stomach. I was so sick, Dutch had to call the hotel doctor in the middle of the night. He was afraid I might die on him."

Hagen paused to let the crowd enjoy the scene he was describing. Then he pointed down toward the practice range. "When I got to the club—we had to take the railroad and an electric street car to get here—my head hurt, my stomach hurt, my whole body was sore.

"I took two aspirin and that got rid of my headache. I went out and hit a hundred balls or so down there and Dutch told me I was well enough to play."

Hagen grinned and shook his head and the gallery chuckled in anticipation. I moved around on the tee so that I could spot Harrison if he came out of the clubhouse. I was half listening to Hagen while fretting over the fact that Cornell was still missing.

"It was hot that summer. Hot and dry, but the ball was running."

Hagen used his driver to point down the first fairway. "Back in fourteen, there was a pond just over the rise and I knew I had to carry that water. But I sprayed the drive, knocked it over there, as I recall." He pointed the driver way right, toward eighteen. "I was so far to the right I didn't even see the water," he added, laughing.

"Here's the strange thing about that day: I was so worried about my aching stomach that I didn't fret over every swing. I didn't worry about whether my next shot would be good or bad; I just played it. The result was I shot sixty-eight and set the course record, and that taught me a great lesson. You never know really what will happen, so you have to be ready to accept whatever comes your way, on the golf course or in life."

Hagen paused, stepped over to me, and pulled several old hickories from the bag.

He splayed out the irons, and they didn't look like much. Compared to the steel shafts we were using, they looked small and ineffective.

"I learned golf with clubs like these, back in Corbett's Glen, near Brighton, New York. I wasn't much older than seven when I crossed Allen's Creek behind our house, walked across East Avenue, and started caddying at the Country Club of Rochester for ten cents an hour.

"I've made a lot of money from golf since those days, and the game has taken me around the world and home again and given me a wonderful life. Just a few years ago, before I retired, I was giving lessons down in Florida for two hundred dollars each, and playing exhibitions for as much as two thousand a round. Not bad for a boy whose father was a blacksmith earning eighteen dollars a week in a railway-car shop in East Rochester.

"We were called homebreds in our day," he said next, "the first American–born golfers to play the game against all those Scottish and English professionals. You might recognize some of our names: Johnny McDermott, Francis Ouimet, Bobby Jones, and your own Chick Evans here."

The Haig paused again as the spectators clapped for Evans and he tipped his cap to the crowd. Then Hagen turned and glanced around at all of us, his eyes sweeping the crowd framing three sides of the tee, taking in, too, all the caddies gathered by the bag rack. It seemed that Hagen was looking at each one of us, pulling our full attention to him with the story of his life and career in the game.

"You know, when I came to your club in August of 1914, I was still thinking of playing baseball for a living. Pat Moran, the manager of the Phillies, had offered me a tryout with his team. I thought I would be leaving golf behind and heading for the major leagues and the Hall of Fame. I wasn't a natural golfer. I didn't have the picture-perfect swing of, say, Bobby Jones. Sportswriters used to say my swing started as a sway and ended in a lurch.

"But my whole life changed here at Midlothian when I won with that swing, beating Chick by one shot, and beating Francis Ouimet, who, as you all know, won the Open the year before, by several more. If I was good enough to beat those fellas, I thought, then hell, I might be able to make a living playing this damn game."

Hagen smiled and waited for the laugh he knew was coming. I glanced around for Cornell and saw Valerie instead. She was staring at me, paying no attention to Hagen. What he was saying was of no interest to her.

"So it's a great honor for me to come here today, at your kind invitation, and present these clubs—the ones I used to win the Open—to the Western Golf Association. But first, with your permission, I'll play one last round with these hickories."

At that announcement the gallery exploded into applause. Hagen nodded, smiling at us all, then gestured that he had more to say.

"I've been trying to write down my life's story, my life in golf really, and I came across a quote to the effect that when a man looks back at his life, and compares it to what he wanted to be, it is always a humbling hour. We never become the person we had planned to be. The problem with backward glances is that you remember more vividly all your warts and misdeeds and failures than your wins and successes.

"Something like that happened to me just a few minutes ago in your locker room." Hagen nodded toward the clubhouse. "I met up with a man I haven't seen since before the war. I knew him in the Bahamas when I played in an exhibition for the Duke and Duchess of Windsor. That man is a caddie here, he says. His name is Harrison Cornell."

The members glanced at one another, nodding, murmuring agreement. Everyone at the club knew Harrison and they kept smiling, anticipating some kind words about the caddie who had improved their golf games that summer.

I was holding my breath. I thought that Hagen was going to tell them what had happened in Nassau.

"What you might not know is that before the war Harrison Cornell was a wonderful player," Hagen continued, "and then when the fighting started he went off to Canada to join their air force, and then to Europe where he was shot down over Germany.

"Harrison reminded me a few minutes ago that he caddied for me in that Red Cross exhibition. And he told me you have a player here at Midlothian who is a better hickory golfer than either one of us.

"Well, today I'm going to give these old clubs another try and see if I can manage myself around your lovely course, and then we'll put them away in a museum where they belong. And while I'm at it, I'll do my best to beat this young kid that Harrison Cornell thinks is a better player then me."

He smiled at the applause and laughter from the crowd. Taking another drag on his cigarette, he gestured and asked, "So where is this fine young hickory player of yours? Who is he?"

There was a moment of silence as the members glanced at one another, wondering whom Hagen meant. I spotted Drew blushing as he stepped slightly forward, ready to be announced.

Hagen turned and pointed to me, saying dramatically, "I'm told it is this caddie right here, Tommy O'Shea." Smiling, he stepped over to me and shook my hand, and then he leaned forward and said quickly under his breath, "Come along with me, son, and everything will work out just fine."

I felt myself in the center of a sudden whirl of attention. Members were applauding, calling my name. I found Valerie's face in the crowd. She was beaming as if I were already victorious; her face was shining like a star.

I didn't know what had happened, what was going to happen, and then Harrison was at my side, having come up out of the pro shop. He was carrying our bag of hickories, and he explained his tardiness: "I wanted to give you a few moments in the sun, Tommy. Now, let's go play some golf."

He seemed calmer now as he shifted the clubs on his shoulder while smiling that wonderful smile of his, which was full of mischief and gall and confidence, as if he—as if the two of us, a broken man from the war and a kid from the caddie yard—could beat the man who had once been the best player of the game.

33

I FOLLOWED HARRISON TO THE MIDDLE OF THE TEE, WHERE HAGEN was shaking hands with Drew McClain. Then the Haig turned and made an announcement to the crowd.

"To make the course closer to the way it was in fourteen, we'll play from the red tees. According to this scorecard, that's six thousand sixty-nine yards, if I'm reading it right. It seems they're making the print on these cards smaller and smaller every year." He looked up, smiling, enjoying his joke with the gallery. He seemed perfectly at ease.

Hagen went back to addressing the crowd now clustering around the red, women's tee, which made the course play several hundred yards shorter than from the men's. He explained the exhibition to the gallery of members and guests. It would be match play, best ball, and the winning team would take away the thousand-dollar prize and the Western Golf Association trophy. In 1946, a thousand dollars was enough money to pay for college for a year.

He and Drew McClain, "your club champion," he said, would play Harrison Cornell and Tommy O'Shea.

"We'll need a caddie," Harrison said, slipping the bag off his shoulder. To me he added, "We can share our sticks—that's allowed under hickory rules."

"I'll loop," I said. There is always arrogance with caddies; they can do it all, play as well as carry their own clubs.

"No, I will," Valerie announced, appearing at my side. Already she had her hands on the bag of hickory clubs. "It's only one bag."

I glanced around and spotted her father standing with the other board members. A frown swept his face as he watched his daughter, seeing her with our golf clubs.

"Girls don't caddie at Midlothian," I told her.

"They do now," she said, giving me a look.

I followed her as Drew glanced our way. Seeing Valerie, seeing me, he broke into a mocking grin. "Gee, O'Shea, you've got a girl carrying your clubs."

As if I were rubbing something off the bridge of my nose, I gave him the finger.

Walking by me, he added, "You think playing a few holes every night on the back side with your hickories is the only place you can learn how to use wooden shafts, O'Shea?"

"Let's see what you learned over at Beverly," I told him so that he'd know I was onto him.

Stepping to the bag, I pulled out the hickory driver and stood beside Valerie. She lowered her head and whispered, "Calm down."

"I am calm."

"No, you're not."

She smiled and added, "You can't lose, O'Shea. You know why? The best players in the world—Hagen, Hogan, Jones, and

Chick Evans—all have five-letter last names—and so do you."

Harrison came up beside us, reviewing the basics, telling me to swing slowly, to try not to crush it, to work the ball left to right. As he talked, all in a rush, he fumbled for a cigarette and lit it. The first puff relaxed him somewhat, but he was clearly not the unruffled, in-control guy I'd spent the last months with.

"Okay, okay," I answered quickly. Getting the jitters on the first tee was common enough, that's for sure. There was nothing surprising about it, even with the best of players; but standing there, waiting for Hagen to finish his remarks, I realized that, between Cornell and me, I was the cool one.

Hagen walked over with his hand outstretched, smiling, and gesturing at the tee.

"Your honors." He nodded to Cornell and me. I took a deep breath. Behind me, Red Denison announced that he would be the official referee for the match, and then he introduced me as if I were teeing off in the U.S. Open.

"And playing out of Midlothian Country Club, our number-one caddie, a recent graduate of Joliet Catholic High School, where he starred for four years on the school's golf team, winner of the state high-school golf championship, and caddie champ for the last five years, Tommy O'Shea."

The applause rose around me. Valerie gave a little salute and then, like a good caddie, moved our bag over to stand to the right of the wooden tee marker. She was ready to watch her player tee off.

What I did next was all from memory and habit and years of playing the game. Everything around me slowed down as I went through all my usual, familiar steps before driving the ball. It was as if I were outside myself, watching myself as I stepped between the red markers. I took a few easy practice swings, listening to the strangely comforting sound of the hickory shaft as it moved.

I found a spot on the fairway where I wanted the ball to land. Then, as I took a longer practice swing, I felt pain knife into my left side where Drew had kicked me. It hurt when I swung the club past parallel on my backswing. I stopped, took a deep breath, and let the pain subside. I glanced at Valerie and, from the look on her face, realized that she understood what was wrong.

I took another swing, cautiously now. Well, I thought, now I'd be playing despite the pain, just as Hagen had back in 1914, when he set the course record. I paused and took another deep breath, and out of the corner of my eye I caught sight of Drew McClain, grinning. He had seen me suddenly hesitate and knew the reason why.

He wanted me to know that he knew. In the deliberate way that I had mastered while playing golf matches, I blocked out the gallery that crowded around. I blocked out the thought of Valerie standing beside the tee, of Hagen and Drew McClain waiting for me to play away. I moved forward, set down my right foot and then my left, gripped and regripped the leather on the hickory shaft, and moved into my easy rhythm.

My bruised ribs hurt and kept me from rushing the hickory clubs, from forcing the shot. My soreness forced me to swing slower, with grace rather than power. Drew McClain didn't realize it, but he had done me a favor by banging my ribs.

I hit a beauty. It was the best drive I had ever had off the first tee at Midlothian with a wood shaft or steel. The ball flew. It did not balloon, nor was it a line-drive screamer. It had a graceful arcing draw that easily carried the ridge in the middle of the fairway, hit the downslope, and ran like a rabbit.

The members applauded in surprise as I stepped forward and retrieved my tee. They had never seen hickory clubs used before, never seen how far someone could drive the ball. They knew I could play, but this shot was a thing of beauty. They were surprised to see that I was more than some kid who looped for them.

I glanced at Hagen. He was clapping, smiling, his nut-brown face glowing in the sunlight. He nodded his approval and, stepping forward, slapped me on the shoulder and said under his breath, "I see our friend has been schooling you."

Harrison was next on the tee, following a glowing introduction by Red.

"Okay, Harrison," I said, "show us how it's done." I was about to say more, when Cornell motioned that I should shut up. He didn't need my advice, though he must have guessed that I was just nervous and needed to talk.

Cornell's drive carried the rise, 180 out and to the left, but somehow he had managed to fade the wood, and the ball worked itself back into the fairway. It would be playable.

He stepped over to Valerie and me in the wake of another round of applause from the gallery of members. He slid the wood back into the canvas bag, winked at Valerie, and then bent down and picked up his burning cigarette as Red announced Drew McClain to the crowd.

"Our reigning club champ and number-one player on the Yale University golf team, Andrew McClain."

The members cheered and Drew tipped his cap and moved to the tee. He knocked his ball 250 yards down but way right. It disappeared in the long rough. I had outdriven Drew and he was buried in the deep grass. As if reading my mind, Cornell leaned in and said, "It's a long match, Tommy."

As the star attraction and the last to tee off, Hagen didn't wait for Red's introduction but went directly to the tee, announcing to the gallery that maybe he was too old to play with the likes of kids like me and Drew. It was all in good humor, all in fun. He was entertaining the members, as he had done so well in his life as a player. He was playing the game, but he was also playing the crowd.

Hagen stopped talking. He took several swings and focused on his game. I had a fleeting, self-satisfied thought that, having seen my drive, maybe he was taking this match more seriously.

"He'll press," Cornell whispered to me. "He'll whack it right."

And that is exactly what he did, driving the ball deep into the rough, so far right that it came to rest on the rise between the first fairway and the eighteenth tee, where the grass was burned dry at the end of the long summer.

"They'll play Hagen's ball," Cornell declared, falling into step as we left the tee. "He's got the better lie."

"What do you mean—don't they both have to play their drives?" Valerie asked, looking puzzled.

"No, it's best ball." I explained that both team members would drive off on each hole, then decide which ball to play out.

"It's strategic golf," Cornell added. "You play the percentage shot on each hole. If a player is good around the green, you want him to play his short game. Most golfers are better with one club than another. Maybe it's the irons or the woods. You play to each teammate's strength."

Looking at Valerie, I slowed my stride so that she didn't have to labor to keep up. Though she talked a good game, she had never caddied before, and she didn't understand what it meant to lug a bag—even a light one full of hickories—several miles around a golf course.

We paused to wait for Hagen and Drew, who had reached the Haig's ball, way right of the fairway. Most of the gallery had

followed Hagen and now formed a half circle around him and
Drew. The match was in the days before the fairways and greens
were roped off to keep spectators away from the players. On that
day at Midlothian, if you counted members and their guests, plus
golf reporters and officials from the Western Golf Association,
there were more than three hundred spectators on the course,
and most of them were crowded around Hagen, laughing at his
jokes and watching his every move.

Drew had picked a club and was setting himself to play off the
bare brown ground. I could see he had a good enough lie,
though his feet were below the ball. He'd need to choke down
on the club to play the shot.

"He's using a mid-iron," Cornell said.

"What's that?" Valerie asked.

"Like a two iron."

"That's too much club," I offered, hoping it was.

"Not from that lie; he won't get enough of it."

As Cornell had predicted, McClain didn't get it all, but he got
enough of the ball that it came back out onto the fairway, carried
about a hundred yards, then ran on the dry short grass and
stopped fifty yards below the pin, giving Hagen an easy pitch
and run into the green.

The gallery burst into cheers.

"That wasn't such a great shot!" Valerie stated, annoyed by
the applause. Drew tipped his hat as if he were a touring player.

Cornell and I laughed at that and I said, "My guess is, the
members didn't think he could even get the blade of that butter
knife on the ball."

Hagen and Drew led the gallery out of the rough while Cornell and I walked another fifty yards to our balls, which were near
each other in the center of the fairway. I had outdriven Cornell
by a few yards and we were both sitting up on the short grass.

"I'll play yours," Cornell announced, making the decision. "When we're on, we'll need your touch."

He pulled the jigger from the bag but didn't rush to play the shot. The gallery was still forming behind us, keeping their distance. They were golfers themselves and knew how to behave on a course, to keep silent and motionless when a player was hitting.

Cornell took out a cigarette, and I noticed that his fingers were trembling as he went to light it. He was nervous, but who would blame him. I glanced around. Several of the members caught my eye, smiled. I smiled back and nodded, and then I spotted Doc Driscoll. He was in the thick of the gallery, but he wasn't watching me or Cornell. His eyes were focused on his daughter.

Playing the shot, Harrison couldn't get comfortable with the jigger. He backed off twice, once to get the alignment, a second time to brush a bug off the ball. Watching him, I kept thinking that he was dressed like a hickory-age player, wearing a tie, a new white shirt, and his familiar trademark panama. He had on a pair of brown leather spiked golf shoes he had rescued from Warren, the locker-room attendant, after some member had cast them off.

Finally he hit the iron without removing the lit cigarette from his lips, letting the smoke drift up by his eyes. He just stepped up to the ball and, moving his hands into a comfortable grip, swung with the smooth grace of someone waltzing in a ballroom.

It was a pretty shot, played with a slight draw, and the ball landed short of the green and ran up onto the putting surface. Silently I kept urging the ball closer, wanting a tap-in for our birdie, but the ball never made the ridge, instead curling to a stop ten feet below the cup. I was left with an uphill putt, which

I knew from experience was against the grain; it would flatten out three feet from the flag and break from right to left at least two inches before it reached the cup. It was about as far from a gimme as you could get.

Valerie handed me my putter. "You can make it," she told me.

"God, you're already learning caddie patter and you haven't even carried my clubs one hole." Since I couldn't hug her, I nudged her with my elbow as I headed for the green, saying over my shoulder, "Get the divot."

"I know. I know," she answered, but before she could reach it, Cornell lifted the slab of dirt and grass and walked back to where he had cut it out of the fairway. He tapped it into place and handed his club to Valerie.

"Nice shot," I heard Valerie tell him, and several members chimed in with praise as the whole crowd of us moved forward, down the fairway to where Drew's ball had stopped and from where Hagen would play his approach shot.

Floyd Ganzer was on Hagen's bag and I watched as he left it and went running up to the green. Floyd was a few years younger than I, a butterball of a fifteen-year-old, a good golfer but a better caddie. As I walked to the spot where Hagen was standing, I couldn't figure out why Floyd was running up to the green. Then I saw him take the flag, ready to pull it when Hagen chipped up. A murmur of anticipation swept through the gallery that fanned out behind where Hagen was standing beside his ball.

I remembered then the story of Hagen at the British Open at Royal Lytham. Hagen had sent an official up to pull the flag when he was still 150 yards away. We hadn't played one hole and he was already trying to intimidate Cornell and me.

"Go ahead, Haig," I whispered, "try and make it." His simple little act of one-upmanship wasn't upsetting me; instead, it made me feel better and more relaxed. Hagen was worried about us. I glanced over at Cornell. He, too, realized what Hagen was doing, and he smiled and shook his head. Neither of us said a word as we stood by the right-side bunker while Hagen pulled a mashie niblick and played his approach.

He didn't make it. It was a chip shot of fifty yards and the ball didn't have enough loft to check up. It came in hot and ran past the flag, leaving Drew a downhill putt of several yards.

Cornell and I walked onto the green. We were playing at a time when USGA rules didn't allow us to clean and replace a ball on the green, only between holes, so I checked to see if my ball had picked up dirt, and then I looked over the putt.

Cornell walked around to the top of the hole and knelt down to get the read of the green from the high side. I did the same from below the hole and asked Valerie to pull the flag. Putting uphill, I didn't want my ball to hit the thick bamboo and bounce off. I wanted it to die in the hole.

It wasn't an easy putt, but the odds were in our favor. Drew had to make his just to tie the hole even if we two-putted, and the down and side hill putt of nine feet was very difficult. Mine was makeable, or so said Cornell when he came to crouch behind me.

Everyone's attention was focused on me, not on the Haig, and I admit I did enjoy it. If anything, looking at the gallery of members calmed me. I think it was because I knew them all and they knew me; out of club pride, they would be pulling for me to make the putt, to go to the tee at two with Hagen and Drew one down.

I told Cornell how I saw it—that the ball would break at least two inches once it reached the second tier. It was against the grain all the way. He nodded and reminded me that the greens hadn't been watered. "So, bang the ball." He stepped away, leaving me alone on the center stage of the first green.

I stood and studied the roll one last time. I held my blade putter loosely in my right hand and picked out a spot five feet ahead
on the line I wanted to take. If I could just get the ball rolling in
that direction at the right speed, the slope of the green would do
everything else.

I didn't look up. I didn't think about anyone or anything but
that ten-footer. I didn't second-guess my decisions about where
to play the ball or how to stroke the putt. I blocked the world
from my mind and took another deep breath. Following the routine Cornell and I had worked out, I stepped up to the putt, took
two measured practice swings, and stroked the ball with the
same cadence and saw it roll over the spot I had selected. I didn't
move. I didn't look up until I saw it take the break that Cornell
and I had determined, and then I watched it curl into the center
of the cup. Dead, solid, perfect.

34

ON THE TEE AT TWO, HAGEN CAME OVER WHILE I WAS USING THE ball wash and congratulated me on the putt. "You stroked it like Bobby Locke," he said. "Do you know who Locke is?" He smiled all the while, watching me with his warm and gentle eyes while trying to make me feel young and inferior. In response, I recounted what Cornell had told me about how Bobby Locke had said that he'd learned to putt from Hagen, playing with him back in South Africa.

Hagen laughed, pleased perhaps that his history was still known, but even as he slapped me on the back he was looking at Cornell, who was standing on the tee, taking in the hole as if this were the first time in his life he had seen it. Then he turned to me and said quietly, "Your partner has had a tough couple of years, Tommy. We need to be easy on him." He pulled a ball from his pocket and said, "I believe your team has the honors, young man."

By now the gallery had fanned out down the left side of the fairway on number two. I walked over to Cornell.

"What did Hagen want?" he asked, not moving his head or looking at me.

"He congratulated me on my putt."

"Be careful. He's going to try and screw up your mind out here."

"Yeah, I know. But he's also being nice."

"That's what I mean. He's being nice on purpose, the bastard. Play your mid-iron and cut it into the green. You'll be short but safe; I'll go for the green with the driving iron."

"Okay," I whispered, trying to calm him down. This was not the time, I thought, to get too excited. Cornell had been lecturing to me all summer, but he was getting on my nerves that day.

I tried to follow Cornell's instructions on the shot, but I totally mis-hit the iron. I forgot everything I had ever learned about hickory and my timing was all off. The ball sliced into the front bunker that guarded the short par-3. I had hit the mid-iron less than 150, a real hacker's drive. I heard the gallery moan. This is the great caddie hickory player, I could imagine them thinking.

I plucked up my tee and stepped aside, wishing to God I had somewhere to hide, but the plateau was framed with spectators. I went and stood next to Valerie as if I were a caddie, not a player. That was my familiar role; that was what I knew how to do.

Harrison didn't comment as he teed up. He was carrying the driving iron. He was still going for the green. Now, a driving iron was too much club for this par-3 that was just 170 from the red tees and with a slope that fell away toward the reservoir to the left. There wasn't a breath of breeze down there.

I had seen enough of Cornell's game to know that he had a natural draw and if he hit any kind of shot, the ball would carry the target and shoot over into the thick grass beyond. Even if he landed short, it was always difficult to get the ball close to the pin on any kind of approach, what with the way the green sloped. There was also a deep bunker beyond, but it was better to be in the hazard than the thick rough.

It was a pretty par-3—and I had learned from years of caddying that it was always the simple, pretty holes that were the most dangerous. That kind of hole has a way of subduing a player, charming him with the contour, a cluster of stately trees, or harmless-looking eyedrop pools of water. Invariably the player pulls a drive into a hazard or out-of-bounds.

That was exactly the situation at the second at Midlothian.

As soon as Cornell stepped to the tee, I noticed a difference in his approach. On the range, on our nightly rounds of practice, he was very deliberate and sure of himself. He teed up and swung, with little time wasted in settling himself on the address, in getting comfortable over the ball. He was the fastest golfer I had ever played with, faster than Drew. He never lacked confidence in how he wanted to play a shot or in his swing.

But that afternoon on number two he seemed not to be able to get settled; he couldn't decide on the correct line. Twice he backed off and stood behind the ball, aligning himself. A slight murmur ran through the gallery when he did it the third time.

Red Denison slipped up beside me and asked, "Is Cornell always this slow?"

I shook my head, keeping my eyes on Cornell, and then he finally did commit himself to the shot. He hit a fine driving iron, played it where he wanted to on the left side of the green. I kept waiting and watching for it to fade, but he had driven it dead straight and the ball hit hard on the front fringe and bounced beyond the green and into the deep rough. That ball was deep in the cabbage.

Drew McClain moved between the markers and scanned the

ground, looking for a smooth place. He bent down, brushed the grass with the backs of his fingers, then teed the ball up high, just as Cornell had taught me to do.

As always, Drew was the best-dressed player on the tee. He was wearing new brown leather shoes with flaps, white trousers, and a blue polo shirt. He never wore a golf cap, and that summer he had let his blond hair grow longer than the crew cuts that had been made fashionable by all the returning servicemen.

There was something else about him that I had never registered, but it seemed so obvious now. He looked like he belonged on the tee and at the center of everyone's attention. It was built into the way he moved through the crowd of spectators, the way he stepped up to his shot; he knew that everyone was watching and waiting for him, and he expected their full attention.

Cornell and I had left the door open for Drew and Hagen. They were hitting into an empty green. I realized that it could turn into a long and humiliating afternoon.

Drew hit a beauty. The ball came in from the right side, hit twenty yards short, and ran down the slope and onto the putting surface. It rolled past the flag, leaving a short putt.

"We'll take it," Hagen declared and led a round of applause for Drew, who smiled, nodding to all, enjoying himself. He glanced my way and smiled.

"I'll putt that one, Andrew," Hagen declared, making a show of returning his club to his bag. "I'm not going to try and beat that drive." Drew smiled, and Hagen added, addressing the members standing near him, "It's a good thing I wasn't playing against this kid when I was trying to win the Open." There was laughter from the members and we moved together along the path that led to the fairway bunker and my ball, sitting up like a lost white egg in the golden sand.

"It's okay," Valerie said. "You won the last hole."

"I'm only as good as my next shot."

"You've made a thousand good shots," Valerie answered. "And you'll make a thousand more, beginning with your next one." She made it sound like an order.

When Cornell and I reached my ball, we saw that it was plugged.

"We'll play mine," Cornell decided, pointing to where it had run into the deep collar behind the green. Walking around the top of the bunker, I knelt to pluck my ball out of the sand, and then I followed him, thinking that I had made the hard putt to win on one and now had to rescue us with a great chip.

The gallery fanned out along the sides of the green. Harrison, Val, and I walked around the edge of the putting surface to where the ball had disappeared. Once I reached the spot, I had to lean over and fan the rough with my hands before I spotted the ball, burrowed into the long grass.

There was no easy way to play the ball with the hickories I had in the bag. I looked at Cornell.

Taking in the lie, he said, "Play the niblick. That will give you enough loft. Don't slug it. Sweep it out. The ball will run, so use the green. You'll be below the hole. I'll make the putt."

I pulled the niblick from the bag. It was just a 9 iron with a fancy name. I needed a wedge—a lob wedge, really. But nothing like a lob wedge existed in the age of hickory or even in the 1940s.

What I was afraid of was leaving the ball in the deep rough. I took a few swings to test the density of the thick grass.

"Don't try to finish the shot," Valerie suggested. "Pop it out. The ball only needs to carry a yard at most before landing on the green."

Cornell smiled. "Our caddie is right, Tommy," he said. "Pop it out, get it rolling."

I took a few more swings and then I stepped back and looked at the green. Both Drew and Haig were on the putting surface, watching me.

As I moved up to the ball, Valerie took the bag away; Cornell, too, stepped back to give me room to play the shot. "Okay," I whispered to myself, "here goes nothing."

In a situation like that, usually you subconsciously dig down too much, swing too hard, but there was something about holding the light niblick in my fingers that kept me from slugging the ball.

I clipped it clean from where it sat down in the long grass, and the ball came out hot, carried onto the green, and ran up to the flag. It would have been six, seven feet beyond the hole if it hadn't hit the bamboo pole in the center. The ball bounced up, then fell back into the cup. Minutes later, Hagen choked on his six-footer; my improbable chip had won the hole.

Walking to the tee on three, I heard the gallery buzzing about my chip-in. Half-a-dozen members came alongside me to whisper encouragement. Here we were, Cornell and I—two caddies—and we had Hagen and McClain two down. The members seemed to be enjoying the shock of it—all except old man McClain.

"Well, it's better to be lucky than to be good," Cornell said.

"You're lucky *and* good," Valerie added, being encouraging.

"Yeah, well, we can't beat Hagen relying on shots like that," I said, knowing what was obvious to all golfers.

I walked up onto the tee, and as I did, there was another round of applause. I should have tipped my hat to acknowledge the spectators, but the acclaim embarrassed me since I knew that I didn't deserve it.

I took a deep breath and looked ahead, up the hill. On the

ridge, most of the gallery were clustered together in their bright summer outfits, as if posing for a class photograph.

Drew moved closer, telling me under his breath that I was one lucky bastard.

"Better lucky than good," I told him, then went ahead and teed up.

"Don't shank it, O'Shea," he added.

I stepped back to settle myself and out of the corner of my eye I saw Val move our bag close to the red marker. She didn't say anything. She was just showing me that she was there for me. I smiled at her and addressed the ball, slowed down my backswing, and ticked off everything Cornell had told me, moving my hands first, swinging slowly, and concentrating on my wrists. I didn't hit a shank. The ball came off the tee low and hard and cleared the crest of the hill as it moved from right to left, landing on the high side of the fairway, where the ground was dryer and the ball would run on the short fairway grass. The reaction from the crowd on the hill told me that my drive had landed safely and was in play.

I stepped away as Cornell came up onto the tee. He nodded okay and took the driver from me.

At that moment, waiting for Harrison to drive off, I must admit I believed that we might pull it off, we might win. Then Harrison swung and the ball went straight left, into the homes that faced the fairway. He was out-of-bounds, a lost ball, leaving my drive the only one in play.

Cornell came back and slid the driver into the bag.

"I cooked it," he said.

I nodded. There wasn't anything else to say.

Hagen didn't do much better, driving his ball way right, but again McClain hit a fine shot down the center of number three. Without even seeing where it landed, I knew that his drive had gone farther than mine.

We stepped off the tee together and McClain kept close by my side.

"What's wrong with your buddy Cornell?" he asked under his breath.

"Nothing's wrong with him," I answered, not trying to lower my voice. Cornell and Valerie were walking ahead of us, and Val glanced back, hearing me, but she kept stride with Harrison, who didn't seem to notice.

"No bullshit, O'Shea. Did you see him, after he duck hooked that drive?" Drew was staring me as we walked and I shook my head, still puzzled. "The left side of his face is twitching."

I moved away from McClain, walking to where my drive had landed in the short rough, 140 from the green, thinking that Drew must be worried about the match if he was trying to needle me about Cornell. Val and Harrison had arrived at my ball and were staring at the lie. When I came up to them, Val glanced back, over Harrison's shoulder, and I saw her frown.

"What do we have?" I asked, trying to sound positive. I stepped around both of them, as if I were going to address the ball, and looked over at Harrison. Drew hadn't been needling me. The left side of Cornell's face was jumping. "Harrison, hey. You okay?"

He stared over at me, nodded his head.

"Sure. Why?"

"Your face," I said. "The left side of your face."

Harrison reached up and gingerly touched his cheek with his fingertips. I stepped closer to him. His face was hidden in the shadow of his panama.

"I'm fine. I'm fine," he said. "Just a little nervous," he admitted. "It's been a while since I've been in a match."

A section of the gallery had gathered around us, waiting politely behind where my drive had landed.

I glanced at Valerie and then back at Harrison. "Okay, let's play golf. What do we have?"

Harrison answered, "I'll play a mashie. It will clear the bunker and run."

I looked up at the green and saw what he meant. It was the right club. Looking across the fairway, I saw Hagen and McClain waiting for us to play our second shot. "Let's go," I said to Harrison.

He pulled the mashie and Valerie moved off with the clubs. I stepped away with her and she stole a quick glance at me. Her eyes were full of worry, and I nodded, as if to suggest that I had everything under control. Which I didn't, but I didn't have time to think about Cornell. We were on the third hole and in the middle of the match.

Hagen, on the other hand, didn't seem concerned. He was across the fairway, chatting up the gallery that had gathered around him, and every few minutes there was another burst of laughter from the crowd.

I looked back at Harrison. He took a few practice swings, testing the grass, getting a feel for how he had to hit the shot. He seemed fine. And as always, Harrison surprised me. He hit more of a punch iron than a full swing, and the ball came out low. I thought it might not carry the bunker that guarded the hole, but it did, running for another twenty yards and stopping short of the putting surface.

As the gallery applauded, I stepped over and congratulated him. Half of his face was twitching violently.

He appeared perfectly calm, however, and he smiled, pleased with his shot.

"Let's keep it up." I slapped him lightly on the shoulder as the three of us followed the ball. Back in the middle of the fairway, the Haig was preparing to hit their second shot into the par-4 green.

I'm not sure what club Hagen hit, but my guess is that it was the spade mashie. In his prime, he was a wizard with that club. But the ball came up short on the green, leaving Drew a long uphill putt.

I fell into step with Valerie. She had taken the long way around the fairway bunker that fronted the green and we were briefly by ourselves, circling the sand.

"What's wrong with Harrison?" she asked.

"I don't know." I kept charging forward. I knew I couldn't worry about Cornell and play golf at the same time.

"Do you want me to ask Daddy?"

"No, thanks. Harrison hasn't played in a match for a while, but he'll be okay," I said, trying to sound confident. I reached over and squeezed her hand.

"I know. I know. We're okay; we're going to do it." She kept smiling.

"We're shooting their lights out."

"Right." She nodded and swung the bag off her shoulder. We had arrived at our ball.

I glanced around. Harrison was approaching. His head was down so I couldn't see his face, but he was smoking, and he had lost his graceful stride. Each footstep was deliberate and heavy, as if he were lugging weight in the soles of his spiked shoes.

I looked down at my ball. It was sitting up on the short grass with less than thirty yards to the green and another ten yards to the flag, which was on the second tier of the green. There were a couple of ways to play it. Hit a pitch and run with a mashie, or chip the ball higher onto the green with a niblick, trying to knock it into the ridge itself, and let it check up. This green was faster than the others on the front nine since it had no shade at all. Besides that, this particular hole had never been kind to me.

There are always certain holes on a course that have a player's number, and this one had mine.

Cornell arrived out of breath, but I saw that his twitching had stopped and that made me feel better.

"What are you thinking?" he asked as he lit a cigarette with the butt of the one he was smoking. His hands were still trembling.

"Chip it up and let it run." I placed my hand on the niblick and waited for Cornell to agree.

He was looking at the shot I had in mind, running his eyes from my ball up to the flag, mentally measuring the distance and the slope. Cornell knew that hole, and he understood how the putting surface was faster than others on the front side.

"It will run," was all he said; then he stepped back, slipping away as if he were part of the gallery and not my partner. I pulled the niblick and took a couple of easy swings and then I stepped back and looked over the shot again, trying to decide where I wanted my ball to land.

The problem with golf is that it churns up a person, burns away at one's nerves when the pressure is on. Golf is a mind game, and there's no way to get away from thinking about all the things that can go wrong on a course. It's a game of walking and waiting. Even the greatest players can eventually lose it.

I shook my head, trying to ease my nerves, trying to refocus on the pitch I had to make. Hagen and Drew had reached the green. They were standing together, talking softly, being friendly with the gallery and each other.

I took another practice swing, waiting to calm down, waiting for the tension in my arms and hands to ease. Small jolts of electricity were still jabbing my arms, as if my fingers were stuck in an electrical socket.

Every time I tried to focus on what I had to do, I had a rush of anxiety about Cornell. I stepped away from the ball again, made motions as if I were being bothered by an insect flying around my face. Up on the green, I knew, no one could see that I was just brushing away hot air.

I took another deep breath, stepped up to the ball, and set myself to play. I tugged at the creases of my pants, making sure that everything was loose and comfortable. I gripped and re-gripped the club, wishing it were my old pitching wedge and not the hickory. Then I reminded myself that the way to play the shot, regardless of the club I used, was to keep my arms close to my body, not break my wrists, let the club do the work, and finish the swing. Like any pitch-and-run or chip shot, this one would depend on feel, that magical and mysterious moment all golfers experience when hitting a soft approach iron with more hope than skill, more luck than talent. Finally, I let it go.

The ball carried the ridge, and while it didn't roll as much as I wanted, it stopped only twenty inches short of the hole. All Cornell had to do was tap it for us to save par.

He didn't need to make the putt. Smiling, Hagen walked over and tapped the ball back to us, nodding his congratulations. They made their two putts to halve the hole and we headed for number four.

35

CORNELL AND I LOST THE NEXT THREE HOLES. WE WEREN'T EVEN in the match. Cornell couldn't get his club on the ball, and there was no way I could rescue us, like on the sixth hole when, with a towering hook, he drove our second shot out of bounds, over the fence and onto 147th Street. After each wildly misplayed shot, a low murmur swept the gallery as the members shook their heads and wondered what was wrong with him. On the greens, he had totally lost his touch.

There was nothing I could do. Standing in the middle of the fairway on four when he topped a spoon, I couldn't yell at him, couldn't even ask what the hell was wrong. He was always the one telling me what to do. I didn't know what to say. By the sixth hole I had stopped giving him words of encouragement when he flubbed a shot. And he stopped apologizing to me. He just walked after each shot with his head down, and smoking one cigarette after the other, stuck in his suddenly miserable play.

Hagen kept his distance, as if he was afraid that his game

might be contaminated by getting too close. In fact, the opposite happened. With every stroke, Hagen got better; he made more-spectacular shots. He went striding down the fairways like a visiting conqueror.

Red Denison came over to me on seven tee when I went to get a drink of water and said flatly that Cornell's play was an embarrassment. "What's wrong?" he asked, staring at me wide-eyed.

"I have no idea." I looked at Cornell, who stood on the tee, staring down the fairway as I had seen him do a hundred times over the summer, taking it all in, deciding how to play his drive. The only trouble now was that he couldn't make a shot. He'd mis-hit shots on the last three holes and after each one went walking off, swearing under his breath. Val was so intimidated that she wouldn't go near him unless I was beside her.

"He looks strange, too," Red offered, following my gaze. "You see his eyes?"

"He was great on the first two holes."

"The Professor said something about him being in a prison camp or something during the war. What do you know about that?" he asked.

Hagen was on the tee, driving, and I avoided Red's question by answering, "Let's play this hole and we'll see if he snaps out of it."

"He's not going to snap out of it, Tommy." He nodded toward Driscoll. "I told the Doc to keep close to him. I think Cornell is sick. In fact, I've always thought he was sick in some way. But the Professor said he was okay, so I let him loop."

Red patted me on the shoulder and walked to the tee, saying, "Do the best you can. You're playing a helluva game yourself with those Patterson clubs."

We were on the fringe of the par-5 seventh green, thanks to

my drive and Cornell's finally hitting a good fairway brassie. Walking up to the green, I asked him again, speaking gently, if he felt okay.

"My timing's off, that's it. It's all in the timing with hickory. Nice and slow, inside out, don't swing from the top. Keep it simple. Let the club do the work. Mike told me that. Mike showed me how." He was mumbling now, repeating himself.

I glanced over at Red, who was walking with Doc Driscoll at the edge of the fairway. Both of them were watching us. I knew that all I needed to do was nod and they would stop the match.

"Everything is going to be okay, Harrison," I said, thinking that we could finish out the hole and then call it quits.

"I told him, Tommy," he said to me next, seizing my arm and stopping in the fairway. We were thirty yards from the green. He looked at me. The whole left side of his face was out of control. "I told Hagen he shouldn't have done that to my wife, Tommy. I told him." He kept shaking his head. "You know I wanted to kill the bastard, Tommy, you know that? And now I can't even beat him on the golf course."

"Easy Harrison." I whispered. I looked over Cornell's head and nodded to Red and Driscoll. They could see in my face that everything had gone wrong.

Play halted as the doctor and the club pro came over to me. Swiftly, as always happens at the scene of a smash-up, the awareness that something was seriously wrong sped through the crowd.

Thick tears were now washing down Harrison's tanned face. I grasped his arm. It was one of the few times that I had touched the man and I was startled by his boniness. Since arriving at the club, Harrison seemed to have gotten stronger. He looked healthier, always neatly dressed in his shirt and tie, his sports jacket and panama. Always the country-club gentleman, never the caddie.

I whispered his name and he stared at me, his blue eyes half hidden in the shadows of his hat, and he said tearfully, "I was a helluva player once, Tommy."

"I know you were, Harrison. You still are."

Driscoll reached us and took command of the moment. Hearing his words, feeling his presence, Harrison didn't resist, letting himself, as if from long experience, be cared for by a stranger.

Valerie stepped to my side and I wrapped my arm around her shoulders. We stood huddled together, stunned, as if witnessing a natural disaster.

Hagen and Drew walked around the big green like spectators coming to view the wreckage. In defense of us all, what was unfolding on that seventh hole was so unpredictable that we didn't have any idea how to respond.

Occasionally accidents happen on the course; a player is hit by an errant ball or suffers heat stroke or has too much to drink. Once, a few years back, after a violent summer storm a groundskeeper touched a downed line and was electrocuted, but none of us had seen anything like Cornell's collapse. We had little experience with mental illness, and posttraumatic stress disorder, part of everyday vocabulary today, was then little known.

Several members came to help Doc escort Cornell to the bench on eight tee. We followed after, like school kids waiting to be told what to do.

There were no phones on the course, so Red sent one of the young caddies running to the clubhouse to summon an ambulance. Mr. McClain asked Valerie and me what had happened.

We shook our heads. Cornell's stories of the loony bin came back to me in a rush, but I wasn't about to share any of them with McClain.

"Stay here," I told Val. "I need to see if I can help." Easing my way through the crowd, I stepped over to Harrison; he was sitting on the wooden bench with Doc Driscoll and Red Denison beside him. Hagen was off to one side, talking to a few WGA officials and, though I didn't know it at the time, a reporter from the *Chicago Tribune*. I would read his account in the next day's morning paper.

Sitting on the bench, Harrison was smoking. The cigarette trembled in his fingers. I crouched down in front of him. He looked at me and smiled.

"Tommy," he whispered, and reaching out, he touched my cheek as if I were a child. "Tommy, I'm sorry I lost it."

"It's okay," I told him.

He shook his head and started to cry. "I get too nervous," he whispered, leaning forward as he always did. "The pressure . . ."

I kept nodding, smiling, trying in the most awkward way to ease his suffering, but I didn't really understand what had happened to him and to so many of our soldiers. They had lived through combat only to come home with their nerves all shot to hell.

"I have to go away for a while," he said, calming a little as he thought of it. "They'll take care of me." He smiled as if sharing a secret. "You know, back in the loony bin."

"Harrison will be fine, Tommy," Doc Driscoll asserted, reclaiming his physician role. "He'll be back caddying, helping all our games. Right, Harrison?" He smiled in his practiced, overly hearty way.

I kept watching Harrison, knowing better. Harrison knew better, too, and neither of us answered. I looked at him and told him again that he would be okay.

He nodded, a look of deep sadness in his eyes.

I heard the ambulance approaching, the distant siren growing louder as it came along the service road, across nine fairway and

the practice range toward the eighth tee. I knew that whatever I
had to say to Harrison Cornell, I needed to say it at once.

"We could have beaten him," I said.

"We had them two down. How did you like that brassie I
hit?" Harrison answered, grinning.

I smiled, holding back my tears, holding myself together. Out
of the corner of my eye, I saw the members moving away, giving
the ambulance attendants room to approach the bench.

Doc Driscoll turned and put his hand on Cornell's shoulder,
telling him that it was time to go. He asked if he could walk to
the ambulance.

Harrison looked blankly at Driscoll, as if he didn't quite understand. Then he looked at me and nodded goodbye. When he
stood, so did I.

"Take care," I whispered. I leaned forward and embraced
him, feeling his slight body against mine. It was as if I was hugging an old man.

Several members called from the crowd, told Harrison to take
care of himself. He acknowledged their good wishes, kept nodding politely, but then he turned to me and said softly, "You
know how I told you everyone in life is someone's caddie?"

I nodded.

He raised a finger, making his final point. "Just do one thing.
Carry your own clubs. Be your own man."

He turned and walked to the ambulance, flanked by Driscoll
and the medics.

To my surprise, a few members began to clap slowly. They
were quickly joined by others, and for a moment, Harrison Cornell was recognized by the members of Midlothian as if he were
a champion finishing up a winning round.

Drew stepped over to me. He had his putter hooked under

his arm, and he was grinning. "I always knew that guy was crazy."

I didn't respond.

"You never learn, O'Shea. You love your losers, don't you?"

"That's why I love you, McClain," I said, and then I walked away from him. I joined Hagen, who was standing with Drew's father and several of the WGA officials, including Chick Evans. I saw a few of the members turn and start to walk back to the clubhouse, as if they realized that the match was over. That's when I knew it wasn't.

Hagen turned to me, smiling sadly, but when he reached to shake my hand, I said quickly, "I'm ready to continue, sir."

Surprised, he said nothing for a second. Then he recovered himself. "That's grand of you, son, but I don't think it would work." He nodded at Drew. "Our best ball against just one player."

"I can hold my own."

Hagen shook his head again. "That's good of you, Tommy, but perhaps, given what's happened, we should just call it a day." He glanced at Red as if asking him to agree.

"We should let O'Shea take us on, Mr. Hagen," Drew said, joining us. "I know Tommy thinks he's as good as you are."

"I don't believe that at all, sir. But, you see, Harrison Cornell told me his story. He wanted to try to beat you, and since he can't be here, I'll do my best to do it for him."

Hagen stared for a moment, studying me. The smooth, cheery look that he'd been wearing since the first tee now slipped away. He looked around the circle, gauging whether Drew or his dad or any of the others knew what I was talking about. Most of them appeared not all that interested. Reassured, he sized me up with a look. I could see that he was judging me, making a decision on whether I was worth his time, and then before he could reply, another voice spoke up.

"Let me help out here. If Tommy is agreeable, I'll finish the round as his playing partner," said Chick Evans, stepping from the mix of WGA officials. He was speaking to Hagen, but it was me he looked in the eyes, and I realized that he, too, knew the story of what had happened in Nassau before the war.

36

"I HAVEN'T PLAYED WITH HICKORIES FOR A WHILE, BUT I ASSUME it's like riding a bike," said Evans, smiling. "Once I start swinging, I should be just fine."

"It would be my honor, sir," I said quickly, still not quite believing that Evans had stepped out of the gallery to help me take on Hagen.

Still smiling, Evans took off his cap and ran a hand through his long, fine white hair. That summer of 1946, he was fifty-six, two years older than Walter Hagen. But, unlike Hagen, Evans still competed in tournaments.

"I caddied for you once," I blurted out, explaining that three summers before, he had played in a foursome at Midlothian and I had carried single just for him, giving up a double so I could say that I had caddied for the great Chick Evans.

"Well, I apologize for not remembering, Tommy." He leaned forward and quickly whispered, "I hope I gave you a good tip."

"You did, sir. A buck."

"Well, let's see what we can do today to earn you some real money. I see you have an unusual caddie." He turned to Valerie, who was standing by silently with our clubs.

I introduced her, but Evans's real interest was the bag of hickories she was holding. "You wouldn't have a Carew putter in there, would you?" he asked. "My first clubs were a Carew putter I bought from my caddying money and an old Morristown cleek my father gave me as a Christmas present."

I explained quickly that the clubs had been left in the pro shop by Jack Patterson when he retired.

"Oh, Jack's, are they? I knew him—a good player. Ah, I see." He lifted the jigger and saw Patterson's name stamped on the club.

"Red told me I wouldn't have a chance to beat Hagen if I didn't have pro shafts from the twenties," I whispered, glancing over at Red.

Evans smiled, glanced at Hagen, and said coolly, "Well, I couldn't beat him back in 1914. Let's see if we can better that today." He pulled the driver from the canvas bag.

"Right!" I couldn't stop grinning.

In Chicago we all knew how great a golfer Evans was. He and Bobby Jones were the only two players to have won both the U.S. Open and the U.S. Amateur in the same year, and Evans had done it first, in 1916. Plus, he'd done it with only seven hickory-shafted clubs.

Evans was also known at country clubs all over America for the college scholarship program he had set up for caddies. After his Open wins in 1916, he made a lot of money from instructional recordings. But if he had kept the royalties, he would have lost his amateur standing. It was his mother who had suggested that he use the cash to fund a caddie scholarship. The idea appealed to Evans, who'd had to quit Northwestern because his family ran out of money.

Now he was slowly swinging the driver, testing the torque, almost as if he were greeting an old friend.

"It's a G shaft," I remarked, showing off the scraps of information I'd picked up from Cornell. Hagen and Evans shot looks at me, both surprised, I guess, that I might know the type of hickory.

"What did you say?" Drew asked, stepping up.

"You wouldn't understand," I said. It wouldn't hurt any if Drew started worrying about what clubs we were playing.

Evans handed Valerie the driver and then pulled out the spoon to tee off the long par-3.

As I stepped away to give him room to loosen up, I saw that Hagen was for the first time ignoring the gallery; he just stood there, watching Chick. A lot later in life I would think back and realize how special that moment must have been for both those men, matching up again at Midlothian in the twilight of their careers.

It was then that Red Denison stepped up and spoke to all of us, suggesting that we call the seventh hole a tie and continue the match. Hagen agreed immediately and gesturing to Chick gave him the honors of teeing off first. We were still two down, but I had a great new partner.

Evans paused to slip the ends of his tie between the buttons of his shirt; to focus himself on playing another round of championship golf against his old rival. It got very quiet on the tee, as it always does when a real player is about to hit. Chick was standing with his feet together, holding the club loosely in his hands.

Then carefully he placed the wood behind the ball, making sure that the sole of the club was flat; only then did he grip the club and move his feet into position. They were square to the target, with his toes pointing out.

He moved then, a slight waggle, glancing once down the line of flight, not picking a point five yards ahead, as Cornell had taught me, but looking down the length of the wide fairway.

He seemed about to swing; then he did something surprising. He forward-pressed his hands slightly ahead of the club head and only on his backswing did he pull his hands back first, and then the club head—the exact technique that Cornell had taught me. He caught the ball square, and it rose off the tee and carried straight for the green forty yards beyond the fairway bunker. Even before it landed short and bounced on, the gallery was cheering. Perhaps they realized that this was the first time in decades that Chick Evans had swung a hickory-shafted golf club. Certainly it was the first time that many of them had ever seen the legendary Chicago player in competition.

Smiling, Evans nodded his thanks as he retrieved his tee. Then he handed me the wood, saying, "Go for it, Tommy. Play like Harrison taught you."

The country-club gallery had regrouped around the tee, and as I prepared to drive, they clapped for me and called out encouragement.

I stood behind the ball, marking the direction, going through the long catalog of advice Cornell had given me all summer, and thinking that even if I played golf every day from that moment until I died, this would be the game of my life, with Chick Evans as my partner, teamed up against the man who had broken Cornell's heart and his life. I stepped up to the ball and hit a screamer.

About 130 out, the ball began to lift with the updraft off the sloping fairway. It also slowly pulled left, and I knew before the gallery broke into applause that my spoon would split the fairway and miss the bunker and run up onto the green. Both of us were on in regulation.

"Wonderful, Tommy," Evans said. "Wonderful." He was beaming his famous smile as I stepped off to the side to wait for Hagen and Drew to tee off. They say that when Evans lost at the U.S. Open in 1914, he looked over at the Haig, smiled warmly, and conceded the tournament.

"Thank you, Mr. Evans," I said, as Valerie slipped the spoon back into the bag.

"Call me Chick, partner."

"Yes, sir. Yes, Chick."

37

WE WON THE EIGHTH AND NINTH HOLES AND STARTED THE BACK side even, and Hagen stepped up to the tenth tee joking that he might not have come to Midlothian if he'd known that he'd have to play Chick Evans one more time. "I wouldn't bet against Chick if I were you," he warned; and then, as if the thought had suddenly popped into his head, he spun around and asked us both, "A friendly bet, fellas?" His eyes swept the crowd, making sure that they heard the offer. "What about a hundred dollars for these nine holes?"

Hagen was all smiles, making light of his challenge, saying that he and young Drew should have odds, playing against the likes of "this famous amateur and Tommy O'Shea."

"Is it a bet?" I asked Evans. I was thinking of Cornell, of how he wouldn't have backed down to Hagen.

"Are you sure?" Evans looked surprised. In 1946, a hundred dollars was a lot of money.

"Yes, I'm sure," I told Evans; and then I added Cornell's

signature line: "It's all about the three-footers. We'll get them on the greens, Chick."

Evans stared at me for a few moments, as if evaluating me, and then he nodded and shook my hand in that polite, old-fashioned way he had, this gentleman from the last century. "You're on, Walter," he said.

Hagen stepped away from his teed-up ball again to get his alignment and then he hit away. The game was on.

Walking off the tee on ten, Drew slid over to my side and said quickly, "Hey, O'Shea, you've got another old-man loser in Evans. You were doing better with crazy Cornell."

"Evans has qualified for the U.S. Amateur every year since he was seventeen," I said. "If you can match that, then mouth off, but until then, keep it to yourself." I picked up my pace and walked with Valerie in the direction of my ball.

"You're right," she said, wanting to encourage me. "Evans can beat them all."

"Sure," I said, once Drew was out of earshot. "Except that he hasn't played hickory for twenty years."

On the par-4 tenth, all four balls had found the fairway, and as we walked toward ours, Evans came up beside me. Hagen was talking, as he had been for most of the first nine, telling stories, remembering the 1914 U.S. Open, when he had beaten Chick Evans by one stroke and begun his great career.

"I remember I was in the clubhouse with a score of two-ninety. I had the tournament won, everyone was telling me, but I kept hearing these cheers from out on the course." He glanced over at Evans and pointed his finger at him. "They were cheering for this fella. Damn, I think everyone in Chicago had come out on the streetcar to watch Evans send me packing to Rochester. Do you remember that, Chick?"

Chick just nodded, not saying a word.

That was Evans's way on the golf course. He wasn't like Hagen, who talked his way around eighteen, the way Lee Trevino did. Hagen needed the gallery to applaud him, but not Chick Evans. He acted as if he were alone on a wet golf course in the early morning hours, keeping score in his head and playing against the course, not another golfer. In that way we were alike, and that was when I realized how we might still beat Hagen and McClain. We had to forget them and play our own game.

I slowed down as Cornell had told me to do when playing with McClain, and, seeing that, Chick Evans picked up my idea and slowed his pace. He did not try to match Hagen's quick pace and patter with the gallery. They surged ahead and the gallery followed them to their next shot.

We looked at our balls. Evans's drive hadn't carried as far as mine but was on a level lie. Hagen's and Drew's balls were together to the far right, and they had both outdriven me. Evans didn't seem bothered. In fact, he was feeling nostalgic.

"I remember coming here to Midlothian when I was ten or eleven," he said, addressing Valerie and me. "At the time, we had caddy matches between clubs and I was the last man on our Edgewater team—that's where I first caddied, when I was eight—and when we got here to the club, I spotted this old apple orchard. It was up there, to the right of your clubhouse. I was very fond of apples and it was a warn day, I recall. I had one too many apples and suffered the consequences. I'll never forget coming up eighteen needing to win for our team and being sick to my stomach." He shook his head, remembering. "It was almost the end of my golfing career before it began.

"Between that and losing to Walter in the Open, I must say, Midlothian hasn't been kind to me."

"We'll change that today," Valerie spoke up. "Come on, you two can do it." She moved our hickory clubs closer to us.

"What do you think?" I asked, watching Evans and waiting for his advice. He didn't say anything at first; he walked up the twenty yards to where my ball had rolled to a stop and then came back to me and stood for a minute staring at our handful of clubs. He asked how I felt about hitting the jigger. We were less than 170 from the two-tier green.

"If you're not sure," he said quickly, "I could give it a try and play your ball."

From Evans's tone of voice I knew he wasn't sure that the jigger, with its small face, would work for me.

Before I could reply, Valerie pulled the club from the bag and handed it to me, saying, "Knock it stiff, O'Shea."

I had to somehow catch the ball clean. Drew would probably hit Hagen's drive into the tenth green, and with their distance off the tee, he had a better chance than I did of getting it close to the pin on the top ledge of the green. He would play a fade off the level lie and work it around the bunker and cascade down the slope to the putting surface, giving Hagen a birdie putt.

Most of the gallery had moved forward to Hagen's ball on the right side of the fairway. Again, Hagen had turned away from us to chat with the members, joking with them as he lit a cigarette. He had even turned Drew, his partner, into a spectator. It was as if Evans and I were playing by ourselves, which was okay with me.

Chick saw me glancing over at the Haig as I swung the club, trying to get ready for my shot.

"That's Hagen's secret, Tommy. He gets his opponent thinking about him, and not their game. He's done it all his life, and that's what made him a great match player."

I nodded, telling Evans how Cornell had always coached me to play my own game, and that's what I was planning to do.

Evans nodded but didn't answer; maybe he was thinking that I didn't have that much of a game to play.

"Watch this," I told him, and set about to prove to Chick Evans, as well as everyone else out on the golf course that August afternoon, that I could play hickory with the best of them.

"Easy, easy," Valerie whispered, noticing that I was rushing.

I set up as Cornell had instructed, focusing my left eye on the ball so that my head was tilted away from the shot. And to that I added a move I had seen Evans do that afternoon. When he played his shots, just before he started his backswing, he kicked in his right knee. I did the same and it helped to free up the right side on my long smooth-cadenced backswing. Coming back to the ball, I didn't drive down or hit against my left side, as I would have with my steel shafts. In the words Hagen had used, I was "clipping the heads off the daisies."

The jigger worked perfectly. I tagged the ball and it flew dead straight to land just where the fairway sloped down. The ball kicked forward, and though I couldn't see where it stopped, I knew it would be on the green or just left of it, pin high and safe, leaving Chick an easy chip to get it close.

Together, with Chick between us, Valerie and I moved a few yards down the fairway, then halted for Hagen and Drew to play their second shot. Evans said quietly to both of us, "They'll play Hagen's."

"Hagen is good around the greens," I added, to show Evans that I did know something about the legend who had beaten him.

"Very good, but not the best of those hickory years," he answered.

"Who did have the best short game?" Valerie asked innocently.

"Well, I guess Bobby Jones did, but at times, I could give him a run for his money."

Drew's long swing worked wonders with the mashie. His shot

centered the fairway, rode the breeze, and came down in the front of the green, but then it took a bad bounce on the ridge and checked up. Hagen and Evans would have similar shots, but Hagen had the longer approach.

"There's a secret to playing approach shots with hickory," Evans said as we walked.

"There is?" both Valerie and I said in unison. Evans laughed, amused by our eagerness.

"What is it?" I asked.

"You're about to see Walter give us all a lesson."

Hagen was twenty yards short and to the left side of the putting surface. The green sloped up, with the pin to the right side and only a few yards from the back fringe. With his pitch, I realized, Hagen couldn't let his ball land short. It would be a long pitch-and-run, and the only club in his bag with the right loft to make the shot work was the mashie niblick.

Sure enough, when he reached his ball, Hagen pulled that club and walked a few yards closer to the green to get a better angle on its two ridges. As he did, the gallery fanned out behind him. We had picked up more spectators on the turn and now, I guessed, more than five hundred members, guests, and reporters were following us.

"His mashie niblick has less loft," Evans commented softly. "I remember that from the Open. His club is less than forty degrees. I never knew why he played with it that way, but watch him. He's a master."

Today's clubs are made with titanium heads and graphite shafts, and there are sixty-four-degree wedges. With one of those Hagen would have hit a full, high flop shot, just like the ones Phil Mickelson made famous. It is an easier game now with hybrid clubs and cryogenically treated faces, adjustable shafts, all the new technology. Back when everyone played with hickory on small, slow greens, they all had to learn how to pitch and run the ball, and to play with clubs that weren't uniform. No two mashie niblicks ever had the same degree of loft, the same size head, or the same shaft length. Every shot had to be handcrafted, as if it were a one-of-a-kind piece of work, which, in a way, they were.

I had been watching the Haig play all afternoon and he hadn't hit two clubs the same way. Each time he stepped up to the ball it was as if he were approaching a new problem, and he had to draw on his history and experience to produce the right stroke.

Hagen moved back to his ball and took a few practice swings. It was the second time that day that he played a short pitch, and I was as curious and eager as the rest of the gallery to see how it would go.

It was the mashie niblick that had made Hagen famous. Moving a few feet into the middle of the fairway to get a better angle on his setup, I saw that he had opened his stance and opened the face of the short iron. He was playing the ball off his left heel and had moved his hands down the shaft and tucked his right elbow in close to his side. He took one quick practice swing, glancing down the slope, looking at the pin. I knew that he was mentally measuring the distance between the ball and where he wanted it to land, and then judging how far and how fast the ball would run. I knew also that he had walked onto the green not only to check the slope but to test the ground, to see just how hard the landing area was. The fringe and fairway up to the putting surface looked rich and green, but Cornell had talked the Duehr brothers into not watering for a few days, just to make sure that the balls would run as well on the hard ground as the rubber-core balls had in the age of hickory, before golf courses had sprinkling systems.

But I was wrong about how Hagen was going to play the shot. He took another practice swing: it was more a quick lift of his wrist and very little swing. Cornell had taught me to bend my knees and keep my legs still on this same shot. Not Hagen. His backswing was flat; he turned his body, broke his wrists, and snapped at the ball. There was no finish, just a quick, crisp smack at impact as the open-face mashie niblick hit the ball first and then the turf. The ball came out low and hard and carried the length of the fairway and fringe, landed on the green up by the pin, and stopped. It didn't run a yard but spun to a halt within feet of the cup.

I had no idea how he had managed to pull that shot off, and I couldn't help applauding along with Chick and all the other spectators.

The gallery was still applauding when we stepped up to our ball.

Evans stood beside our ball and studied the lie and then the distance to the green. Valerie set down the bag and looked expectantly at us both. Like the good caddie she was becoming, she kept quiet, taking her cues from her players.

Chick said softly, "When I was first learning to play the game, back at Edgewater, I used to practice run-ups early in the morning before school. I hated it when the elevated railway replaced the old Chicago and Milwaukee Railroad tracks because all those people would watch me from the train windows."

Then he asked me what I thought, whether he should use the mashie niblick or the pitcher, which was another forty-five-degree-loft club that Patterson had in his bag.

We were ten yards from the edge of the green, another twenty yards to the flag. From our angle it was mostly a level shot, and since the cup was cut on the far side, there was plenty of green to work with. It was a clear shot and, unlike Hagen, Evans had no rise to worry about. I knew that, of all the Midlothian greens, this one was the slowest. That was one reason why Hagen's ball had checked up so quickly.

Cornell had taught me two pitch shots with the mashie niblick and the niblick. One was a simple knockdown, hitting the ball with a descending stroke and taking a thick inch of divot in front of the ball so that it would die once it hit the green; the other was to cut the ball, working across the line and hitting more under the ball than down on it. "Cut the legs off it," Cornell kept reminding me when we had practiced.

Evans pointed down at the ball and asked me what I saw.

It was a good lie in short grass, but the blades were growing away from the target, which meant that the club head would get snagged in the grass on the downswing; Chick would make weaker contact, and the ball would come up short of the pin. When I said all this to Chick, he just nodded.

We both understood that if we were playing with steel, Evans would use the sand wedge, play the ball back in his stance, take a short, slow backswing, and hit behind the ball so that it would pop up. He'd aim for the fringe as the ball would run on the green. But we didn't have the luxury of a wedge.

"So what do you think?" Evans asked again.

"A cut shot with the mashie niblick."

He nodded, adding, "I'll play it left of the pin and let it work to the flag." He knew, as I did, that a cut shot always jumped right.

"This green is the slowest on the course," I told him. Then Valerie and I stepped back and gave him room to play.

"Let's see what I remember from those early-morning practice sessions at Edgewater," Chick commented, as if talking to himself, and took a few more careful practice swings.

The ball came out low and hot off the short, dry fairway grass and carried to the green. Chick had played it well left, and when the ball hit the putting surface it hopped right and took the roll straight for the flag. My heart was in my throat—I was thinking that he had been too strong—but the ball had landed well short and the ball stopped five feet from the cup.

"Okay, good," I said encouragingly to Evans, but both of us knew that he hadn't played it that well and had left me with a tough putt.

Valerie handed me the putter, whispering, "Knock it in, O'Shea."

"I'll do just that, Driscoll," I answered, trying to sound confident.

To my surprise, that is just what I did. I knocked in the five-footer and quickly fished the ball out of the cup, recognized the applause of the gallery by tipping my hat, and grinned at Val and Chick.

I moved a few yards away from the cup, giving Drew room to look over his short putt, but I didn't move off the green. I wanted to hover by him. I wanted him to be well aware of me, and that my ball was safely in the cup.

McClain stepped around to check the line from both sides of his short three-footer, the toughest putt in golf. When he walked by, I commented offhandedly, as if just giving him a word of encouragement, "Bang it in there, Drew."

McClain knew as well as I did that the tenth green was habitually slow, but he didn't know that it hadn't been watered and so was faster than he realized. I hoped my phrase *bang the ball* would catch in his subconscious and make him do just that: bang the short putt past the hole. He did. His putt never had a chance.

38

CHICK AND I HAD WON THE TENTH WITH OUR PAR FOUR AND with the flow of the gallery, we moved to the par-4 eleventh, now one up.

Hagen walked off the green with us, congratulating me on my five-footer. "You've learned your Bobby Locke putting lessons well, Tommy. What else did Cornell tell you?" he asked as we crossed the wooden bridge over the small creek.

He meant, of course, about golf, but all I said was, "A lot," and walked away from him.

Then I heard him say to Evans, "You still have a problem getting up close to the cup, Chick."

I looked around. Evans was smiling but not responding. I kept my eye on both men, and when we reached the tee and the two of us stepped up between markers, I asked Chick what all that had been about.

Evans smiled wryly and said, "Oh, Walter is having a little fun. He was talking about the Open. I was one shot off the lead going into eighteen. He had finished up and I hit the best drive of the tournament, over two-seventy and a foot short of the green. I needed to chip in to tie. My chip came up short by a foot and I finished a shot behind him."

I nodded and said nothing; I pulled the driver from the bag. It was our honors, and Chick had suggested that I always hit first. I knew why: if I was wild off the tee, he had the experience to play safely so that we weren't out of the hole.

Valerie stepped over as I was teeing up. "Are you upset?" she asked.

I shrugged. "I didn't think it was very gentlemanly for him to remind Chick about losing the Open, that's all."

"You and Drew do that stuff all the time."

"That's different. We're kids. We've got nothing at stake but a couple of bucks. Chick lost his chance at the U.S. Open when that chip came up short. I bet he's thought about that shot a hundred thousand times since then."

"Don't let it bother you, okay?" she said. "Remember what Cornell said about swinging slow."

I kept nodding, registering some of what Valerie was telling me. I knew what she was doing—trying to make up for the fact that Cornell wasn't with me.

I took a deep breath and then another, and then shook out my arms and did all the other small things that Cornell had taught me to do on those late-night practice rounds. Then I drilled the driver low and hard and over the left edge of the fairway. The ball landed safely and kicked twenty yards forward, disappearing over the ridge. It was so good that Evans didn't even bother to tee off.

"I'll play yours," he said; then he added, "I'm not sure how many good hickory drives I have left in me, so I'd best conserve them."

We halved the hole with pars on eleven, but then on twelve, the short par-3, I cooked my mid-mashie and pulled it left into the green-side bunker. Chick pressed his tee shot, trying to get close, and ran his ball into the long grass beyond the hole. Both Hagen and Drew were on the green, Hagen within two feet. Drew putted out and we were back to even. Walking off the tee, Hagen turned to Chick and joked, "You should have been getting lessons from Cornell, like our Tommy here." He was grinning, enjoying himself.

Heading to thirteen, I walked over to Chick and started apologizing. He stopped me and said simply, "We're in this match, Tommy, and it begins now." His words left a nice chilling effect in the air, as if someone had just opened an icebox door. Clearly, the back nine wasn't going have any more reminiscing about the El train and the apple orchard.

I knew what had changed his mood: Hagen. Up till now, Evans had been ignoring his old competitor's needling, but now he was angry. He responded not in words but by switching our pecking order. He drove off first on thirteen. We need a change of luck, he told me, but he also said that he wanted me to use my strength. He felt that I was being too careful, trying to place my drives, not bang them.

"I'll get one ball in play, and let's see you use that young body of yours to pound out those tee shots," he told me.

"Cornell taught me to swing nice and easy; he said hickory wasn't for slashers."

Evans nodded, agreeing, but then he explained how I could swing the Cornell way and still bang it. "Widen your stance an inch or two, and on the backswing keep your right elbow close to your side and your left arm straight, and keep behind the club head. Let the club do the work. Feel the swing in your fingers. Hickory is played with your hands. The club will tell your fingers where they are in the swing. Don't think about just banging the ball as far as you can. Concentrate on your hands and play."

And that's what I did. I focused on my hands and the club head and swung away and outdrove Hagen and Chick and Drew, even though he hit one of his longer drives of the day.

I could see the surprise in Hagen's eyes when I stepped off the tee. He smiled, but in his eyes I saw the look people get when they realize that they are coming up against the real thing, whatever the game.

Golfers know that there comes a moment in the round when players retreat within themselves and begin to focus on winning. Now it happened with all of us walking off the tee on thirteen. Hagen went striding down the middle of the fairway. No more chatting with the gallery, at least on that hole.

"What's happening?" Valerie asked when I fell into step with her. The gallery surged by us as they rushed to keep pace with Hagen and Drew. Evans was walking with several of the WGA officials, so she and I were alone.

"It's not an exhibition anymore," I answered. "It's a real match."

"What's the difference?" she asked.

"Hagen thought it would be a cakewalk, taking on Cornell and me, but he didn't count on Chick Evans."

She fell silent, as if she, too, understood that it was a contest on the back side. She wasn't just my girlfriend looping for me on a special day: we had a golf match to win.

When we reached Hagen's ball, we paused, standing off to one side, while Hagen and Drew decided which of their two balls they should play. They chose to play Drew's. Red Denison moved over beside me and whispered, "Hell of a shot, Tommy."

I nodded thanks and he smiled and said, "When are you going to thank me again for giving you Patterson's old hickories?"

"When we beat him." I gestured at Hagen.

"Keep hitting them like that and you might."

"I'm just sorry Cornell's not here to help me."

Red nodded at Evans and, lowering his voice, added, "I'm not sure you can beat Hagen, but you wouldn't have stood a chance with Cornell as your partner."

"We had them two down the first two holes, Red," I reminded the pro.

"Thanks to your play, not his."

We reached Chick's ball and I'm sure he had already decided what to do, but he asked what I thought anyway. He was always respectful of his partner, even though it was just me, a kid who hadn't won anything in his life but a state high-school championship and a couple of caddie tournaments.

"Let me get up around the dogleg with a draw with your ball," I said. "You can get us close with a pitch-and-run. Your short game is better than mine. I'll make the putt, promise." I smiled, feeling at that moment that I was in control of my game as well as the match.

The lie was tight and I placed the spoon carefully behind the ball. The loft was greater than twenty-two degrees degrees, giving it the lift of a 4 wood. The fairway was wide. I had plenty of room to maneuver the ball around the dogleg, but I wanted to keep it close to the bend so that, beyond the trees, the ball would catch the fairway and run.

The plan was better than my execution. I played it too close to the trees; plus, I caught the ball on the toe. My ball never made it to the corner. It dived into the cluster of trees edging the left side of the long par-5 and disappeared into the thick grass. We'd be lucky to find it, I thought next, let alone give Chick a shot at the green.

Hagen, hitting Drew's ball, played a beautiful little driving iron that drew nicely around the corner of the dogleg and scooted toward the green. It was the shot I had wanted to make. Drew had eighty yards left, an easy pitch to the flag. Chick was dead in the weeds.

We were all square in the match but I knew that my wayward fairway wood meant we would lose thirteen. Even with everyone looking, including the officials from the WGA and others, we couldn't find the ball; it was buried somewhere in the grass that grew long and wild in the span of trees at the corner of the dogleg.

After five minutes of searching for the lost ball, we were about to concede the hole and move on to fourteen, one down to Hagen and McClain, when Valerie cried out, "I've got it."

The ball had carried farther than we'd thought, and though it was buried, Evans had a shot at it. He looked up from the lie, smiled at Valerie, and said to me, "You've got yourself a great caddie, Tommy, in this young woman, what with her finding this ball."

"She's the best," I said.

"If only you could play this one for me."

"Hit it stiff, Mr. Evans," Valerie advised.

Chick laughed and pulled the niblick from the bag. Most of the gallery had paused on the fairway, wide of where we were, though Hagen walked over as if to inspect the lie and then stopped. He shook his head and looked worried, and I was thinking then that he was trying to intimidate Evans, who appeared not to notice or be concerned with anything more than making the shot from the deep rough.

He played the ball back in his stance and gripped low on the niblick. The only way he could manage to pop the ball out of that cabbage was to hit down. Hit it hard. And hope. Chick did get it out, but barely. The ball ran twenty yards toward the green and stopped in the middle of the fairway fifty yards from the green. I had a shot, but we were already laying three.

"The best I could do," Chick said, slipping the niblick into the bag as we waited for Drew to play up. Drew had a perfect lie in the middle of the fairway and he hit a lovely pitch onto the green: the ball held. Hagen had a simple enough birdie putt inside of ten feet on the small flat green.

I had practiced enough chips around that green over the last few weeks that I knew exactly how to play the pitch-and-run and how the ball would react on the green. Valerie didn't even have to tell me to knock it close. I was playing a shot that I could do in my sleep.

I pitched to the fringe, not the green. I knew that this hole was faster than most, and the ball hit in the thick grass and spun up to the hole. The gallery framing the green thought at first that the shot didn't have the speed, but I knew from my many nights of practicing that once it hit the hard surface it would roll. And it did, straight for the pin, banging into the bamboo and dropping for a birdie.

Chick was closer to the pin, but he let me have the pleasure of the long walk up to the green with all the members applauding; there, without removing the flag, I bent down and scissored the ball between my fingers and lifted it out of the cup. The reaction from the gallery was more of a roar than a cheer and they kept applauding as I stepped to the side. I couldn't keep from grinning. It was as if I were a kid on Christmas morning.

All afternoon Hagen had been just going up to the ball and putting. Now he was taking his time. He even had Drew step over to help read the line. What I knew about the putt on this side of the green was that it looked as if it should be played two inches left of the cup to take the slope—but it didn't break as it appeared. Standing beside Evans on the fringe, I whispered that course knowledge to him, saying that Hagen would miss the putt.

"I wouldn't be so sure, Tommy. Remember, he saw how your ball reacted coming across the green."

Chick was right. Hagen drilled the lengthy nine-footer to match my birdie. We were still even heading to fourteen.

39

HAGEN PICKED UP HIS CHATTER AGAIN ON FOURTEEN TEE, TELLING the gallery that when he last played at Midlothian, in 1939, the trees had not been as tall or the hole as tight. He looked at Chick and in his bantering way asked how he had played the hole back in 1914.

Chick stared down the length of the tight, tree-lined opening that burst out into a wide landing area of smooth grass. We couldn't see the green. Then Evans said, raising his voice so that the gallery framing the tee could hear and understand him, "I believe the wind was against me that day. I drove two-ninety off the tee and ended up in the bunker on the left side, missed a sixteen-footer for a birdie."

I smiled to myself, thinking that this was the way with golfers. They never forgot a round or how they had won or lost a match.

Hagen grabbed the crowd's attention again. "I birdied this hole once in the Open, on the first day, when I shot my sixty-eight." He glanced around and, feigning ignorance, asked the members if that record still stood.

As a chorus of voices assured him that, yes, he still held the course record, Evans just smiled and shook his head.

"What's happening?" Val whispered.

"Hagen is trying to put Evans in his place," I said under my breath. "He's reminding Chick and me that he holds the course record. He's trying to intimidate us."

"That's not fair!" Valerie declared. "What can you do about it?"

"We can beat him at his own game, that's what we can do." I stepped over to Chick; he was staring down the length of the fairway, as if trying to recapture—visualize, as we might say today—how he had played the hole decades before.

"Let's not go for it," Chick suggested when I approached. "Those two will, and they're both wild. The chances are they'll bunker their drives or come up short. We'll play conservatively, and have a niblick left."

I knew he was right, but it wasn't what I wanted to do. "I want to go for it. I can drive this green," I said, trying to sound more confident than I was.

"We need to get one ball in the fairway and have a safe shot at the green," he reminded me.

"You do that," I told Chick. "I'll go over those trees." I reached for the driver but Evans shook his head. "There's no need to announce ourselves. Let them play their game; we'll play ours." He spoke calmly, lowering his voice, and I heard enough of an edge to his tone to know that Hagen had upset him with his comment about the course record, reminding Evans again how he had beat him. Still, Evans was enough of a gentleman that he wouldn't say anything in the middle of the round, or later, I knew, when interviewed by the press.

Hagen and Drew weren't wild off the tee. Neither of them

went for the green. Both played safely into the middle of the wide fairway, leaving a short iron to the target for their second shots. Hagen, I guessed, would have Drew play up so that he could putt. Chick had mentioned that Hagen's strategy would be to keep the putter out of Drew's hand since he'd blown the three-footer on ten.

Evans teed off and faded a spoon around the dogleg. He was short of the other two balls in the flat fairway and left of the bunker, but with his drive, we, too, had an open shot to the pin. I set up to go for the green, playing my ball between the markers but as far back as I could. I needed all the wood I could get to reach the green at fourteen, but Patterson's driver had an eight-degree loft and I couldn't get the ball up fast enough to clear the top corner trees of the dogleg. I pulled the brassie, which had a few more degrees of loft. I was strong enough to whack the brassie as far as the driver, if I caught it right.

Stepping between the markers, I saw Drew grinning. He knew that I was going for it, and he was thinking as well that it wasn't the percentage shot. It was clearly a gamble, but we had one ball safely in the fairway, and even as I stood judging the line to the green, I kept wondering why Drew hadn't also played for the green, what with Hagen safely in the fairway.

The trick for me was not to cook the brassie. I kept thinking of what Cornell, and now Chick Evans, had said: to focus on my fingers on the shaft, to follow the club head and not force the shot. I was kept, too, from overswinging by the pain in my side from when Drew had kicked me. There was no way that my body would let me power the shot off the tee.

I stepped back and got the angle, picked the spot where I wanted the ball to clear the trees. All I had to do was hit it high and straight, and the wind and the right angle would get me close or on. By cutting the corner of the dogleg, I knew I had less than 250 yards to the green.

When I stepped up to play, I saw, out of the corner of my eye, Drew cross his legs. He had positioned himself so that all of his movements would catch my attention. I backed off the drive as if to suggest that I didn't have the right angle; then I motioned to Val to bring the clubs out onto the tee, as if I were thinking of switching woods, and whispered to her what Drew was doing to throw off my swing.

She thought for a moment and then said, "I'll go stand in front of him. I'll block him from your sight."

"Good thinking, Driscoll!" I grinned. "Don't say anything. Just block him."

I turned back to the ball and studied the angle over the trees, giving Valerie time to move into position. She stepped in front of Drew, as if she were only a caddie doing her job, and successfully shielded his movements so that I wasn't distracted by them. Knowing that she was there helped me, made me feel that much more confident and sure of myself and what I had to do, which was swing within myself and drive over the top edge of the tall poplars. That's exactly what I did. The ball rose like a hot-air balloon, higher and higher, easily clearing the leafy trees. While I could not see the entire flight of the ball, I knew it was on line, and then a cheer came back up the rise and I knew the ball was safely on.

When we reached Hagen and Drew's balls down in the fairway, I understood why they both had played safely off the fourteen tee. Hagen wanted to play Drew's ball. He wanted to be sure that they would be close to the pin. He was 110 at most to the top tier where the pin was cut, and when he pulled his niblick, Hagen was clearly concentrating. There was no conversation with the gallery. He took several drags on his cigarette, smoking thoughtfully.

I moved closer to enjoy the show. I was feeling great, having made the green in one. Chick and I were sitting in the catbird's seat.

Once finished with his calculation, Hagen tossed down the cigarette and addressed the ball, his eyes never leaving the target. He gripped down two inches on the shaft, moved his body closer to the ball, played it back, and opened his stance. It was a three-quarter shot; on the backswing he took the club outside the line, breaking his wrists immediately, and when his hands were just above his waist, he started his smooth, quick downswing, clipping the ball off the turf without a divot. It came out low and hard, as if this were a British links course and he was trying to play it under the wind. But there was no wind on that lowest point on the Midlothian course, and I saw by the flight that his shot would hit high up on the green. And if it did, it might fly the green. It did hit into the rise of the green, but with Hagen's cut action the ball checked up, took one forward bounce, and came back to the hole, leaving Drew a gimme birdie.

Walking up to the green, I knocked their ball away, giving them three, and pulled the flag and handed it to Valerie and walked down the rise to where my drive had stopped. I realized Chick had at best a lag to the cup. There wasn't much of a chance that he could nail the putt.

Chick Evans, who his entire great golfing career had the reputation of being a poor putter, nevertheless sank the uphill lag putt for an eagle and we were one up going to fifteen tee.

40

WE PLAYED THE SHORT PAR-3 FIFTEEN IN REGULATION, HALVING the hole, and headed to sixteen tee and the last three holes. The gallery continued to grow on the back side. The match was attracting more members and all the kids from the caddie yard, and when we reached sixteen green, some motorists on 147th Street joined in. They pulled their cars off the two-lane road and stood up against the wire fencing to watch as all of us, players and spectators, approached the green.

Both of our second shots on the par-5 had come up short. Drew was away, with a long, sixty-yard pitch to the postage-stamp green. Chick's fairway wood had caught the shallow bunker to the left of the hole, and when I approached our ball, I saw that I was not only in the sand but close to the front lip of the bunker. The only good thing about it was that the ball wasn't buried. I had a chance to play it out safely, but getting it close to the cup would be all luck.

Chick came up beside me and looked at the lie. We hadn't been in a bunker all day.

"You know how to play sand?" he asked calmly, studying the lie.

"I think so. I practiced some with Cornell."

"You'll have to hit the niblick," he said, as if thinking out loud.

"I know." I turned to the bag. Valerie was watching me, her eyes full of worry. I winked and pulled out the niblick, and said to Evans, "I'm going to hit the short-jump-out explosion."

That caught Evans's attention. "You know how to play it?"

"I think I can. Besides, I have nothing else, not where the ball lies."

I turned around to see Drew and watched him play a pitch-and-run. He hit it too hard. The shot landed hard and ran across the green and off, leaving Hagen a long chip or putt to make birdie.

I stepped into the sand and moved around behind the ball to check the line and distance. Val put the bag down and grabbed the rake. Evans moved out of my line but he didn't move away.

"What do you think?" I said, realizing that he wanted to share his knowledge of how to play an explosion shot.

"Don't open the face. Stand ahead of the ball so you swing down. And take a full swing. Aim a full inch behind the ball. The ball will jump out fifteen feet or so. It will run, and you'll need that—the flag is fifty feet from where you're standing. Remember, you have to hit the sand back of and under the ball with a downward chop, so the force of it carries the ball. Don't try and finish the shot; bury the club head."

Evans took his cap off and ran his fingers through his hair. Other than that, I would have had no notion that he was nervous. He had learned in a lifetime of match play to keep his emotions in check—a lesson that Cornell had been trying to teach me.

I addressed the ball, setting myself forward on the shot, picking a spot an inch behind the ball where I would bury the niblick. Now all I needed was the courage to take a full swing, not a halfhearted one.

I swung hard and the ball popped out. It carried farther than I had imagined and, with a spray of sand, landed on the green and bounced toward the flag. My distance was okay, but I had set up wrong, too far left. Chick had a putt of seven to eight feet for our birdie.

I stepped out of the sand, wiping it off my arms and pants, and walked up to the fringe and waited there for Hagen to try to make birdie from off the green.

Hagen pulled his putter and stepped onto the green and studied the line, carefully moving around, circling the shot. He was leaving the flag in and leaving it unattended. If his putt came in hot, it might just hit the thick bamboo and drop.

When Hagen went back to his ball, there was no hesitation, no rethinking his decision. He stepped up and, with his famous wide stance, putted from off the fringe. The ball bounced on the thick grass and I thought then that it would be knocked off line. It was hit hard and coming straight downgraid to the cup. If it missed the thick bamboo pole, it would run another six or seven feet beyond the hole, but it didn't. The ball hit the flagstick squarely in the middle with a sharp whack and dropped for a birdie. The gallery circling the green exploded with surprise and delight, thrilled that once again, and after all those years, Walter Hagen was playing like the great champion that he was. As much as I hated to see the ball drop, I tipped my cap to him. There were players who always found a way to win, and he was one of them.

We now had a tester just to tie the hole and stay one-up. I had hoped—seeing Hagen play Drew's ball off the fringe—that we would walk off sixteen with a two-hole lead.

"Knock it in," I told Chick, thinking at the same time how weird it was that I was the one encouraging the great golfer.

Evans nodded and together we studied the line—Chick on one side of the hole, I on the other. We switched sides to look at the seven-footer and Chick asked me what I saw.

"It's dead straight," I told him. There was nothing tricky about the putt. It was only a question of getting the ball on line and judging the speed. This late in the season, all the greens were hard and dry, baked by the summer sun, and while they had been rolled that morning, I knew that the grass was bumpy from so much play all summer long.

As the gallery watched, waiting for Chick to step up, all I could think was how quiet it was on sixteen. It was almost as if we were playing alone. There was hardly a breath of air that hot afternoon, hardly a sound from the spectators.

Evans still did not step forward to finish the hole, and I wondered then if the long afternoon and the stress of being caught up in a tense match might be too much for him. Evans hadn't come to Midlothian to play, to compete again with Walter Hagen. I took a deep breath. There was nothing I, or any of us, could do to stop what was about to happen. I realized that the whole match, and perhaps my whole future, hung on this simple seven-foot, dead-in putt.

I looked at Valerie and saw that she had closed her eyes. She couldn't bear to watch. When Chick stroked the putt, the blade putter striking the ball sounded like the echo of a distant bell. He drove it straight at the center of the hole, taking the break out of the putt, and the ball clicked into the metal cup as if someone had just locked the door on the match.

Walking toward the seventeenth green, I said to Valerie that these two U.S. Open champions—Hagen and Evans—were showing Drew and myself how the game was played. "Compared to them," I said, "we're just two country-club hackers."

41

"THIS IS FUN, RIGHT, BOYS?" HAGEN ASKED DREW AND ME ON THE seventeenth tee. He was fitting another cigarette into his holder as we waited for the gallery to fan out down the left side of the fairway.

I smiled, not knowing what to say, but Drew began to babble about how he liked the competition and had matches like that all the time at Yale. I watched Hagen watch Drew. Hagen had the eyes of a hustler, steady and cold, and you could feel him taking the measure of Drew. As Drew rambled on about his big matches with Harvard, I wondered if he knew that Hagen had never finished elementary school.

I knew that Drew's frantic talk was all nerves. I had played enough matches against him, and caddied enough for him, to know that the pressure was seeping into his cockiness. Hagen, on the other hand, had gotten quieter on the back side.

Evans teed up and took several swings. Then, just as he prepared to hit, looking down the open fairway, aligning the shot, but before he could address the ball, Hagen said casually, as if he were simply telling the temperature, "Since you fellas are up, what about doubling the bet?" He spoke loudly enough for the gallery and the WGA officials to hear him. Now the match would cost me more money than I had saved up for college.

Evans paused, then said nicely, "Our pleasure! Right, Tommy?" He was all smiles. But I had begun to notice how Evans hid his anger under his good manners. It was clear to me, and I am sure it was to Chick as well, that Hagen was trying to break our composure by raising the bet, figuring that I, for one, wouldn't be able to stand the pressure.

Then Chick stepped up and hit a good one. The drive reached as far as the bunker to the right side of the fairway and ran another twenty yards into the middle of the fairway, a good 280 down the 411-yard par-4. My drive caught the fairway bunker, and when I stepped away from the tee, Chick just nodded and said that we'd play his ball. We were all right, he said. His ball was sitting up in the middle of the long fairway.

Once again, Hagen sprayed his drive, sending it into the deep rough on the right side; but Drew's tee shot was perfect, shorter than Chick's but also in the middle of the fairway.

Hagen didn't even bother to pick up his ball. Instead, he deliberately fell into step with me as we walked down the cut path to the fairway. I guessed that we were finally going to have it out about Cornell.

He began by saying quietly, "He's going to be okay."

I nodded but didn't speak. I stared ahead, watching Chick and Drew walking and talking together. My guess then was that Hagen wanted me to start thinking about Cornell and lose my concentration.

"The pressure just got to him," Hagen said, his voice sympathetic. "He's had a tough time these last years."

"It didn't seem like anything ever bothered him," I answered.

Hagen asked me then if I had ever heard of Johnny McDermott. I shook my head, and Hagen said, "Not many people have, and it's a shame. McDermott was our first American winner of a championship. He won the U.S. Open in 1911 and again in '12. Then he went over to play in the British Open in 1914, but got delayed and was too late to tee off. On his way home, his ship collided with another one and sank. He spent a day in a lifeboat before he was rescued.

"When he got back to the States he found out he had lost all his money on Wall Street, so he took a job as golf pro in Atlantic City. He was twenty-three at the time, and had to quit playing tournament golf.

"A few years later he started to have mental breakdowns and his family put him in a hospital. He played golf only one more time in his life, shot par for eighteen, and never played again."

Hagen shook his head. "Golf makes human beings out of us all, regardless of how good we think we are."

"Harrison had his plane shot down," I said, defending him. "He didn't just go crazy."

"Well, there were wild stories about him that I heard down in the Bahamas."

"Cornell told me he found your Red Cross medal in their bedroom."

Startled, Hagen stopped walking. I stopped walking, too, and waited for him to answer. The gallery, hugging the rough, moved ahead on their own, without ropes or marshals.

"Unfortunately true, Tommy. Gwendolyn was very kind to me when I was in the Bahamas, and I gave the medallion to her as a keepsake. Unfortunately, it caused a misunderstanding between them. I had just left Nassau. Harrison, as I recall, was pulling military duty, and later in the day he confronted his wife at the country club. I'm told she drove off in a huff and wrecked her car on one of those twisting island roads. What happened to her was a terrible shame."

Before I could ask another question, he added, "Did I make love to her? I'm sure Harrison told you I did."

He stared at me for a moment longer. "You deserve to know that much, Tommy. The answer is yes; but I wasn't the first man to share her bed. She was an unhappy young woman and those were wild times on the island among people who were too rich, too young, and living useless lives."

"Cornell didn't lead a useless life, Mr. Hagen. He was a pilot in the air force and helped defeat the Nazis. That's more than you did, sir. You were off playing golf with the Duke and Duchess of Windsor." And with that, I turned and walked off, leaving Hagen to play their second shot to the seventeenth green.

My gut was churning with what I had said to Hagen and I was briefly dizzy with emotion. Valerie at once saw how shaken I was. Whispering, she asked me what Hagen had said. I shook my head and told her it was too complicated to discuss with her now. I was thankful at the moment that I wasn't hitting first. Standing in the middle of the fairway, with the gallery pressing in and the sun blazing, I was having trouble focusing on the game.

I turned toward Hagen and watched him play up to the green. Playing that match with Hagen, I could see why he drove Bobby Jones crazy; after his wild drive, his second shot on seventeen—playing Drew's ball—was a laser. It landed short and kicked forward. I saw it roll onto the green and then curl down toward the flag. Drew had a putt left for a birdie.

My cleek into seventeen never had a chance. It was the worst shot I made that afternoon, the worst I had made since I had picked up the hickories. I couldn't focus. I couldn't bear down. I couldn't do any of the things that Cornell had drilled into me. My mind was whirling with everything Hagen had said about Cornell and Nassau, and what I had said to him. Hagen had managed to break my concentration.

The long iron off the level fairway sprayed right and into the green-side bunker. Chick pitched it safely on, but I didn't even regroup for that putt and missed it as well. Drew and Hagen two-putted to win with a par and even the match.

42

EVANS DIDN'T RUSH OFF THE GREEN FOR THE EIGHTEENTH TEE. HE took his time and I knew why: he wanted to talk to me alone.

He smiled, retrieving our ball and handing it to me and our putter to Valerie, and said nicely, "We have to do it now, Tommy."

I nodded.

"It's my mistake," he said next. "I shouldn't have let Hagen talk to you back there. He got you all turned around."

"I guess," I said, now realizing what Hagen had done. I was embarrassed that I hadn't seen it coming.

"He wasn't the greatest match player in the world without having a few tricks up his sleeve," Chick remarked.

"He was talking to me about Cornell," I said.

"Of course, but it wasn't about this match, which is most important, given all the money we've wagered."

I nodded. "Okay."

"We have one hole to go," he added, "and we're all even."

"I won't let you down, Chick." And I didn't mean to.

In the U.S. Open of 1914 at Midlothian, Walter Hagen birdied the short par-4 eighteenth hole every round of the tournament. It was a feat that has never been matched in U.S. Open history. The eighteen was a short finishing hole, only 287 yards long, and drivable. Teeing off, Hagen's drive finished in the shallow front left-side bunker, but Drew's ran up just short of the front entrance to the hole, leaving an easy pitch-and-run to the pin cut that afternoon on the back ridge of a green that sloped severely from back to front.

"Drive first," Chick said when we moved onto the tee. "And get on. You have the distance." It wasn't a request; it was an order.

I did hit a lovely drive off eighteen, but I didn't have the length. I didn't even reach Drew's drive. Chick did no better. Trying to make the green, he played for a draw, hoping to catch the fairway and run up, but his drive was hit too perfectly. It rode the right side and ended up in the rough, short of the bunker, and buried in the long grass.

We needed to play my drive, and we had a pitch-and-run up the slope. It was a shot that Chick Evans had been making for years, a shot that he owned, as we say that day; and walking up eighteen fairway, I was feeling pretty good. We could win, I told Val.

The final green was encased with gallery. They stood three and four deep on the slope between the putting surface and the rambling white clubhouse. The film cameramen had moved to the first tee, which was a high platform that looked down over the gallery. A round of applause began slowly and then grew louder as we moved closer and closer to our drives. It was as if we were onstage, finishing a drama, and in many ways I guess we were.

Hagen took off his hat to the applause, as did Chick Evans, and even Drew, but I was too embarrassed to accept the recognition and stopped beside my drive, back again to my role as a caddie. Chick walked up to Valerie and me and without hesitating pulled the niblick.

"I think I've been here before," he joked, recalling the Open.

"Well, this time, chip it in."

Evans turned to Valerie and said politely, "Young lady, go up and take the flag, please."

A moment of panic swept through me.

"No, I'd better get it." I had a sudden vision that she wouldn't do it right, that the chip might hit her or the pin and we'd be penalized.

Valerie looked straight at me and said calmly, "I'm the caddie, Tommy. I'll take the flag." She shoved the bag of Patterson's clubs into my arms and walked onto the green, holding her head high and striding across to grab the flag and stand ready for Evans's chip. Taking the flag, Valerie received a bigger round of applause than any of us.

By this time it was close to five o'clock. A breeze had picked up, and with the sun beginning to lower, I remember thinking how lovely it was there in the shadow of the clubhouse on the final hole of that final match. And I thought, too, that I would even enjoy it more if I were just in the gallery and not having to play the hole and win.

Hagen was going to play Drew's ball, which was safely in the fairway and a few yards ahead of where Chick was getting ready to chip. Hagen and Drew stood on the fringe and waited for

Chick's ball to land to see how it would react on the green, what the break would be like.

I told Chick what I knew about the eighteenth—that even playing uphill the ball would run, and while it looked like a fall off to the right, there really wasn't one. He nodded and I moved the clubs away so that he could play the shot.

It seemed like forever before he addressed the ball. People in the gallery who had been speaking softly to one another, exchanging comments and observations as they watched the four of us, now fell silent as Chick settled himself. I am sure that more than one, including me, of course, wanted Evans to chip the ball in for an eagle, to make the shot he hadn't in 1914, and win the hole, win the match, and finally beat the great Walter Hagen.

In some ways I think that Hagen himself might have enjoyed the irony, but it didn't happen. Chick hit a great chip. The ball ran up the slope and stayed on line, as I knew it would. Evans had followed my advice about the green. Valerie quickly pulled the bamboo pole but the ball slipped by the hole and rolled another four feet, leaving me a tricky downhill putt. I knew from experience that it wouldn't be easy to make.

I carried the clubs around to the far edge of the green, pulled the putter, and laid the bag on the fringe. When I looked up, I saw the Professor. He had locked the caddie shack and come to watch us finish. I smiled and he nodded. I could see in his eyes that he was pleased that I was out there battling the likes of Hagen, but he would not, of course, admit that to anyone, least of all to me.

I stepped onto the green as Hagen played. He had learned something from watching how Chick's ball reacted, and he knew that his chip wouldn't fall away from the cup. He played it straight for the hole, and seeing it come up the rise, I thought at first that he might hole the pitch, but he had played the ball too far left on the ridge. Ganzer, now on the flag since Hagen was hitting, pulled the pin and stepped away. The ball slipped by the left edge of the cup and ran another three feet and stopped in my line of putt. I was stymied.

The gallery groaned as they saw what I saw. Hagen smiled slyly, as if he had planned that shot, and shook his head. I stepped back to the bag, dropped the putter, and pulled the niblick. I kept thinking: Of all the ways to lose a match, and all that money . . .

"Can you play the stymie?" was all Evans asked, arriving beside me.

"Yes," I said, and then I added, "but not well."

"You only need to clear the stymie. The ball will take the slope and run."

The truth was that I had never made a chip with a niblick, even when I practiced with Cornell, who was magical with the club. I knew how to use a wedge for stymies, but the niblick didn't have the loft.

Hagen and Drew had stepped aside, giving me the stage. I could see Drew whispering to Hagen. He was suddenly relaxed, and I knew that it was all because he was sure I couldn't make it. He would tap in his three-footer and win the hole, win the exhibition.

I took a few more short practice swings, trying to get myself to imagine the shot and how I would make it.

I looked once more at the ball, and the slope, and thought of all the stymies Cornell had made when we practiced on the back nine. For him, it was almost an art form, something he had learned in Scotland.

Behind me, a low murmur ran through the gallery. They were restless and eager for the match to be over. It had been a long day and only these shots remained to be made or missed.

"You can make it," Valerie whispered as I stepped away from the bag and walked onto the green. I didn't even bother with judging the roll. My only hope was to clear their ball and be on the right line.

I stepped up and took a half-dozen practice swings to calm myself. Even then I wasn't calm, but I also realized that I never would be. I tried to image Cornell, thought about how he was always so casual and relaxed with the niblick. I stepped up and played the hickory the way I had seen Cornell do it a hundred times, the way he had taught me: a short and stiff wrist/arm-action stroke with no follow-through.

The ball popped up, cleared Hagen's ball seven inches in front of me, landed hard, and sped down the slope. Only the cup got in the way.

Behind me, the audience ringing the green roared up in a single loud cheer of both shock and praise. Valerie jumped into my arms. She was so happy that she was crying.

I managed to move off the green, to shake hands with Chick, who then raised both our arms to quiet the crowd. Drew had a putt to make and halve the hole.

McClain stood over the ball and studied the line. I knew that he was just trying to calm himself down so that he could make the shot. He stood looking down at the short three-footer, gauging the break. But there was no break, I knew. He needed only to tap the ball; it would roll in on its own.

It was very quiet on the green. With my nerves calm and my heart no longer pounding, I felt for the first time the intense pressure of the members pressed together to watch Drew putt. They seemed to be collectively holding their breath. It was as if all the air had gone out of the afternoon.

Drew carefully and softly stroked the ball, terrified as I knew he would be by the speed and the downhill. The ball moved slowly at first, then picked up speed. Drew waited for it to take the break, but there was no break and the ball slipped by the cup on the right side and kept rolling. The final hickory-club golf match played at Midlothian was over. Chick and I had won on lofting a stymie, the shot that Harrison Cornell always called the prettiest one in golf.

Epilogue

What comes back to me most vividly now, after all these years, is the warmth of the members who rushed to embrace and congratulate me as we exited the green. They wanted to demonstrate, in whatever hasty way they could, their happiness at our triumph; to share in the success that was all of ours, those of us who were part of the Midlothian Country Club.

In making his presentation of his hickory clubs to the Western Golf Association that evening at the banquet, Hagen would remark, half kidding, half in farewell to the game, that when he had first played golf as a caddie he never would have thought that he'd be beaten by such a spectacular shot as mine to lose a match on the final hole. He said that it was a perfect way to end his career.

When Chick Evans and I stood up that evening to accept the trophy and $1000 victory check, Chick made the surprise announcement that would change my life. He began by mentioning Harrison Cornell, telling the audience of members how Cornell had caddied for him at Edgewater Country Club that summer and told him about an amazing caddie, Tommy O'Shea, who had a gift for playing with hickories. Because of Cornell, Evans said, he was giving his share of our winnings to the Evans Scholarship Fund, and then he announced that the Scholarship Committee was awarding me an Evans Caddie Scholarship to Northwestern University for that coming fall.

There was a brief moment of stunned silence, and then, en masse, the roomful of members stood and applauded our victory and my college scholarship.

After that evening I would see Chick Evans from time to time when caddies were invited to WGA functions at Golf, Illinois. And I also played golf with Chick many times later in his life. He died in 1979 after having competed in a record fifty consecutive U.S. Amateurs in his long career, playing his last rounds of competitive golf in 1967 at the age of seventy-seven.

As for others who were part of that amazing summer, time and tragedy have touched all our lives. Jimmy Leamer, the Professor, never did retire, nor did he have a life away from the caddie yard. A new caddie to Midlothian found his slumped-over body in his old wicker chair on a quiet Friday afternoon in midsummer of 1952.

The country-club members held a wake and funeral for Jimmy, which was attended by many of the former caddies he stewarded. Then his ashes were sprinkled over the front lawn that faces the open terrace and stretches down to the eighteenth green. That way, members, as he had often joked, would have to walk over his body when they finished a round.

Red Denison, who had been so helpful and kind to me in those last days of that summer, was not rehired by the Midlothian Country Club at the end of the 1946 season. I never found out if it had anything to do with the fact that he had given Jack Patterson's clubs to me rather than Drew.

Billy Boyle kept working at the men's bar, trading rumors and stories with new generations of members, retelling, I'm told, the events of that August of 1946. I imagine that his telling became more dramatic and he played a larger role in Hagen's time at the club with every new telling.

The Duehr brothers retired as the superintendents of the golf course, and Ed's two sons, Mel and Mitch, took over as grounds-keepers, until they, too, retired in 1997. They were, again to the members' credit, made honorary members of the country club.

You must wonder what happened to Clare Farrell. After she left our barnyard that summer morning, I did not see her again for almost a decade, and then we met by chance downtown on State Street in Chicago. She had graduated from Smith College and stayed out east, but she came back to visit every so often. I had returned from the Korean War, and one day we passed each other on the street.

It was Clare who recognized me at the intersection of State and Madison and called out my name. She was more beautiful than ever, so much more sophisticated. She lived in Washington, D.C., she said, had gone to graduate school at Georgetown University, and was working in the State Department as a Foreign Service officer. She was home to see her family after a two-year assignment in Nice.

While we stood on the downtown Chicago sidewalk and talked of places I had barely heard of, I stood in awe, realizing then, having lived through a war of my own, that Clare had been right about us. I was not the right person for her and the life she had envisioned back when we were kids working at the club.

After that chance meeting, I never saw Clare again. In her late twenties she married another Foreign Service officer, and then after children and a divorce, she remarried, and rose in the ranks of the State Department to become one of America's first women ambassadors. When she was still in her early fifties, she was flying to visit a refugee camp somewhere in Africa and her plane crashed in a violent storm somewhere in the mountains of western Ethiopia. I'm told that there is a plaque in the lobby of the State Department in Washington, D.C., with her name inscribed with other ambassadors' who died in service to America. I keep promising myself that someday I'll travel to Washington to see her name written in marble on the State Department wall.

As for Drew, he finished college and then went on to Yale Law and returned to Chicago to work with his father in the family firm. He kept up with golf, and from time to time I would read in the small print of the *Tribune* sports pages that he had won a pro-member tournament or had finished fairly high up in a state amateur event. He never became the player we all thought he would be.

Valerie and I were invited to his first wedding, shortly after he passed the bar exam. We were not invited to his second wedding or, for that matter, his third.

He is still a member at Midlothian and from time to time we spot each other on the country-club drive when I'm leaving for the office and he is coming out to play a round of golf. We wave.

As for myself—well, I never became a medical doctor. Thanks to the Evans Scholarship and the support, anonymously, of several country-club members, I earned a degree in business from Northwestern University.

In my senior year of college my dad died of a heart attack, and Mom and I were left to manage the farm. One of my professors, Dr. Michael McCaskey, who taught real estate Law, suggested that I go into business with my brothers. We started a construction company and built a model home on some back acreage, with the idea of creating a subdivision. I followed his advice and found a career.

Valerie and I were married in the summer of 1952.

I still had another year in the air force and I wore my captain's uniform at the wedding. Dr. Driscoll swallowed his pride and his Episcopal heritage to walk his daughter down the aisle of St. Christopher's Catholic Church. He came, over time, to respect me, my business acumen, and his daughter's decision, especially when the grandchildren arrived.

I formed a real estate development partnership with my brothers. We bought more farmland out in the direction of Oak Forest and Tinley Park and built additional subdivisions as more and more Chicagoans began to move south, out of the city.

Then, twenty years ago or so, when we had to put Dr. Driscoll into a hospice, we moved back to Valerie's childhood home.

Today, when I leave that house and pull out onto the narrow drive in the mornings, I drive slowly down the length of the tenth hole, glancing through the trees to see who might be playing on the back side. It's a caddie's reflex, watching for players.

I drive up past the new practice range where once the club's private railroad terminal was located, and go by the new clubhouse, which imitates, in loving ways, the grand old clubhouse built at the turn of the last century.

It has all changed, of course. The gravel parking lot is now paved. The caddie shack is gone; but still standing, though all overgrown with weeds, is our old caddie handball court, my initials slapped on with red paint. Sometimes I'll stop and remember shooting craps behind the court's high wall, out of sight of the Professor up in the shack, sitting there with his books and vodka waiting for the phone to ring, a call for another caddie to be sent up for a member waiting to tee off.

And then I'll ease down the country road, driving over the narrow bridge by the reservoir, and remember the morning when

I spotted Harrison Cornell walking down the private drive as if he were late for an important appointment.

But that is all that is left of my memories of the country club, and they come from another age. Though Val and I live within a short chip shot of the tenth green, I never joined Midlothian Country Club. Instead, my brothers and I took farmland west of Tinley Park and turned it into a public course.

We named it Harrison Hills, and for many years players were entertained and treated to stories by the honorary pro at the club, Harrison Cornell himself, who on his good days would also give lessons on how to play golf with hickory clubs—the way the game, he always said, was meant to be played.

A STORY OF GOLF, LIFE,
and the people who guide us along the way

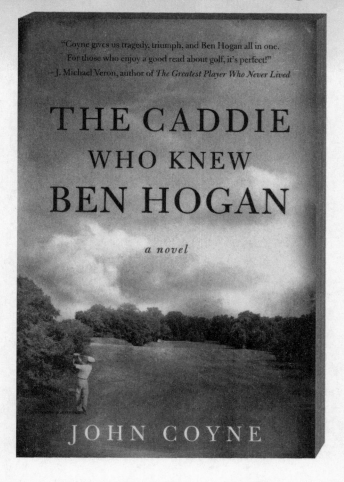

"Coyne gives us tragedy, triumph, and Ben Hogan all in one.
For those who enjoy a good read about golf, it's perfect!"
—J. Michael Veron, author of *The Greatest Player Who Never Lived*

THE CADDIE
WHO KNEW
BEN HOGAN

a novel

JOHN COYNE

Invited by the anniversary committee, Jack Handley returns to the country club where
he caddied as a young boy. Speaking to its members, he recounts the historic summer
of 1946 when Ben Hogan visited the club to play in the Chicago Open. Full of
Hogan anecdotes, memories from a golden era of golf, and the story of a young boy
changed by life, love, and tragedy . . .

**"A terrific blend of golfing lore, PGA tournament drama, and
country club soap opera . . . the results rank with
James Dodson's nonfiction."** —*Publishers Weekly*

St. Martin's Griffin
www.stmartins.com

THOMAS DUNNE BOOKS